THE VILLA NEXT DOOR

BEVERLEY HARVEY

BLOODHOUND
— BOOKS —

First published in 2025 by Bloodhound Books.

www.bloodhoundbooks.com

Print ISBN: 978-1-917705-19-6

CHAPTER ONE

MAY

Standing on the doormat dripping, Emma peels off the cold wet layers. The walk to school had been a chore, not least because she'd slept poorly thanks to the storm that had raged all night, leaving her fractious and fuzzy-headed.

She'd left Callie at the school gates, said hello to her friend Mel and a couple of the other mums, then walked home on pavements slick with fallen horse chestnut blossom, spurred on by the thought of a flat white and a toasted teacake.

Now, bending to retrieve the few items of post, Emma passes through to the kitchen where the breakfast pots await her. She's about to cast the collection of damp junk mail into the recycling bin when a glossy A5 postcard addressed to Mrs E. Burrows stops her in her tracks. She studies the photographs. The most eye-catching one depicts a sandy cove being lapped by clear turquoise water, while other enticing images portray a sparkling swimming pool set within a lush tropical garden.

Deciding that it's an ad for a Mediterranean resort, Emma's hand is poised over the bin when the words *prize* and *competition* leap out at her. Intrigued, she scans the copy.

Congratulations, you have won first prize in our super summer competition! boasts the headline.

Emma reads on, waiting for the catch – the call to action inviting her to ring some suspicious-looking overseas phone number to claim her prize: in this instance, an all-expenses paid three-week holiday in a whitewashed villa on the island of Menorca. And there it is, she notes with a degree of cynical satisfaction as she reads the words *call your participating travel agent to claim your prize. Don't miss out!*

Emma scoffs. *As if.*

She recalls last year's disaster of a staycation. A week in Devon, which had barely seemed like a break at all, what with Ryan constantly checking his emails and fielding work calls as the three of them trudged between the hotel and the beach, battling wind and rain for five days out of seven. It had felt more like an endurance test than a holiday.

'Never again,' Ryan had said through gritted teeth on the drive home. 'Next year, I don't care how much it costs or what else is going on, we are flying to the sun and for at least a fortnight.'

With a pang of longing, Emma gazes at the photographs. *No wonder people get sucked into these scams*, she thinks, flipping the card over and rereading the copy for a second time.

The telephone code of the named travel agent is a Cranbrook number and relatively local. She frowns, a fragment of hope stirring – not that she can remember even entering the competition.

She goes to the fridge, pins the card to the door with a magnet bearing the motto *I can and I will*, with the sole purpose of mentioning it to Ryan later.

Ryan arrives home from the office looking tired and deflated. Emma waits until after the three of them have eaten and Callie has been bathed and tucked up in bed before raising the subject of the competition.

Ryan glances at the flyer and reads a few lines of the copy, his mouth set in a thin straight line. 'It's a scam, Em,' he says, 'throw it away.'

'How though? I mean, I thought that at first, but where's the catch?'

'When did you enter the competition?'

Emma shrugs. 'I can't remember doing one.'

Ryan raises an eyebrow. 'Well, there's your answer. You can't win a competition you haven't entered.'

'Yes, but listen.' She takes the card from Ryan, her eyes shining with hope. 'I looked online this afternoon and the travel agent mentioned is a real one. A proper ABTA registered company in Cranbrook. Why would they involve themselves with scammers?'

'Bless you, Em.' Ryan inclines his head. 'Because these people are clever. They know how to make things look legit, how to clone telephone numbers so it looks like you're ringing a proper company.'

'I know, but what if it's real? What if we're about to pass up a free luxury holiday? Why don't we drive over there at the weekend? Then we'll know for sure. And if the agent has never heard of this so-called competition, we'll go for a drink in a country pub – one with a nice garden.' Emma sighs and rakes back her hair. 'Assuming it ever stops raining.'

Ryan puffs out his cheeks. 'Okay. But don't get your hopes up.'

Emma pours two glasses of Shiraz and places them on the kitchen island. 'Yes, I know it's only Monday,' she says, 'but I've been so cold and miserable today. I feel the need.'

Ryan raises his glass and takes a long swallow. 'We both need a holiday, competition or not. Em, I can't keep going at this pace. I mean, I don't resent the extra work while Paul's off recovering from major surgery – my life's a breeze compared to his – but there are only so many hours in a day. Roll on June when he's due back in the office.'

Emma nods. 'Well, maybe we should book something, a couple of weeks in the sun.'

Ryan's shoulders sag. 'I'm not sure I can get away; it would only compound the problem.'

'I disagree,' Emma says. 'Think how much more productive you'll be after a proper break. Love, it's not just about work, you and I need some quality time together.' *After everything we've been through*, she adds silently.

There's a beat, a moment's tension while the two of them absorb the significance of her words.

'I'm not trying to guilt trip you,' Emma says, seeing the wariness in Ryan's eyes, 'but after everything that happened last year, we need to...' she trails off, searching for the right words. 'We need to reconnect as a couple,' she finishes gently.

Ryan's eyes are downcast; he swirls the wine in his glass then takes a sip. 'Em, there isn't a day goes by where I don't regret—'

'Of course, and I know that. But we need a change of scene, time to relax – and to find each other again.'

She picks up the promo card, strides to the fridge and re-pins it to the door. 'Look, it *might* be dodgy, but promise me you'll keep an open mind. We'll drive over there, find out about this so-called prize and if it's not real, we'll see what special offers they've got on this summer.' She gazes longingly at the photograph in all its shimmering aquamarine glory. 'God, Ry, what I wouldn't give to lie on a beach like that for two weeks.' She sighs.

CHAPTER TWO

JULY

Emma can see the tension in Ryan's jaw and the whiteness of his knuckles as he grips the wheel.

'There's a good chance we'll miss our flight,' he says, his voice low. He glances in the rear-view mirror to where Callie is scrolling on her tablet and singing softly to herself, comfy in her car seat and blissfully unaware of her parents' angst.

Emma tucks a strand of caramel blonde hair behind her ear and peers at the satnav. 'This thing's predicting a twenty-two-minute delay, so if we can just get past this hold-up, we'll be fine,' she says with more conviction than she feels.

Ryan frowns. 'Let's hope so. Anyway, if we miss it—'

'Which we won't—'

'Yeah, but if we do, we'll sort it. We'll get the next flight out. I've moved heaven and earth to take time off work and we are having this bloody holiday if it kills us.'

Emma grimaces at Ryan's choice of words. 'Which is a distinct possibility the way your blood pressure's shooting up. Love, there's no point stressing yourself out. We've been looking forward to this trip for months, let's not jinx it before we even get there. I still can't believe we won a free holiday – I've never won anything in my life,' she says, recalling their trip to Fly High Travel that drizzly Saturday afternoon in May.

The woman behind the counter, a strawberry blonde in her late thirties with a clipped accent and a brisk manner, had examined the printed card in considerable detail.

'Well, I'm pleased to say it's not a scam,' she'd said with certainty. 'Looks perfectly authentic to me. You see this QR code? That tells me it's linked to a children's charity. You must have donated at some point and been entered into a prize draw without realising.'

'Ah, that makes sense,' Emma agreed. 'I'm always donating small amounts – mainly through Facebook.'

Ryan had been unconvinced. 'Are you sure?'

'Absolutely. It's a brilliant prize. You'll be staying in a small villa complex about half an hour from Mahon, for up to three weeks. There's no restriction on dates and all you have to pay for is the flights.'

The flare of a horn jolts Emma back into the car and she scans the horizon for evidence of roadworks or an accident, but there's nothing other than the Monday morning crush as they approach the turn-off that switches them from the M25 to the M23 bound for Gatwick.

She eyes the monotonous grey-green undergrowth to her left and the static line of cars ahead, her thoughts drifting to their destination.

Seventeen nights in a whitewashed villa, in a quiet Menorcan village. In the ten years she and Ryan have been together – eight of them married – it is by far the longest break they've ever taken.

Emma had been thrilled when Ryan had not only agreed to book the holiday, but then surprised her by taking an extra three days' unpaid leave on top of the two weeks she'd hoped for.

Now the glorious Mediterranean sunshine is within touching distance, so close she can almost feel its warmth on her pale, freckled shoulders.

Her lips curve into a smile as she pictures the three of them relaxing on pine-fringed sandy beaches, Callie squealing with delight as she splashes in the shallows of the warm sea. She imagines herself, supine on a sunbed, wearing one of her new bikinis, a cold drink in one hand, her Kindle in the other, as she escapes into one of the bestsellers she's downloaded for the trip.

With a ripple of excitement, she considers the quality time the three of them will spend together: relaxing, sleeping in late, sunbathing and swimming in the villa's pool – albeit a shared one with the two other villas on the development.

'Shame it's not a private pool, just for us,' Ryan had muttered once the travel arrangements had been made.

'Oh, I don't mind sharing,' Emma said, talking it through with him afterwards. 'There might even be another child for Callie to play with. I don't want her to be bored or lonely.'

At last, the car lurches forward as Ryan accelerates.

'Finally,' he says, turning to her with a triumphant grin. 'Looks like we're off on our holibobs after all.'

It's almost two o'clock when they land, and the sun is at its peak. Stepping down from the plane into a shimmering heat haze, Emma's heart contracts at the sight of Ryan gripping Callie's hand as he steers her down the steps and towards passport control.

It's the first week of the school holidays and the straggling lines are lengthy. Regardless, they are soon passing through baggage reclaim where the usual bunfight for bags is chaotic but brief.

'That was almost too easy,' Emma says, watching Ryan load their holdalls onto a trolley while she shoulders her handbag and holds Callie's hand tightly.

'Well, don't speak too soon. We need to sort out the hire car next – let's hope it's a decent vehicle.' Ryan scans the area. 'Yep, over there. That's the company we booked through, I recognise the logo.'

He strides towards a desk where a fifty-something man with an air of quiet patience is working through the line of tourists.

Emma's pace is brisk beside him but Callie resists, her little face flushed. 'Mummy, I need to *go*,' she says in a stage whisper.

'Okay, darling, we'll leave Daddy in charge of the car and see if we can find a loo.' Emma looks around and spots a sign for the restrooms. 'Meet you back here in five,' she tells Ryan.

By the time the girls return, refreshed and smelling of pine-scented handwash, it is to find Ryan looking puffed up and pleased with himself having negotiated a free upgrade.

Why am I not surprised? Emma cringes inwardly, knowing how much Ryan likes to get his own way.

Outside, in the company's parking bay, Ryan eyes the sleek new-looking SUV. Then there's a hurried signing of paperwork conducted in a booth the size of a telephone kiosk, where a booster seat for Callie is produced and Ryan is issued with instructions about petrol and insurance.

Once the transaction is complete and the operative has returned to his post, Ryan's expression is smug. 'You see, Em? Sometimes it's worth being assertive. This car's bigger and newer than the one we booked – and for the same price. Right, let's get this holiday started,' he says, loading their bags into the boot, his good mood evident.

After twenty-five minutes of following the satnav through remote villages dotted along rural, undulating roads, they arrive at the small coastal resort of Cala Savannah.

'This is it, girls. We just need to find the villa complex now,' Ryan says, his eyes darting between the satnav and the road ahead.

Emma smiles. 'It's so pretty here, and I'm glad there are facilities – we don't want to have to get in the car every time we need a pint of milk or a bite to eat,' she says, taking in the sea views glimpsed between huddles of white rendered villas to one side, and the small parade of shops, bars, and cafés on the other.

Frowning with concentration, Ryan doesn't answer. He brakes sharply, almost missing the sign for Santa Martina, the name of the development.

'Hey, we're here,' he says, slowing to a crawl as he drives beneath an arch and along a smooth tarmacked road that leads to a lush tropical garden filled with palm trees, bougainvillea, and hibiscus shrubs.

As they near three whitewashed villas, a swimming pool comes into view; a flash of sparkling topaz, flanked by weathered planters filled with lavender, scarlet geraniums, and succulents in dusty shades of green and grey.

'This place is stunning,' Emma breathes. 'I wonder which house is ours?'

'We're in no. 2 and from what I can remember, it's the middle one. The travel agent said we'd find the key in the door.' Ryan grins. 'How lovely is this? Not bad for a free holiday, eh?'

Emma reaches across and squeezes his forearm, her eyes shining. 'It's beautiful – we won't want to go home.' She turns to

Callie, who's wide-eyed in the back of the car. 'What do you think, sweet pea?'

'The flowers are so pretty, Mummy, I love it. Can we go in the pool?' Callie says, releasing her seat belt seconds after Ryan has mounted the villa's driveway and switched off the engine.

Emma smiles. 'Of course, but let's get inside, unpack and have a look around first, shall we?'

Stiff from travelling, she exits the car and stretches. Throughout the drive, the air con has kept them cool, but now the balmy warmth hits her. 'I think we all need a nice cold drink,' she adds, butterflies fizzing in her stomach as they walk up the path to the villa's green front door. As expected, the key is in the lock.

Once inside, there's an instant drop in temperature as they pass through the tiled hallway and into a spacious open-plan area that serves as kitchen, dining, and sitting room. Even with the heavy drapes closed against the sun, Emma can make out the eclectic blend of traditional Spanish and contemporary styling.

She walks around, opening the curtains, letting the sunlight flood in. At the rear, a sliding glass door opens onto an attractive patio equipped with rattan furniture. Over a low whitewashed wall, a patch of scrub separates the end of their garden from the beach beyond.

In the living area, two huge leather sofas form an L-shape around a low glass table piled with magazines, a jigsaw, and several board games. An additional leather armchair, an old-fashioned mahogany sideboard, and a wall-mounted TV complete the set-up.

The kitchen is a little dated but charming and practical, its blue and white spriggy tiles cheerful against ivory marble worktops and dark wood cabinets. There's a reassuring citrussy smell of cleaning fluid, and a vase of white chrysanthemums atop a dining table flanked by four chairs.

Emma opens the fridge, touched to discover a bottle of cava, half a dozen cans of orange Fanta and two litres of still water. On a worktop sits a large packet of crisps.

'But where do we sleep?' Callie asks, skipping out to the hallway, now strewn with bags thanks to Ryan's trips back and forth to the car.

'That's everything,' he says, breathlessly pushing his dark hair from his forehead.

Emma makes a face. 'I'm sorry, love. I should have given you a hand. Hey, let's go and look at the bedrooms,' she says, ushering Callie upstairs where two large shuttered rooms, each with its own en suite bathroom, spur from a tiled landing. The beds are made up in cheerful blue gingham, with a rattan chair in the corner of each room as well as a white painted wardrobe. Delicate seascapes adorn the smooth walls. The effect is rustic, calm, and welcoming.

Callie frowns. 'My room has two beds in it and there's only one of me.'

'That's okay, you can use it to put things on if you like. I expect a lot of visitors who come here have more than one child.'

Callie sighs and crosses her arms. 'Maybe *I'll* get a brother one day.'

'Maybe,' Emma says, catching Ryan's eye and mouthing *where did that come from?* over their daughter's head. She changes the subject: 'Right, who wants a drink and some crisps in the garden?'

Outside, they gather around the table. Emma sips sparkling wine and watches Ryan and Callie as they sit, dark silky heads bowed over their devices while muttering to each other contentedly. Simultaneously, they both look up, relaxed smiles reaching their cocoa-brown eyes. Laughing, Emma shakes her head.

'What?' Ryan asks. 'What's funny?'

'You two: peas in a pod. I'm just thinking how lucky I am, having you both to myself on this lovely island. It's so peaceful here and I can't wait to explore the beach tomorrow, and have a swim in the pool.'

'Yep, it's pretty perfect,' Ryan agrees. He gets up. 'Refill, madam? It's not like we're driving anywhere tonight. I thought we could walk to the pizzeria we passed on the main road.'

He goes inside and returns seconds later with the bottle of cava and another can of orangeade for Callie.

'We're lucky,' he says, topping up Emma's glass. 'There's always a risk when you go on holiday that it won't be like the photos, but if anything, this place is better than I expected.' He takes a handful of crisps, leans in, and lowers his voice. 'I wonder who we've got next door.'

'I haven't seen any signs of life; maybe it's just us.'

'Well let's hope we don't get a stag party or something,' Ryan says, filling his mouth with crisps. He crunches and swallows. 'Because the only thing that could spoil this place is if the neighbours aren't nice,' he adds, licking salt from his lips.

CHAPTER THREE

Emma awakes with a start, a sense that something is off, but as the room falls into focus around her, its white walls dotted with cheerful seaside prints, she remembers where she is. Beside her, Ryan is still asleep, his handsome face half buried in the pillow, lips parted as he emits gentle snores.

From across the landing, she can hear the whine of electronic sound effects and wonders how long Callie has been awake.

She gets up, reaches for her robe – a new floral print kimono, bought specially for the trip – and pads to the bathroom. The woman who greets her in the mirror is more dishevelled than usual. She pulls back her shoulder-length hair and twists it into a claw at the nape of her neck before splashing cold water on her face in an effort to de-puff her blue eyes.

Then she tiptoes past Ryan and goes into her daughter's room.

Callie beams at her. 'Mummy! Can we go to the beach? I'm ready, look,' she says, throwing back the covers.

Emma stifles a giggle. 'That's great, sweet pea, but I think your swimming costume is on inside out – see, there's the label.'

Callie frowns. 'I dressed in a hurry.'

Emma sits on the edge of Callie's bed and peers at her iPad. 'So, what are you watching?'

'Nothing, I'm playing my frog game. You have to find as many as you can; they hide under the lily pads, see?'

Ruffling her daughter's hair, Emma leans in and inhales her warm biscuity smell.

'Mummy, are you listening to me?'

'Yes, darling, of course,' Emma answers. 'How about we go downstairs for some breakfast?'

The evening before, at Ryan's suggestion, they'd walked for ten minutes into the village, where they'd bought basics in the *supermercado* before eating at one of the local restaurants. Watching the diners gathered around weathered oak tables lit by tea lights in rustic red jars, they were encouraged to find at least half were Spanish, borne out by the buzz of convivial conversation.

Hungry from travelling all day, they'd made short work of the pasta and crisp green salads they'd ordered, but within ten minutes of finishing, Callie had crashed and was lolling against Emma, her eyelids flickering.

'We need to get her home. She's exhausted, poor poppet,' Emma said, signalling to the waitress for the bill.

After paying up and adding a generous tip, Ryan had hoisted Callie into his arms and carried her back to the villa. She'd barely stirred as, together, they'd tucked her into bed, hovering for a moment, besotted.

'I don't think I'm far behind her,' Emma said, stifling a yawn as they crept downstairs.

'It's been a long day, but a good one,' Ryan said. 'Why don't we have one last drink on the terrace? We can crack open the red we just bought... come on, just a small one. We are on holiday after all.'

The atmosphere had shifted subtly then, Ryan nudging Emma towards the loveseat made for two, their thighs touching as they sipped the wine.

'You look beautiful tonight. A bit like on our first date,' Ryan said, setting his glass down on the table and cupping Emma's face. He brushed her lips with his own, pulling back a little as if seeking permission, before kissing her again, harder, and more insistently.

Emma felt herself tensing up. 'Darling, I'm sorry, but I'm just too tired... and a bit drunk, if I'm honest.' She got up, avoiding Ryan's gaze. 'Do you mind if I go up?'

He gave a resigned little shrug. 'Babe, of course not. I'll finish my drink, then follow you.'

But by the time Ryan had crept into bed beside her, Emma had fallen asleep.

Callie is finishing her cereal when Ryan appears, wearing cargo pants, yesterday's black T-shirt and a sheepish grin.

He rakes a hand through his hair. 'We got any paracetamol?'

Emma gets up and retrieves a blister pack from her handbag. 'That bad, eh? Must admit I'm a tiny bit worse for wear myself. Here, take two. I'll make some coffee. I found a lovely old-fashioned stovetop percolator and some ground coffee in a tin. The owner's left us all sorts of things that will come in handy.'

Ryan sits at the table beside Callie, who is eyeing up the brioche buns and peach jam bought last night, along with a dozen or so other essentials.

'Have one, sweet pea,' Emma encourages. 'Just brush your teeth well afterwards, okay?'

Callie's shoulders sag. '*Then* are we going to the beach?'

'Soon,' Ryan says. 'Bun, teeth, then you can sit and play with your tablet for half an hour and let your breakfast go down properly while Mum and I relax with a coffee.'

Forty minutes later, after everyone has washed and dressed, breakfast has been cleared away, and a canvas bag has been packed, they head out into the communal garden in search of the track that will lead them directly to the beach.

'Good morning!' calls a husky female voice.

Emma pivots towards the sound to find a woman emerging from the house next door. A few steps behind, a man waves from the open door of no. 3.

Emma glances at Ryan before waving back. 'So much for being alone here,' she whispers, then, louder: 'Morning!'

The woman, a spry, tanned sixty-something, offers Emma a slim, weathered hand. 'Hello! I'm Maxine – but call me Max, everyone else does – and this is John, my husband. When did you arrive?'

Emma shakes Max's hand. 'Hi, Max, John. I'm Emma, this is Ryan, and this is our daughter, Callie. We arrived yesterday afternoon. I didn't know there was anyone else here. I hope we didn't disturb you.'

'Oh, we were out with friends last night, on the other side of the island. I expect you were in bed by the time we got back... bit of a late one for us.' Max eyes the canvas bag, their shorts, and flip-flops. 'Anyway, I can see you're bound for the beach, so I won't hold you up. If there's anything you need, please ask – we're usually around.'

'Oh, right. Do you live here?' Ryan asks.

Max nods. 'Most of the time, although we keep a flat on the Kent-Sussex border, just in case. We semi-retired here a few years ago.'

Ryan inclines his head. 'Ah, not far from us; we're from

Kent, too. Not that it compares with living here. This is a beautiful spot. Can you direct us towards the beach, please? As you can imagine, *someone's* keen to have a swim in the sea.'

Max reaches out and lightly brushes Callie's cheek. 'Bless you, little one. You enjoy every minute,' she says, her tone indulgent.

John points towards an area of dense foliage. 'You'll find the beach path over there; go past our house, past the bin store – there's a gap in the bushes, you'll see,' he says.

Emma smiles. 'Great, thanks. Well, no doubt we'll see you later. Maybe we can have a drink together one evening if you're around?'

'We'd love that, just give us a knock,' Max says, her blue eyes lighting up.

Moments later, Ryan walks ahead while Emma steers Callie past two fetid smelling dumpsters and onto the shadowy beach track. Then the thicket of trees ends as abruptly as it began, and it's as though they've stepped through a portal into another world as a small horseshoe of fine white sand and turquoise sea comes into view.

On the far side, music pipes softly from Juan's Café, a rustic bar with a modest seating area. Beside it, a mahogany-skinned man who looks north of seventy, sits beneath a blue and white striped canopy, poised to hire out sunbeds and umbrellas to tourists.

Emma breathes deeply and gazes out at the ocean. 'It's so beautiful here.'

'Yes, it's perfect. I'll get us a couple of sunbeds, shall I?' Ryan says, signalling to the older man who flies into action with surprising speed and agility.

'Now that's sorted,' Ryan says, once they've spread themselves out and established a makeshift camp, 'who's up for a dip?'

Collapsed on sun loungers, hair in wet tendrils, saltwater evaporating from their bodies, they watch Callie making patterns in the sand with shells she's collected at the water's edge.

Ryan smiles at his daughter and lowers his voice. 'Bloody hell, Em, what did you go and say that to the neighbours for?'

'Say what?' Emma shields her eyes from the sun.

'You know, inviting them for drinks. Now we're going to be stuck socialising with pensioners for the rest of the holiday. Honestly, you and your big—'

'I was just being polite. I doubt they'll even remember. Anyway, I don't suppose we'll see much of them.'

Ryan shakes his head. 'They live right next door; we'll be bumping into them all the time.'

'Does it matter? They seem nice,' Emma says, trying to keep the exasperation from her voice.

'Daddy!' Callie calls, holding up a tiny pink shell. 'Look at this lovely one. Can we go in the sea again? Please, can we?'

Emma raises her eyebrows. 'Yes, *Daddy*, stop moaning and go for another paddle, will you?'

Ryan gets up, muttering under his breath, brushes the sand from his damp shorts and swoops in on Callie, picking her up and running into the sea, play-growling as she squeals with delight.

Smiling to herself at the sheer luxury of some peace and quiet, Emma reaches into the canvas bag for her phone and is surprised to find it's almost twelve thirty.

An image of Mrs Guthridge pops into her head, who, at eighty-seven years old, has had exactly the same shampoo and set every Tuesday at twelve thirty since Emma joined the salon as receptionist three years ago.

For the first three years after Callie's birth, she'd loved spending every waking hour with her daughter, but when a local couple had recommended a great – and affordable – pre-school where their own kids were happy and thriving, it had been a game changer.

Ryan's approach had been pragmatic. 'Don't worry about the money, just find something local that's enjoyable and will give you interaction with other women, preferably two or three days a week. You're an amazing mum to Callie and a brilliant wife, but you need to focus on *you* for a change.'

Emma frowns, remembering. He'd made it seem like therapy at the time, tried to make it all about her, but as usual, Ryan had had his own reasons for giving her something else to think about and to occupy her time.

A fleeting image of a woman's face slides into her mind: a swish of long copper hair; pale, luminous skin; full lips curving into a seductive smile—

She jerks upright, her thoughts interrupted by Callie's squeals. Shielding her eyes, she watches as Ryan dunks Callie in and out of the water, making aeroplane sound effects. Callie, who at six is small and light for her age, is shrieking with laughter until Ryan lowers her to the sand and raises his hands in submission before walking back up the beach.

'Your turn! I'm knackered,' he says, throwing himself down on the sunbed, while Callie scampers after him.

After a few minutes, Ryan looks towards the bar, which is little more than a wicker shack with a row of high stools lined up around a central serving area, and a dozen or so umbrella shaded tables and chairs where a handful of people sit.

'Shall I get us all a drink?' he asks, hunting in the bag for his wallet.

Emma nods. 'Please. What do you fancy, Cal?'

Ryan strolls up the beach towards the bar, his lean, muscled shoulders and back already darkening from the sun. Emma eyes a group of young adults who are relaxing on a rug, noting the way two women stare after him, lowering their sunglasses as they exchange a few words in Spanish.

Her heart sinks. Even here. On this beautiful, tranquil, and sparsely populated beach, Ryan still manages to attract female attention.

Does she imagine that Ryan slows his stride, turns, and smiles at the women before continuing towards the bar? She watches his brief exchange with the male bartender before he returns, carefully balancing a stack of cardboard cups, three cans of pop and a foil-wrapped ice cream for Callie.

'Ooh, thank you, Daddy,' Callie says, her eyes lighting up as she takes the ice cream from him.

'Two Diet Cokes and a Fanta for madam,' he says. 'It's not a bad little bar, actually. They do toasted sandwiches, portions of chips, a tuna salad thing... there's even a loo.' He pauses. 'Not that I checked it out, but you know... useful.'

Emma opens her cola and takes a sip. 'Cheers, Ry. I love it here: golden sand, clear water for bathing... what more could we ask for?'

'And all because of a random competition.' Ryan raises the cola to his lips and gulps greedily, head back, eyes closed against the sun, reminding Emma of an old TV commercial. She glances at the group a few metres along the beach and is irritated to find the same two women who'd noticed Ryan earlier are paying close attention, nudging each other and speaking in low husky Spanish, unaware of her existence.

Feeling hot and slightly peeved, Emma blows out her cheeks. 'Actually, can we go back to the villa? I don't want Callie to get sunburnt on our first day – that would be a disaster.'

Ryan hiccups, excuses himself, and looks at his daughter. 'Really? She's not even pink and she's plastered in Factor 50.'

He grins. 'And anyway, she takes after me; she's only got to look at the sun and she's—'

'All right, well to be honest, I'm getting a headache, and I'd like to walk back if that's okay?'

Ryan's forehead puckers in sympathy. 'Sorry, Em. Why didn't you say?' He turns to Callie. 'Right, trouble, you heard your mum; how do you fancy lunch back at the villa and a swim in the pool?'

'Cool,' she says, licking the last of her ice cream.

CHAPTER FOUR

The headache had started out as a white lie, but as they walk back towards the villa, Emma's temples begin to throb.

Callie, in swimsuit and flip-flops, her limbs already turning golden, skips ahead towards the patch of scrub dotted with sparse pine trees and rocks.

'Wait for us, please – not too far,' Emma calls.

Ryan frowns. 'She's fine, it's not as though she can get lost and there's nobody here but us.'

'Why do you always have to disagree with me?' Emma snaps.

'I don't,' Ryan says, looking hurt. 'Em, are you okay? You seem a bit off.'

'I'm fine,' Emma says, feeling anything but. They walk the rest of the track in silence, rejoining Callie on the approach to the villa. As they pass the neighbouring house, they see Max and John sitting side by side on rattan chairs, their faces angled to the sun.

'Hello again.' Emma waves without breaking her stride.

Once inside the coolness of the villa, a wave of relief washes over her; she touches Ryan's forearm. 'Look, I'm sorry. I know you and Callie were having fun and it's our first day and everything, but I'm not as hardy as you in the heat and it takes me a while to acclimatise.'

Ryan smiles. 'We don't mind, do we, Cal? We could all do with a break from the sun. How about I make us all a *sandwich de jamón*,' he says in a silly faux Spanish accent.

Emma laughs. 'Thanks, sounds good. We can sit in the garden, under the awning.' She turns away, regretful that she has let a moment's insecurity and jealousy change the course of their day.

'How's your headache now?' Ryan calls from the kitchen as he butters crusty bread and slices tomatoes thinly. Callie hovers beside him, passing utensils and taking food from the fridge.

'It's lifting, thanks,' Emma says, joining them. She encircles Ryan's waist from behind. 'I'm sorry, it was just the heat. Hey, that looks like a fabulous sandwich,' she says, winking at Callie and filling three glasses with bottled water.

They carry lunch into the garden, and sit under the striped awning, enjoying the peace until Callie shrieks, startled by a gecko as it crosses the terrace, almost grazing her bare toes in its hurry to escape into the undergrowth.

Ryan laughs. 'He won't hurt you, sweet pea. Geckos are shy and timid – he couldn't wait to get away from us.'

Callie looks doubtful. 'Is that true, Mummy?'

'Yes, he was scared of us, couldn't you tell?' Emma turns towards a rustle and a quiver of foliage. A face peers through, startling all three of them.

'It's just me,' Max sings, her disembodied head poking through the branches of a bougainvillea. Amazed, Ryan and Emma's eyes meet.

'Everything all right?' Ryan asks.

'Absolutely fine,' Max says. 'But I heard you chatting and

wanted to invite you for drinks and nibbles this evening, if you're free?'

Ryan hesitates. 'That's very kind, but we haven't decided what we're doing yet,' he blusters, glancing at Emma.

'So, let me take the weight off. I'll make something light, salad and something or other. I've got some gorgeous local wines and plenty of gin, so there's no need to bring anything. Shall we say seven o'clock?'

Ryan's eyebrows shoot up. 'Well—'

'Perfect. That's settled then.' Without waiting for an answer, Max withdraws her head so the branches spring back like a window shutting.

'What just happened?' Emma mouths.

The rest of the day passes in a languid blur as the three of them relax by the pool on sun loungers. Emma settles back, stretching her pale limbs beneath the gentle afternoon sun and tries not to dwell on their privacy being compromised by the older couple next door.

Callie has found her inner mermaid and is practising breaststroke under Ryan's doting gaze.

Hearing her daughter's gleeful squeals and Ryan's encouragement, Emma gets up, squats by the pool, and runs a hand through the water. 'Well done, sweet pea,' she says, proudly. 'Carry on like this and you won't need armbands by the time we go home.'

Ryan wades to where Emma crouches and takes her hand. 'Have a dip with us.'

Emma pulls away. 'No thanks, the water's a bit cool for me. Maybe tomorrow.'

Callie squints her eyes against the sun. 'Aww, come on, Mummy. It's lovely once you get used to it. Look! Watch this.'

She submerges her head so her bottom sticks up like a little duckling's.

Emma laughs and claps as Ryan reaches for her again, tugging at her arms. 'Okay, okay, I'm getting in!' she cries, half falling, half jumping into the pool.

Emma strikes a flattering pose. 'How do I look?'

'Bloody gorgeous,' Ryan says in low voice. 'Are you sure we have to go to this awful drinks thing tonight? I'd much rather have you to myself.'

'Me too. But to be fair, it might *not* be awful and even if we make an excuse and cancel, we've still got Callie to feed and look after, so down boy,' she says, her tone playful.

Nevertheless, Ryan's approval pleases her. She smooths down her cherry-print halter-neck dress and stands tall in her matching scarlet wedge heels. In addition, she's applied smoky eye make-up and a layer of self-tanning lotion, which has given her a healthy glow as well as a confidence boost.

Already sun-kissed, Ryan looks more handsome than ever. A ripple of desire catches Emma off guard.

'Mummy, can you help me, please?' Callie pipes up from across the landing, breaking the spell.

'Coming, sweet pea.' Emma goes into her daughter's room to find her torn between two outfits: a striped cotton sundress, and her favourite jeans and 'Little Miss Trouble' T-shirt. Emma coaxes Callie into the latter, on the basis that there could be midges in their neighbour's garden, and later, a chill in the air.

Shortly after seven, they walk next door, with Ryan clutching a bottle of red wine in one hand and a carton of juice for Callie in the other.

Max ushers them in, resplendent in a gold and purple maxi dress worn with gold sandals and a jangle of glittering bracelets.

Emma is taken aback. 'Wow, you look amazing, Max. I'm sorry, I didn't know we were dressing up.'

Max bats suspiciously long eyelashes. 'Oh, any excuse... one gets *so* bored with shorts and trainers.'

John greets them through a cloud of spicy aftershave; he too has made an effort and is sporting a ruffled cream shirt and a deep blue cravat.

At once, Emma sees the couple for who they are: bold, stylish, and judging by their furniture and the original artwork hanging on the walls, wealthy.

'Welcome, and thank you for these,' John says, graciously accepting the wine and juice from Ryan before disappearing into the kitchen and returning seconds later to take their drinks order.

Soon, they are sipping gin and tonics in Max and John's attractive back garden.

Ryan raises his glass and nods his approval. 'Cheers. This is lovely, and quite different from next door. Loving this Moroccan style; we could be in Marrakesh.'

Callie's eyes widen. 'It looks like a fairy tale.'

Emma agrees, taking in the mix of lapis blue and terracotta floor tiles, the exotic pewter and glass lanterns ready for lighting after dark, and the wind chimes that stir on the early evening breeze.

At the centre of the terrace sits a firepit, surrounded by a stone eating area and low comfortable seating bedecked with colourful silk cushions. The effect is Moorish and decadent.

John points to the sky. 'You wait, little one: it's even prettier after sunset.' He swirls ice around his glass and takes a sip. 'Hope you don't mind, but Max has invited some friends from the village. They own the boutique next door to the pharmacy on the main road.'

'No of course not, the more the merrier. You've both gone to so much trouble,' Emma says, feeling wrong-footed and embarrassed. She and Ryan had turned their noses up, thinking the evening would be boring and suburban, eking out small talk, but it's becoming clear that Max and John are anything but dull.

'Ah, do excuse me, I hear the doorbell.' Max glides into the house and returns with two tanned, silver-haired men in their fifties, and a third much younger man with dark shoulder-length hair and a slight round-shouldered stoop. The older pair, both stylishly dressed and liberally endowed with an exotic fragrance, swap hugs and kisses with John and Max.

'Emma, Ryan, these are our dear friends, Colin and Arturas, and this is Teddy, Colin's nephew.' Max says. 'He's only visiting, aren't you, dear?'

Teddy mouths hello, looking as though he'd rather be anywhere else, while Colin and Arturas shake hands and gush how *wonderful* everyone looks.

'And if you haven't visited their shop on the main road yet, you really must – it's fabulous,' Max says completing her introduction.

Joining in, Ryan grimaces. 'Well, that's all I need; an excuse for my wife to spend more money.'

'Hello, lovely to meet you,' Emma says, knowing that Ryan is merely playing to the gallery. 'And don't worry, if I see something I want, I'll pay for it myself.'

There's a ripple of polite laughter. 'Now that's fighting talk where I come from,' Colin says, in a distinct north-west English accent.

Arturas turns to Callie: 'And who is this adorable little angel? What's your name, poppet?'

'Go on, darling, say hello,' Ryan tells Callie, who has become inexplicably shy.

'This is Callie,' Emma says, 'she's six and a half.'

'And not often tongue-tied,' Ryan adds.

'Bless her, it's a lot to take in – five adults she's never met before,' Max says warmly. 'Right, I must away to the kitchen, or we'll be eating at midnight.'

After sunset, flushed from local gin and Spanish white wine, their stomachs full of Max's delicious chicken and apricot tagine, the adults lounge around the firepit, mesmerised by the flames.

'Excuse me, I'll just check on Callie,' Emma says, getting up and padding into Max's spare room, where her daughter dozes beneath a cosy throw, cuddling a plush lavender scented mouse made by Max.

A pang of guilt rips through her: *what exactly is happening here?* It's only their second night and, somehow, they've become embroiled with the local expat community and welcomed as friends; people who seem nice enough, but with whom she and Ryan have absolutely nothing in common and under normal circumstances would not even be on their radar. This is *not* the intimate family holiday they'd planned.

Callie stirs, releases her grip on the mouse and throws an arm above her head.

'Love you, angel. We'll go home soon, I promise,' Emma whispers, bending to kiss Callie and tucking the blanket around her. Her head spins slightly as she straightens up. *Note to self: no more alcohol this evening.*

Tiptoeing back to the party, she hears raucous laughter.

'Still asleep?' Ryan asks, as Emma takes her seat beside him. 'We've just been swapping stories about how we all met, and I've admitted to asking you out three times before you said yes.'

Max winks at Emma. 'There's nothing wrong with playing hard to get. Make 'em work for it, I always say.'

Emma's smile is tight; she hesitates, remembering. 'Yes, it's true. I turned Ryan down at first, because he's so good-looking I was worried he might be a player.'

'And is he?' Arturas asks, a glint in his eye.

Emma tilts her head. 'No,' she says after a pause that seems a fraction too long. 'He's a brilliant husband and father, and Callie adores him; she's a total Daddy's girl.'

Laughter erupts, except from Max, who silently watches Emma, her expression unreadable.

CHAPTER FIVE

The morning after John and Max's get-together, Emma leaves Ryan in charge of Callie and walks into the village. She buys a white geranium in a terracotta pot, and a boxed orange and almond cake dusted with icing sugar.

Pleased with her gifts and enjoying the feeling of the sun on her face, Emma returns to Santa Martina and knocks on her neighbours' door.

John answers, still in his bathrobe, his sparse white hair standing on end.

'Morning, John, how are you both?' Emma says.

Appearing behind him, Max rests her chin on his shoulder. 'Fit as fleas, thanks for asking. How are *you*, Emma, dear? I'm afraid it was another late one – we seem to be making a habit of them recently.'

'It was a bit, but we had a lovely time, thank you,' Emma says. 'You're an amazing cook, Max, and a brilliant hostess. Anyway, just a quick visit to thank you properly and to say we're planning to explore the island over the next few days, so we may not be around much.'

John's face falls. 'Oh, that's a shame. We were rather hoping—'

'Well, have a *gorgeous* time,' Max cuts in. 'And be sure to hit the shops in Mahon; what it lacks in size, it makes up for in charm.'

Emma nods. 'So I've heard. Mahon is certainly on our list. Well, thanks again for a lovely evening. These are for you.' She hands over the plant and the cake. 'I'd better go – make sure Ryan's not giving Callie ice cream for breakfast or caving in to some other daft demand.'

Pleased with her pre-emptive strike, Emma trots to their villa and finds Ryan and Callie still dawdling over breakfast.

'It's not that I don't like them – gosh, I hope we've got half their energy at their age,' Emma tells Ryan over coffee. 'I just wanted to manage their expectations, so that last night doesn't become the norm, you know, where we end up seeing them most evenings.'

Ryan is impressed. 'Go you, Em. I didn't know you could be so manipulative.'

'Manipulative? God, I hope *they* don't think that.'

Ryan laughs softly to himself. 'Oh, I'm sure they don't.'

By Friday morning, after two blissful days spent exploring the island, discovering breathtaking coves and swimming in the warm topaz sea, Emma longs for something other than the feel of sand between her toes.

'Like what?' Ryan asks after the breakfast things have been cleared away and all three are washed and dressed.

'We could take a look at Mahon,' Emma suggests. 'I was reading about it in the guidebook and it sounds quite lively.'

Callie makes a face. 'But, Mummy, I want to practise my swimming. I'm getting really good at it.'

'You are, darling. You're like a little mermaid.' Emma bends to cup her face. 'Bless you, sweet pea, you're so brown, you look like a local.' She straightens up. 'Okay, so how about we do both? Daddy can drive us into Mahon, we'll look around the city – maybe have tapas for lunch – and then head home for swimming mid-afternoon.'

Ryan nods. 'Sounds perfect. What do you think, Cal?'

'Yes!' Callie says, her eyes shining.

'Now that's what I call great timing,' Ryan says, swinging into a newly vacated parking space as they drive into the port of Mahon.

Emma gets out of the car and unbuckles Callie from the back seat. She puts her bag on her shoulder and takes her daughter's hand. 'Look at the boats, sweet pea. Aren't they beautiful?' She nudges Ryan and lowers her voice. 'I have a feeling you'll end up carrying her before the day's out; I read online that it's quite a hike into the old town.'

Ryan shrugs. 'It's fine. We can check out the historic landmarks, then wander round the shops for an hour or two before they close for siesta. Then we'll head back this way and have a bite to eat overlooking the marina.'

'You've got it all worked out, haven't you?' Emma says, pleased that Ryan is taking charge of their day out. 'I'd like to get Callie some cute local sandals if we see some – maybe I'll even treat myself to a pair.'

'How about I treat you both.' Ryan takes Callie's other hand as they approach the ancient stone steps up to the town centre. 'Right, girls. Off we go – last one to the top's a loser,' he says as they begin the ascent.

The winding narrow lanes pulse with life as tourists clamour for gifts and souvenirs, and local people go about their daily lives. The scene is a shifting assault on their senses as the pungent smell of seafood in the fish market gives way to the delicate scents and vibrant colours in the flower quarter, before waves of jasmine, ginger and patchouli compete in the rustic homeware stores.

It isn't long before they discover a street lined with shops selling Spanish-made leather goods.

'Ooh, look!' Callie squeals, pointing to a display of bejewelled children's sandals.

Fifteen minutes later, they leave the shop, Emma clutching a carrier bag containing matching shoes for herself and Callie.

'Daddy, you should have got some, then we'd all be the same,' Callie says earnestly.

'I'm good thanks, Cal. My sparkly-shoe days are over,' he says, ruffling her hair.

As the streets quieten and the shops turn their signs from *open* to *closed*, they begin their descent towards the port. As Emma predicted, Callie is tired by the time they reach the harbour. 'It's okay, sweet pea,' she says, 'we can all have a rest while we eat lunch and watch the ships come in.'

Soon they're seated at one of the portside restaurants facing the marina, tucking into delicious tapas and drinking zesty cloudy lemonade. Yachts of all sizes bob gently in the inky water, while overhead a thin bank of cloud floats like an island in a cobalt sky. As they watch, a cruise ship glides into view, eclipsing the horizon and surprising them by its sheer scale as it docks further round the port.

'Come on, trouble, I'll give you a lift,' Ryan says, raising Callie onto his shoulders as they make their way to the car an hour later.

Emma stifles a yawn. 'Why is being on holiday so tiring?'

'It's because we're finally unwinding properly. We really needed this break,' Ryan says.

Back at the villa, Callie is flushed and crabby. She throws herself down on one of the sofas, having dozed during the twenty-minute journey home.

'We need to wake her up, get her going again, or she won't sleep a wink tonight,' Emma tells Ryan as Callie turns her face away, saying she wants to sleep.

'Come on, stinker, snoozing's for wimps,' Ryan teases. 'I thought you were going to beat me at swimming later?'

Callie shakes her head.

'She'll come round, it's been a busy day,' Emma says before jogging upstairs to freshen up and change. She reappears in a blue and white bikini, a diaphanous black sarong tied around her waist. 'Right, who's joining me?' Emma asks, adopting a flattering pose.

Ryan wiggles his eyebrows suggestively. 'You're looking hot,' he says quietly, then louder: 'We'll see you by the pool in ten minutes, won't we, Cal?'

Dressed in a polka-dot one-piece, Callie skips towards the pool and thrusts a pair of semi-inflated armbands into Emma's lap. 'Help me get these on, Mummy – I'm going in,' she says, bouncing on the balls of her tanned bare feet.

Emma laughs and looks up at Ryan, who is in swim shorts ready for a dip. '*Please*, madam. Anyway, Daddy will blow them up, he's got more puff than me.'

Callie chunters to herself and hands the limp water wings to her father, leaving Emma to settle back against the sunbed, but before she can get comfortable, she's distracted by the low rumble of an approaching vehicle. For reasons she can't fathom, its arrival creates a prickle of unease along her spine. She sits up and shields her eyes against the sun, expecting the car to stop outside Max and John's villa. Instead, it glides straight past, stopping abruptly at the end property before mounting the adjacent drive.

She prods Ryan's calf with her foot and jerks her head towards the neighbouring house. 'Looks like we've got company.'

Ryan frowns. 'So I see.'

'Come *on*, Daddy, *please!*' Callie says.

'Okay, okay. Stop being a little tyrant, it's not nice.' Ryan finishes blowing up the armbands to their required volume and helps his daughter into them. 'Last one in's a chicken,' he says, squawking as he jumps into the water, while Callie laughs happily and leaps in after him.

Keeping her sunglasses on, Emma angles herself towards the neighbouring property and watches as the car – a white hatchback, typical of most hire firms – disgorges a family of four: two adults of around forty; and two little boys who look close in age.

The woman, tall and lean, her chestnut hair in a messy updo that emphasises her angular profile, turns to Emma and waves.

Emma smiles and waves back, conscious she has been caught staring. The woman's partner, stocky in build, his round face framed by a nest of chaotic brown curls, herds the two boys into the house. He too turns to smile and wave. Emma watches as both adults empty the car before shutting the front door of the villa behind them.

'Okay, Cal, Daddy's had enough for now,' Ryan mutters, heaving himself out of the pool. 'You swim and I'll watch for a bit, okay?' He returns to the sunbed and gropes for a towel, leaning down to kiss Emma. When she recoils, it's a reflex because he's dripping cold water all over her, nothing more, but she sees the surprise and hurt in his eyes.

'Sorry,' she says, reaching for him. 'You made me jump, that's all. Hey, I wonder what our new neighbours are like,' she whispers as they break apart.

Frowning, Ryan glances over at their house. 'Mmm, I had hoped it would be just us and the old codgers next door. Now we'll have to be sociable with new people.'

Emma laughs. 'Don't be such a misery guts! Anyway, they look nice enough and they've got children, so maybe the boys will be company for Callie.'

Ryan grunts and towels himself dry.

CHAPTER SIX

They'd managed well enough with the local shops all week, buying bits and pieces from the village supermarket as and when, but with a limited choice of products and prices that are surprisingly high, by Saturday Emma longs for the security of a *big shop*.

Ryan is not convinced. 'I don't want us to get bogged down with cooking. I love that we're mostly grazing on salads and tapas.'

'I know, but I want to get a few basics for Callie, the stuff we always have in at home, not to mention things like laundry gel and cleaning products.'

Ryan sighs. 'In that case, we need to find a bigger supermarket. I'll have a look in the ring binder the owners left us; it's stuffed with local info so there's bound to be something useful in there.'

Forty-five minutes later, having identified a hypermarket on the outskirts of Mahon, the Burrows are by the car just as the new arrivals stream out into the sunshine. The same woman who

Emma had secretly watched the day before waves and strides over.

'Hiya, I'm Sheena.' She smiles. 'This is my husband Jack, and our sons Leo and Lucas.'

At five foot five, Emma feels dwarfed by the stranger, whom she estimates to be at least five nine. Her face, angular from a distance, is fine-boned close-up, and her wide-set green eyes are a striking contrast to her long chestnut hair, which today she wears loose. It's a relief when her smile reveals white but slightly snaggle teeth that save her from looking too flawless.

'Nice to meet you, Sheena. I'm Emma and this is Ryan.' Emma nods towards him as he pauses awkwardly by the driver's door and raises a hand. 'And this is our daughter, Callie. Say hello, sweet pea.'

Callie's gaze is one of starry-eyed wonder. 'You look like a princess,' she breathes.

'Do I?' Sheena looks mildly embarrassed. 'You look lovely, too.'

Callie inclines her head. 'Are you going to the beach?'

Sheena glances towards Jack and the boys. 'We are.'

'And do your children like swimming?' Callie asks.

'They both love the water,' Sheena says, her expression bemused, 'but only Leo can swim. Lucas is only five and still learning.'

Callie claps her hands. 'Like me! I'm getting good though, aren't I, Mummy?'

Emma nods. 'You are. Anyway, Miss Chatterbox, get in the car, please – we can talk about your swimming prowess later.' She turns to Sheena, her smile sheepish. 'Sorry about the twenty questions. Meanwhile, we're off to find a big supermarket – wish me luck!'

'Oh, right. Will you try the hypermarket near Mahon? We went there as soon as we arrived. I read on Tripadvisor that the resort shops have really put their prices up since Brexit, so we stocked up on our way from the airport.'

Emma swallows. 'Gosh, that was very organised of you. I think you're right about the prices in the smaller shops. Right, better go, hopefully see you later. Have a lovely day.'

'Thanks, you too,' Sheena says, stepping away from the Burrows' drive and returning to her family.

They are speeding along the now familiar route towards Mahon, saying little and enjoying the scenery. It's only ten thirty and already the sun is high and searingly hot.

'Thank God for air con,' Ryan says, fumbling with the dial.

'You said it, not that I'm complaining.' Emma gazes at the parched fields flashing by. She turns to Ryan. 'Sheena's nice,' she says, keeping her tone light.

'Yeah, she seems okay,' Ryan says.

'She's very good-looking, don't you think?'

Ryan makes a face. 'Not especially. She's tall, I'll give you that.'

A silence descends. 'Wonder where they're from,' Emma says, breaking it.

'At a guess I'd say London or at least the south-east, judging by Sheena's accent.'

Emma nods. 'Wonder what *he's* like?'

Ryan frowns. 'Who, her husband? Love, why are you so interested?'

'*Because*... if they're a nice family, Callie can play with the boys, and we can have an occasional drink with Jack and Sheena in the evenings.'

Ryan purses his lips. 'I thought you didn't want to socialise while we're here. Are you bored with my company already?'

39

'Of course not. I just thought she seemed... you know, chatty, friendly.'

'Two words: high maintenance,' Ryan says, glancing at Callie in the rear-view mirror.

Emma's eyes widen. 'Wow. That's not fair. We only met her for two minutes, and she didn't strike me that way at all.'

'Believe me, I've met enough women like her through work and that's exactly what she is, I guarantee it.'

'Ry, we know nothing about Sheena, or her—'

'Ah, here's the turning,' Ryan interrupts, giving Emma a warning look. He lowers his voice. 'Best not to say any more in front of little ears.'

An hour later, Emma and Ryan are filling the SUV's capacious boot with salad, vegetables, pasta, cereals, biscuits, spreads, and sauces – many in a range of brands they recognise – as well as a dozen utility products and toiletries.

'Anyone would think we're here for another month,' Ryan says, forcing the last few items into the boot.

'It's only what I buy most weeks at home,' Emma tells him, buckling Callie into her booster seat.

'Well, no wonder we're always broke,' Ryan mutters, reversing out of their space and exiting the car park in the direction of home.

Soon they're unloading the car, just as Sheena, Jack and the boys file past, this time looking flushed and out of sorts.

Sensing a problem, Emma's tone is hesitant. 'Hello again. How was that?'

'Rubbish. I got stung,' the taller boy whines.

Jack ruffles his son's hair. 'Mate, if you will flap about near wasps... I did warn you.'

Sheena pastes on a bright smile. 'He'll be fine. He's not

allergic. Just a bit sore and upset. Jack's heading to the pharmacy in a minute to get something to put on it.'

'Really? Oh no, don't bother. I've got Savlon, plasters, antihistamine tablets, the works. Hold on a sec...'

Pleased to be able to help, Emma darts inside, jogs upstairs and goes straight to the ziplock first aid bag she'd put together the night before they left.

'I knew this would come in useful,' she says, handing Sheena the bag. 'Here, take what you need and pop it back to me whenever.'

'Are you sure? Thank you, that's so kind.' She brushes Emma's forearm, and their eyes lock for a second. 'We mums need to stick together. I won't forget this. Right, kids, inside. Let's get Leo patched up; maybe we can use the pool later.'

Emma watches as Sheena corrals her family into the villa next door, before going inside to unpack the shopping.

'Wow, Callie's got the hang of that.'

Emma jumps at the sound of Sheena's voice. 'Hey, you startled me. I didn't hear you coming.'

Sheena lets out a little yelp of laughter. 'Jack called me stealthy the other day – must be the yoga or something.' She waves to Callie, who is swimming up and down the pool with a quiet determination. 'Well done, Callie. You'll have to teach Lucas.'

'How's the patient?' Emma asks, recalling Leo's tear-stained face an hour earlier.

'He's fine, thanks to your brilliant first aid kit, but it's knocked him back a bit. He takes things to heart, does Leo. My youngest is the opposite – absolutely fearless and not always in a good way.'

'Really? Funny how siblings can be so different. Not that I'd know, having just the one.' Emma's focus returns to Callie. 'Hey, that's brilliant, sweet pea. Maybe tomorrow you can try a few strokes without armbands?'

'Yeah, so far,' Sheena continues, dragging a sunbed closer, 'Lucas has managed to fall from a climbing frame and break his arm, swallow one of his milk teeth, and get bitten by a Jack Russell terrier.' She pauses. 'Doesn't bode well for his teens, does it?'

The two of them giggle. 'Sorry, I shouldn't laugh,' Emma says. 'I'd be mortified if Callie hurt herself. Ryan's always telling me I'm overprotective as it is,' she frowns, 'like he can talk.'

Sheena raises dark shapely brows. 'What's he up to this afternoon?'

'Ryan? I left him having forty winks; well, that's what *he'd* call it – more like forty minutes by now. I'll go and get him in a minute. How about Jack and the boys?'

'Oh, they're coming. I said I'd line up some sunbeds. It seemed easier than the beach somehow, after the wasp sting and everything. Which reminds me, I must return your first aid kit.' Sheena pauses and puffs out her cheeks. 'I'm sorry, we're kind of disturbing your peace, aren't we?'

'No, don't be daft. It's a nice big pool and we knew we'd be sharing. To be honest, it'll be nice for Callie to have company.'

'Mummy!' A brown-haired little boy wearing water wings and swim shorts runs at Sheena and hurls himself into her arms, his dad and brother loping at his heels. Realising that Sheena is not alone, he turns to stare first at Emma, then at Callie, a smile spreading across his face.

'Look, Mummy, that girl is swimming,' Lucas cries, pointing at Callie who waves back at him.

Soon, Lucas and his father are both in the pool, their teeth chattering from the momentary chill as they splash about, getting used to the water.

Leo sits beside Sheena, his shoulders hunched, his expression sullen. 'It hurts,' he moans softly.

'Babe, try and think about something else. I promise you, by the morning you won't even remember you got stung. Now why don't you get in the pool with Daddy and your brother... take your mind off it. Go on, love. Don't spoil things for Lucas.'

Grudgingly, Leo joins his father and brother in the pool, studiously ignoring Callie, even when she politely introduces herself.

Lucas on the other hand has doggy-paddled himself right up to her and is demanding she watches while he pretends to dive.

'Ooh, I can do that, too,' Callie says, holding her nose and shoving her head and shoulders under the water.

Sheena cackles. 'I think Lucas might have met his match.'

Laughing with her, Emma stretches and gets up. 'Do you mind watching Callie while I pop inside for a second, only Ryan'll be so crabby if I leave him asleep.'

'You make him sound like a toddler, but yes, of course.' Sheena giggles, gets up from her sunbed, and peels off her shorts and T-shirt to reveal a well-cut scarlet one-piece.

Emma grins. 'Cheers. I'll be two minutes,' she says, thinking her new friend would look at home in an episode of *Baywatch*.

CHAPTER SEVEN

As one long sun-filled day melds into the next, the Burrows fall into a routine of visiting the beach one day and hanging out at the pool the next. It's a gentle pattern that suits them, particularly as Callie and Lucas have become firm friends, competing against each other in the water and chatting away like an old married couple when they think nobody is listening, leaving their parents shaking with mirth. Even eight-year-old Leo has cheered up, occasionally joining in with the younger kids or reading his boys' adventure annuals while the adults chat or sunbathe.

It surprises Emma just how much she enjoys Sheena's company on poolside days, to the point of wondering if she might be neglecting Ryan and excluding him from conversations. She says as much after a morning spent laughing at Sheena's featherbrained anecdotes, interweaved with sharing confidences about family and friends back home.

Unperturbed, Ryan is quick to reassure Emma that he's happy if she's happy. 'Anyway,' he adds wryly, 'Jack's a top bloke so there's always plenty for us to talk about.'

Emma agrees. 'Yes, I like him. He's nice; they all are,' she says, relieved that Ryan has dropped his original *don't get involved with the neighbours* stance, and that he appears to be enjoying Jack's friendship as much as she appreciates Sheena's.

Sheena yawns and stretches languidly. 'Hey, guess what? I met the old couple who live here yesterday and they seem lovely,' she says as the two women relax on sunbeds and all three children splash noisily in the pool.

Emma sits up and angles herself towards Sheena. 'Max and John? Yes, they're a great couple, aren't they? To be honest, I feel a bit guilty about them.'

Sheena shifts position and pushes her sunglasses up into her hair. 'Why?'

'Because the day after we arrived,' Emma glances around and lowers her voice, 'they invited us to their place for a so-called snack and ended up putting on quite a lavish meal. I mean, it was kind of a big night. It wasn't just us; a couple who own one of the boutiques on the strip were there, too, with their nephew. Poor thing was like a fish out of water, bless him. Anyway, Max had obviously gone to a lot of effort. And since then, we've barely acknowledged them.'

'What are you two whispering about?' Ryan says, tuning into the conversation.

Sheena winks at Emma. 'Wouldn't *you* like to know? Go on, Emma.'

'Well, it sounds daft now, but at the time, we both felt a bit... under pressure? No, that's not the right phrase really, but we'd only just got here and they're older than us, and we didn't want to create an expectation, you know?'

'Yeah, I get it.' Sheena nods. 'Tell you what though, why don't you and I organise drinks and nibbles for all of us by the pool one evening – maybe even tonight? Then it's not too claustrophobic as it's on neutral territory. What do you think?'

'Sheena, that's a brilliant idea. We could send the boys out for stone-baked pizzas and just throw some salad and crisps together,' Emma says. 'Oh, and plenty of wine and gin – Maxine loves a tipple, I can tell you that much.'

'Perfect. First job is to find out if Max and John are free.'

Emma gets up, blots her glistening face with a towel and reaches for her sarong. 'No time like the present,' she says, tying it into a makeshift halter-neck before striding in the direction of John and Max's villa.

By seven thirty, the stage is set: Ryan and Jack have borrowed a mismatched collection of garden furniture from their respective patios, before duly walking into the village and returning with a stack of freshly made pizzas, along with a crate of salad, ready to be washed, diced and dressed, and served in big ceramic bowls.

'Don't forget these.' Ryan waves two bags of potato chips, each the size of a small pillow.

'Wait, we need music,' Jack says, disappearing inside and returning with a smart speaker and his phone. Moments later, Ibiza chill-out sounds fill the early evening air.

Emma, manning the makeshift bar, looks up to see Max and John emerging from their villa.

Max is all smiles. 'Buenas tardes, my lovelies,' she says, her long black and tan dress swishing at her legs as she walks. 'What a marvellous idea, thank you for this.'

'It was Sheena's idea, but I've been meaning to do something to thank you for the lovely dinner you made,' Emma says.

'We loved having you,' John says, placing a bottle of Bombay Sapphire gin on the table. He winks. 'A small contribution.'

Emma is touched by their generosity. 'Thank you, but you shouldn't have.'

By now, all six adults have congregated around the drinks area as Emma and Sheena mix gin and tonics for Max and John, fill glasses with cava for each other, and hand stubby bottles of Spanish beer to Jack and Ryan, who stand shoulder to shoulder, chests puffed, bickering good-naturedly about football.

Nearby the children glug cola, enjoying the novelty of eating dinner outside. Callie, never far from her tablet, is soon showing Lucas and Leo her favourite games and puzzles as the three of them crowd around the screen.

Two drinks in, the couples sit down, happy to relax as the alcohol begins to take effect. The conversation butterflies from one topic to the next, light and increasingly irreverent and amusing.

As dusk falls, Sheena is first to mention the children's bedtime. 'If I don't get the boys down soon, tomorrow will be a bloody nightmare,' she tells Emma under her breath. Then louder: 'Come on, kids, bedtime for little ones.'

There's a hail of objections from all three children, but Sheena is having none of it.

'Leo, Lucas, if you're not in bed within fifteen minutes, you can kiss goodbye to swimming tomorrow. It's that simple.'

Callie runs to hug Emma and beams up at her. '*I* don't have to go, do I, Mummy?'

'I'm afraid you do, sweet pea, or you'll be too tired to play tomorrow, like Sheena said. Come on, say goodnight to everyone.' Emma catches Sheena's eye. 'Shame. Just when we were getting started.'

Sheena's eyes glitter with mischief. 'The party's not over – not by a long chalk. I thought we could stick Callie in with the boys and take it in shifts. I'll go first, then someone can relieve me in half an hour and so on. Ryan can carry Callie back to her own bed later. Job done.'

Emma hesitates. 'I don't know... won't the kids see it as an excuse to mess around?'

Right on cue, Lucas yawns, staggers as though drunk, and hangs on to Jack's thigh for support.

Sheena nods towards him. 'Lucas is shattered; I bet they all are. I reckon they'll pass out within ten minutes.'

With a tightness in her chest she recognises as guilt, Emma creeps back to the party having tucked Callie in beside Lucas, who'd sweetly lain his head against her shoulder.

'She'll be fine,' Sheena said. 'I'll be in the next room, and someone can relieve me in thirty or forty minutes. Now *go*. Relax, have a drink, woman; you're on holiday.'

Emma returns to find Ryan holding court. He opens his arms. 'Hey, gorgeous, what are you drinking? We were about to start the dancing; Max is going to show us how it's done.'

Max's expression is coy. 'I may do... given the right motivation – and the right music, of course.'

'*Oh*. Well, what's it going to be? I like a challenge,' Jack says playfully.

Max indicates the smart speaker. 'Does that thing play the Rolling Stones?'

'That *thing* will play anything I tell it to.' Jack reaches for his mobile phone and begins to scroll.

A moment later, John and Max are strutting and twirling, urging the others to join them.

Ryan draws Emma close. 'Look at these two,' he whispers. 'Hope we're like them at their age.'

'I do, too,' Emma says, realising Ryan may be a little drunk.

'Come on, Jack! Shake a leg,' Max cries, moving

rhythmically, her arms waving over her head like a sixties go-go dancer.

Jack raises a hand. 'Oh, no. Not me – Sheena's the dancer in our family.'

Ryan hiccups loudly. 'Lame, mate, very lame. I insist you dance with my wife while I nip to the loo.' He detaches from Emma, pinching her bottom through her thin sundress before heading indoors.

Jack shrugs, laughing awkwardly. 'You heard the man. Shall we?'

Embarrassed and a little bit tipsy, Emma follows Jack to where the older couple are twisting and shaking with considerable vigour as the Rolling Stones' familiar riffs fill the air.

She smiles encouragement as Jack stomps his way through a series of uncoordinated dad dance moves, noticing for the first time how handsome he is, despite the slight paunch and his unkempt hair and beard.

'Jack, I'm sorry, I've realised I don't even know what you do,' Emma says, reverting to small talk.

Grinning, Jack holds his hands up in submission. 'I'm an accountant, but don't let that put you off. I'm a right handful once I get going.' He laughs, reaching for Emma, jerking her towards him and catching her off balance so she has to steady herself against his broad chest. Soon they are throwing shapes and singing along with Mick Jagger, while howling with laughter.

'Hey, what have I missed?' Ryan says, rejoining the group. He smiles at John and Max as they continue to gyrate, then is startled as Emma, steered by Jack, almost slams into him. 'Whoa, hello! Someone's going for it tonight.' There's a note of amusement in his voice.

Soon they are shuffling as a group, egging each other on,

caught up in the music, until Jack abruptly stops dancing. 'Right, I'd better relieve Sheena. Have fun, you two,' he says, weaving towards his villa without a backward glance.

Emma flashes Ryan a desperate look. 'Do you think he's a bit too drunk to babysit? I mean, what if something happens and one of the kids is ill—'

'Em, relax. If anything happens, he'll come and get us, won't he? Jack's a responsible adult who loves the bones of those boys. You don't think for a minute he'd put them, or Callie, at risk, do you?'

Ryan resumes dancing but is distracted by something over Emma's shoulder. She turns to watch Sheena glide towards them in a cloud of exotic fragrance.

'Wow, you look amazing,' Emma says, taken aback as she eyes Sheena's white lace mini dress and the gold gladiator sandals that accentuate her brown toned legs. With the moonlight on her face, and strands of silky hair caught by the evening breeze, she looks bewitching.

Sheena rolls her eyes dismissively. 'Ahh, thanks. I changed cos I felt a bit frumpy in my shorts, and you and Max look so glam I thought I'd better raise my game.' She laughs and takes Emma's arm without acknowledging Ryan. With a pang of dismay, Emma can see him trying not to stare, while failing spectacularly.

Max's eyes sweep over Sheena's outfit and she nods her approval. 'Well, don't *you* look a picture!'

There's a lull in the music. 'Someone else's turn to choose,' Max says, tottering towards a seat, fanning a hand in front of her face. John follows, stopping by the bar area to top up both their drinks.

Soon Emma, Ryan and Sheena are moving rhythmically to an old-school *Ministry of Sound* compilation that Ryan has put on.

'Oh, I love this, turn it up,' Sheena says, her movements becoming more sensual.

Max gets up stiffly. 'Time for us to hit the hay,' she calls over the music. 'Thanks so much for a lovely evening. Goodnight.' She and John wave, then walk the few steps home arm in arm.

Now, without the buffer of Max and John, the shift in atmosphere is palpable. Ryan is openly gaping at Sheena, hypnotised by her graceful dance moves, leaving Emma feeling foolish and increasingly surplus to requirements. She glances at her watch and discovers forty minutes have passed since Jack went inside to watch the children, meaning it's either her turn or Ryan's.

She chews her lip. As little as she wants to leave her drunk husband alone with Sheena, she's loath to come across as the bossy jealous wife and make an idiot of herself. It feels like a no-win situation.

Thinking of sweet and affable Jack, she takes the lesser of two evils: surely nothing will happen on his watch.

'My turn to watch the kids. I'll send Jack out,' Emma announces, her smile stretched and forced.

'Okay, love,' Ryan says, his gaze still on Sheena who is barely moving now, her eyes closed and her head thrown back as though in a distant reverie.

Once inside Jack and Sheena's villa, the music is a soft drone, and as Emma's eyes adjust to the dimness, she finds Jack slumped on the sofa, mouth open and snoring like a wart hog.

So much for watching the children!

She pads upstairs and is relieved to find all three little ones asleep in the back bedroom, Callie's arm thrown across Lucas's chest, while Leo is starfished on the bed opposite.

Castigating herself for what she is about to do, yet powerless to stop herself, Emma tiptoes to the front bedroom with its view of the pool terrace. Then, with Sheena's heady perfume still hanging in the air, she goes to the window and peers out.

Illuminated by the pool lights and a few remaining candles, Emma can see Ryan and Sheena as they slow dance, their bodies pressed together as they sway to the music; Sheena's slender arms draped around Ryan's neck, laughing with abandon, head thrown back, mouth open.

Emma's breath comes in tight, painful gasps and nausea roils in her stomach.

'Please, God... not again, not here,' she whispers into the dark.

CHAPTER EIGHT

It's gone eight o'clock when Emma surfaces. Leaving Ryan asleep, she pulls on shorts and a vest, puts her head around Callie's door and finds her sleeping, then goes downstairs to make tea.

Clutching her mug, she puts the front door on the latch and wanders barefoot to the pool terrace where the only clues to last night's gathering are a handful of burned-down candle stubs and a few garden chairs askew.

Grateful for a moment's solitude, she sits sipping the hot tea and tries to clear her head.

Last night had started well enough, with all six adults in high spirits and the children playing harmoniously together. But later, after Max and John had gone to bed, alcohol had taken its toll, leaving Jack passed out indoors when he should have been watching the children, and Ryan and Sheena smooching like teenagers at a school disco.

With a queasy feeling in her gut, Emma recalls spying on them from Jack and Sheena's bedroom window. She'd watched, with mounting dread, heart racing, mouth dry, for a few minutes, before snapping back to herself, knowing that it was up to her to break things up, and with as much decorum and nonchalance as she could muster if she wanted to keep the peace and spare everyone's blushes.

So, she'd marched outside and pasted on a good-natured grin as she approached Ryan and Sheena. 'Hey, I think it's time we called it a night. Poor Jack's fast asleep on the sofa and I'm dead on my feet, to be honest.'

Ryan, slow to react, had staggered slightly, then spread his arms; loose, drunk arms that told her he'd been using Sheena as much for support as for affection. 'Sure, whenever you're ready, love,' he'd said, a languid smile spreading across his boyish face.

Sheena, on the other hand, had been much more lucid. 'Jack's asleep? Oh for God's sake. He just *goes*, always been the same. Life and soul one minute, then zonk.' She'd mimed sleeping standing up before grabbing Emma's arm. 'Men, bloody hopeless. Don't worry, *we'll* clear up *and* sort the kids.'

Then leaving Ryan to weave unsteadily back to the villa, Emma and Sheena had collected up the debris, blown out the candles and between them, gently extracted Callie from Lucas's embrace before Emma had carried her daughter home.

'It's okay,' Ryan said, hovering at the bottom of the stairs, his expression sheepish. 'I'll take her up. I'm not that drunk, just tired.'

Moments later, with Callie tucked up in her own bed and Ryan passed out in theirs, Emma had lain awake, mulling over the night's events.

Had she jumped to conclusions, seeing flirtations where there were none? After all, she and Jack had danced together earlier in the evening and at times, it had been quite physical. In addition, neither Ryan nor Sheena had looked the least bit guilty or caught out when she'd reappeared and abruptly ended the evening.

Conversely, Sheena had been brilliant: going around collecting rubbish and tidying up as though she'd gained a second wind – not the behaviour of a woman busted for flirting with someone else's husband.

Sleep had claimed Emma soon after that; her final thought being that it wasn't Sheena's fault Ryan had form. To be fair to her new friend, it wasn't anybody's problem but her and Ryan's. What was done was done. Emma had forgiven him – or at least compartmentalised his behaviour and moved on. No way would she let something that had happened almost two years earlier impact on a much-needed family holiday.

Feeling calmer and more upbeat, Emma drains her cup and wonders how late it is and who else is up. She stands, rotates her shoulders and stretches while gazing at the pool. The surface ripples gently, stirred by a light breeze. At the far end, where the water is at its deepest, something catches her eye: something dark and compact.

Emma walks around the pool, then squats to peer into its depths. There, on the tiled bottom, is Callie's tablet. 'Shit,' she says aloud, 'how the hell did *that* get there?'

'Darling, I'm not cross, I promise. Just tell me; what was your tablet doing in the swimming pool?' Ryan asks, his tone patient.

'I already told you, Daddy, I don't know!' Callie says, her voice high-pitched with frustration.

Emma throws Ryan a warning look: if Callie has any clue how her tablet ended up under water, she is not sharing it.

Emma had wasted no time in retrieving it, of course, before drying it thoroughly, first with a towel then with a cool blast from her hairdryer. But still Callie's tablet remained resolutely dark and lifeless.

Ryan, mildly hungover after their late night, had shaken his head. 'Love, forget it, it's gone. These things happen. I'll get her another one when we get home. It's not the expense – although they're not cheap – I just want to know what happened and I don't know why Callie won't tell us.'

Gently, Emma tries again. 'Sweet pea, could you have dropped it by accident when you were showing it to the boys last night, while the grown-ups were talking?'

'No, Mummy. I *said*, I don't know how it happened. It wasn't me,' Callie repeats, her cheeks growing hot beneath her tan.

Ryan opens his arms and gathers his daughter in. 'It's okay, baby. I'll buy you another one when we get home,' he croons, stroking Callie's hair until she wriggles from his grasp and runs upstairs to look for another toy to take outside.

Emma waits until Callie is out of earshot. 'What do you think?'

Ryan shrugs. 'Honestly? I suspect one of the lads next door swiped the tablet off her and threw it in.'

Emma gasps. 'What! Why do you say that?'

'Because Leo's a whiny little kid at the best of times, and I think he's got a spiteful streak. I was watching them playing together last night – Leo snatching stuff off the younger ones. He's got a real sense of entitlement.'

'Ry, he's only eight. That's a terrible thing to say about a child.' Emma puffs out her cheeks. 'Still, if you really think that's what happened, we need to speak to Jack and Sheena, see if we can get to the truth.' She clams up as Callie returns, clutching two small sparkly figurines.

'Are we going to the beach today?' she asks.

'Yeah, soon.' Ryan nods. 'I just need to pop next door – say hi to our neighbours. Why don't you and Mummy sit in the garden for a bit, eh?'

'Okay, Daddy.' Callie skips out of the back door, muttering to her toys.

Emma frowns. 'Love, for goodness' sake, be tactful. You can't just barge in and accuse Leo of throwing Callie's tablet in the pool. If it goes down badly, it could ruin the rest of our holiday – theirs, too.'

'What do you take me for? I'll just ask the question, that's all. If it was an accident, I'm sure Leo will own up and apologise.'

Emma's head begins to throb. 'Maybe we should say nothing, just leave it, you know?'

'Like I said, I'll knock on the door and just ask, okay?'

'All right. Who will you speak to? Jack or Sheena?' *The woman you were all over like a rash last night*, she adds in her head.

'What a weird question. Whoever answers the door. Now, give me five minutes and then we'll head out to the beach.'

Five minutes pass, then fifteen, and after forty minutes, during which time Emma has cleaned the kitchen surfaces, bleached the sink, and made a fresh pot of coffee in an attempt to keep busy, Ryan returns, his expression closed.

'Well?'

'Surprise, surprise, both Leo and Lucas deny all knowledge. Sheena asked them right in front of me and they both said they hadn't touched it. Then again, they would say that, wouldn't they?'

Emma shrugs. 'I don't know, would they? Guess we'll never know. So, how are Jack and Sheena this morning? Did they enjoy last night?' she asks, keen to change the subject.

'Sheena said she did. I didn't see Jack; he's in the village picking up a few bits.'

'Oh, okay. But you were gone ages.'

Ryan feigns surprise. 'Was I? Sheena offered me a coffee. I thought it only polite to say *yes*, seeing as I'd practically accused her kids of wrecking Callie's tablet.'

'Ah. Shame, I've just made a pot... don't suppose you'll want another one?'

'No thanks, I'll be wired if I do.'

Emma looks away. 'Of course. So, did you chat much? To Sheena, I mean?'

Ryan frowns. 'A bit... nothing memorable. Em, what are you getting at? I thought you liked Jack and Sheena.'

'I do, they're a nice couple. I just wondered what you talked about, that's all.' Emma can feel the heat creeping into her cheeks.

'No, you're worried. I can tell. You're checking up on me.' Ryan glances towards the garden where Callie sits chatting away to herself. He lowers his voice. 'We've *got* to get past this. It's been ages since...' He closes his eyes, allows his head to loll back. 'Don't you think I regret what happened, every single bloody day?'

'Do you though, Ryan? Or do you just regret that I found out about it?' Emma hisses as tears spring into her eyes. 'Tell me this – and I want the truth – do you fancy Sheena? I wouldn't blame you, she's gorgeous... tall, skinny, with really cool hair and—'

'No, I don't fancy her. I said I didn't, so just stop it, will you?'

'Ryan, I saw you together last night. Dancing. Did you kiss her? I mean, you looked close enough to.'

Ryan's eyes widen. 'What? No, *of course* I didn't kiss her. And you can hardly call it dancing, we were just... you know, shuffling about. Emma, there's only one woman I fancy and that's you. Now are we taking Callie to the beach today or are we going to spend hours raking over old wounds and hurting each other again?'

'Beach,' Emma whispers, wiping her eyes and going off to change.

CHAPTER NINE

Relaxed and happy after three hours of sunbathing and splashing around in the warm sea, Emma grasps Ryan's hand as the three of them trudge home along the stony track.

As they pass the rancid smelling bins on the edge of the development, Callie holds her nose dramatically and feigns gagging.

'It's just rubbish, silly, same as at home,' Emma says.

Ryan grimaces. 'But she has a point; it stinks in this heat.'

Emerging into the lush communal area, they find Max and John in their garden, each wielding secateurs in one hand and what looks suspiciously like a G&T in the other. On the ground between them sits a small mound of browning plant debris. The couple wave and raise their glasses as the Burrows wander past.

'We should say hello,' Emma says, breaking her stride and going over to their plot, with Ryan and Callie at her heels.

Ryan grins. 'Now *that* looks tempting – might join you later,' he says, eyeing their drinks as they sparkle in the sunlight.

'Yes, do join us. John, fetch two more glasses,' Max instructs grandly.

Emma laughs. 'Thanks, Max, but he doesn't mean right

now,' she says, eager to avert a misunderstanding. 'For one thing, we all need a shower.'

Max waves a hand. 'It's only sand. Lovely get-together last night. It was kind of you young people to organise something. We enjoyed having a bop, didn't we, John?'

John nods. 'You've still got it, my love.'

'Gosh, they start early,' Emma says once Max and John are out of earshot and they're approaching their own front door.

'That's the expat lifestyle for you,' Ryan says as they dump sandy flip-flops and beach bags by the entrance. 'And anyway, what's that expression? It's five o'clock somewhere?'

Emma turns her attention to Callie. 'Right, trouble, straight upstairs. Swimsuit off and I'll be up in two minutes to shower with you, okay?'

'Okay,' Callie says, taking the stairs. Moments later, she lets out a piercing scream. 'Daddy!'

Alarmed, the two of them rush upstairs and into Callie's room, where she stands rooted to the spot, eyes wide with shock. 'Mummy! Look, a big mouse and I think he died,' she wails, pointing to her bed.

'Oh Christ,' Ryan says, disgust evident on his face. 'Emma, take her down, will you. I'll sort this.'

'What's wrong with mousey? Why did he die?' Callie sobs, unable to look away, despite Emma's efforts to block her view of the poor dead creature.

'Emma, please! Go downstairs, both of you.'

'Come on. There's nothing we can do for him.' Emma ushers Callie down the stairs and out of the house, her instinct leading her as far from the source of upset as possible.

Outside, she finds Sheena hovering, her expression quizzical.

'Hiya. Everything all right? Only I thought I heard a scream.'

Emma shakes her head. 'We're fine, or we will be... Actually, Sheena, you couldn't keep Callie for ten or fifteen minutes, could you? I'll explain later.'

'Of course,' Sheena says. 'Callie, come and say hi to Lucas and Leo; they're having crisps and lemonade in the garden. Would you like some, darling?'

Thank you, Emma mouths gratefully, before diving back inside to where Ryan is attempting to eradicate all traces of the rat.

'How the fuck did that get in and why did it have to expire in Callie's room – never mind her actual bed? Jesus! Of all the disgusting things—'

'Where is it?' Emma asks, feeling sick to her stomach.

'It's double bagged in the back garden. I'll take it to the bins in a minute, but first we need to fumigate the whole bloody room.'

They strip Callie's bed, then Emma puts the sheets on to wash, setting the dial to hot. Afterwards, she runs a bucket of soapy water and mops the whole of the first floor thoroughly.

'You know they cause Weil's disease, don't you?' Ryan says. 'So, I'm not sure I want her sleeping in there again.'

Emma shudders. 'I know it's gross, but it'll be fine once everything's been cleaned properly. We'll put her in the other bed, just to be sure.'

Within half an hour, all evidence of the rat has been removed and the room smells clean and citrussy. 'I'd better go and get her,' Emma says. 'It was good of Sheena to take her at no notice like that.'

'It was and I'm sure we'd do the same if something weird happened to them,' Ryan agrees.

Next door, it is Jack who greets Emma, concern etched on his face. 'Hey, come in. All sorted? Callie told us about the, er... big mouse.' He mimes air quotes and waves Emma through to the living room, where Callie, Leo and Lucas are huddled around the coffee table, engrossed in a lively game that involves stacking weirdly shaped objects until they topple. To Emma's relief, Callie shows no outward signs of trauma.

In the adjacent kitchen, Sheena, who has started prepping the boys' tea, beckons Emma over.

'Just so you know, I explained to Callie that poor mousey was very old and that her bed must have looked like a nice comfy place to rest.' She glances to where the children are playing and lowers her voice. 'We had a few tears, but then she forgot all about it. Awful for you though; must have been a terrible shock.'

'Yeah, you could say that. Ryan's fuming.'

Sheena bites her lip. 'I'm not surprised. Hey, if the two of you need to decompress, Callie's welcome to have tea with the boys – it's only fish fingers, chips, and salad.'

Emma frowns. 'Are you sure?'

'Yes, of course. What's one more little mouth at the table? And Lucas will *love* it. I swear he adores Callie.'

'Then, thank you, that's really kind,' Emma says. 'Tell you what, why don't Ryan and I have the boys tomorrow evening? Give you and Jack a break.'

Sheena looks chuffed. 'Really, you'd do that? Thank you, that would be lovely.'

Then Emma glances across at her daughter and does a double take. Embarrassed, she covers her eyes. 'Oh my God, look at her. Still in her grubby swimming costume! She was about to jump in the shower when the rat thing happened. I'll just pop next door and get her some clean clothes – two ticks.'

Emma trots to their villa and returns moments later, clutching a neat pile of clean clothing for Callie, before helping her to change in the downstairs cloakroom.

'There, all fresh and comfy again,' Sheena says. 'Now you and Ryan can relax and get your breath back after a nasty shock. Have fun, see you when we see you, okay?'

Showered and fragrant, Emma and Ryan wander into the village, pausing outside a bar where people are drinking wine in the early evening sun.

'I could murder a drink,' Ryan says, eyeing a tray of cold beers as they are carried past.

'Me too.' Emma sighs. 'What a weird and quite horrible day.'

'You're not wrong. Shall we?' Ryan walks up to the entrance, signals to the waiter and orders a beer for himself and a glass of white Rioja for Emma. He gestures towards a free table. 'Maybe we can get some tapas; don't think I can stomach a proper meal tonight.'

Emma nods. 'Tapas sounds great. Poor Callie. First, we find her tablet under water and completely ruined; next, a dead rat turns up in her bed! You couldn't make it up. I only hope there's no lasting damage. An experience like that could scar her for life.'

'What I want to know is how both incidents happened.' Ryan scowls, takes a glug of cold beer and sets it down, licking his lips.

'Cheers.' Emma raises her glass and takes a sip. 'Sheena told Callie that the big mouse was old and that her bed looked like a cosy place to rest. If only *that* were true.'

Ryan scoffs. 'That thing was putrid. I reckon someone killed it and put it in her room.'

'Love, that's ridiculous, as if anyone would do such a thing. For a start, the house was locked and nobody could get in.'

'Ahh, you don't know that. What if a disgruntled maid or cleaner put it there to make trouble for the villa's owner... you just don't know what people get up to.'

Emma shakes her head. 'Ryan, that's horrible. And a bit far-fetched. It's more likely that there are rats on the beach and that someone put poison down to get rid of them.' She pauses, unsure of where she's going with her theory. 'And... and then some poor creature staggered into our back garden in its death throes, waddled upstairs and died.'

'Oh, so you're going with Sheena's theory?'

'We should ask Max and John tomorrow – they'll know if there's been an infestation recently. It wouldn't surprise me if there are rats hanging round the bin shed.' Emma shudders. 'The seamy side of our holiday paradise. Ry, can we please change the subject – the whole thing's creeping me out.'

'Of course.' Ryan downs the rest of his beer and reaches for a menu.

CHAPTER TEN

The following morning, Ryan stands at the front door, watching the rain fall. 'Great. That's all we need,' he says.

Emma leans against him and looks up at the slate sky. 'It's fine. It'll blow over by this afternoon, you watch. We can't complain; the weather's been perfect since we got here.'

'Yeah, I guess.' Ryan raises his hand to John and Max as they emerge from their villa, looking smart and purposeful. They wave back before getting into their car and pulling away smoothly.

'Wonder where they're off to,' he mutters, shutting the front door and sitting heavily on one of the leather sofas. 'That reminds me, I need to speak to John about the mouse.'

Callie's eyes widen in horror. 'Daddy, don't! It's too sad – I don't want to think about him.'

Emma shoots Ryan a look of disbelief. 'I'm with Callie; we don't need to talk about it, do we? Now, how about we play a nice board game, or we can watch a DVD – there's quite a selection in the—'

The chime of the doorbell cuts her short. She glances at Ryan, who shrugs and gets up.

Eavesdropping, Emma stiffens at the sound of Sheena's voice, noting the way Ryan's tone brightens at once.

There's a brief exchange of pleasantries as their voices draw closer. 'Yeah, why not? Sounds good... come through,' Ryan is saying, a relaxed smile on his face. 'Em, Sheena wants to invite you somewhere.'

Sheena bounces into the room. 'Hiya, Callie,' she says before turning to Emma. 'I just thought, as it's raining, if you haven't got plans, there's a spa I'd like to visit. Do you fancy coming with me? I picked up a flyer in the village the other day. It's in a hotel, quite smart. There's a gym, an indoor spa pool, as well as an outdoor pool, and a beauty salon. I thought we could have a little workout then get our nails done, or even a facial. Only if you fancy it though, obvs.'

Feeling trapped under the weight of Sheena's enthusiasm, Emma hesitates. She pictures her, toned and trim in workout clothes, parading her flawless body in the gym, while other women stare enviously...

'That sounds lovely, Sheena, but I'm not really one for the gym, and I haven't got any kit here,' she says, finding her voice.

Sheena is undeterred. 'No problem, I've got a spare set. Oh, go on, it'll be fun.'

Emma glances desperately at Ryan, willing him to step in with a valid reason why she shouldn't go off with Sheena, but none is forthcoming.

She puffs out her cheeks. 'Okay, thanks. I'll keep you company if you like. And as you say, a manicure would be good.' She glances at her short practical nails. 'I could certainly do with one.'

Sheena gives a lady-like little fist pump. 'Yay! Oh, that's fab.' She leans over and nudges Ryan, who hovers, his expression bemused. 'Hey, you know what that means... the daddies are in charge.' She shakes her head in mock despair. 'Oh my God, you want to keep Jack company? Share the load, so to speak.' She laughs and starts for the door. 'Give me a knock when you're ready, Emma. I'll drive. It's only twenty minutes from here,' she calls, letting herself out.

'And breathe,' Ryan whispers. 'Look, I know what you're thinking, but she's right; it *will* be fun. And don't worry about the gym, just have a walk on the treadmill, do some hand weights and then hit the beauty salon – if they can squeeze you in, of course.'

Feeling slightly railroaded, Emma shakes her head. 'Sheena's sweet, but she's a bit forceful. Still, I guess I'm committed now. Are you sure you're okay looking after Callie for a few hours?'

Ryan grins. 'Don't you worry about us.' He raises his voice. 'We'll be fine hanging out here, won't we, stinker?'

Callie nods vigorously. 'Oh, *yes*, Daddy.'

Sheena rattles along at a little over the speed limit, windscreen wipers going full tilt, and chatting all the while. 'Ooh, this looks posh,' she says, sounding impressed as they drive into the spa hotel's car park full of expensive SUVs and sports cars. She laughs. 'And look at us, slumming it in a hire car.' She gives Emma's forearm a little squeeze. 'Ah, thanks for coming. I'm so pleased you did. Your face when I knocked, I thought you were going to blow me out. Right, got your kit?'

Touched by Sheena's show of friendship, Emma smiles back. 'I've got *your* kit – thanks for the loan. I'm afraid you'll have to remind me how everything works once we get inside; can't remember the last time I was in a gym.'

'That's handy then. Did I mention I used to be a fitness instructor before I had the kids?' Sheena grabs her bag and gets out of the car. 'Anyway, it was just an excuse to escape for an hour or two. Know what I mean?'

Emma nods, unsure what Sheena is pleased to escape *from*.

They enter through sliding doors that part to reveal the hotel's pale luxe interior.

'Hola.' Sheena beams, marching straight up to the reception desk where a reed-thin blonde woman, who looks more Scandinavian than Spanish, greets them cooly.

'We'd like two half day spa passes, please,' Sheena says.

The receptionist raises one immaculate eyebrow. 'Are you a member, madam?'

'No, but I picked this up in town.' Sheena fishes a printed flyer from her bag. 'It says here: *day guests welcome*.'

The blonde gives Sheena a curt nod. 'Indeed. Non-residents may stay for up to five hours and the price is one hundred and seventy-five euros, per person, which includes a complimentary mocktail in our spa bar and a luxe goody bag upon departure.'

Emma conceals her horror. She hadn't planned on spending so much, particularly on a jaunt that was practically forced upon her with a woman she hardly knows. Embarrassed, she clams up, expecting Sheena's reaction to match her own.

She's shocked when Sheena produces her debit card without missing a beat. 'Yeah, fab. Whatevs. Stick us both on that, please.'

The receptionist smiles serenely, thawing somewhat now that money is about to change hands. 'Perfect, Mrs Havers,' she says, reading the name on Sheena's bank card. 'My name is Lenna. Please ask if I can help you with anything during your visit.'

Emma starts to protest, but Sheena is already keying in her pin number.

'Thank you, ladies,' Lenna says. 'Please, go through those

doors and turn right. Juan or Mariska will meet you and give you a brief tour of our spa area. Have a great day.'

Sheena arranges her toned limbs into an elegant pose and settles back against the lounger. 'I'm blissed out.' She sighs. 'How about you?'

Emma closes her eyes and inhales the scent of lavender and eucalyptus that fills the air around them. 'I must admit, I feel super relaxed,' she says, her lips curving into a smile as she considers the events of the last two and a half hours.

At Sheena's suggestion, they'd kicked off with a forty-five-minute workout in the hotel's state-of-the-art gym. At first, Emma had felt foolish and clumsy beside her glamazon friend; a feeling that soon passed because from the moment they'd stepped into the air-conditioned space, with its rows of treadmills, static bikes, cross trainers and up-to-the-minute weight machines, Sheena had been nothing but supportive and encouraging.

'That was *so* much better than I expected,' Emma said afterwards, her face flushed and her limbs tingling from exertion as they headed to the changing rooms together. After showering, they'd put on bathing suits and entered the hushed fragrant spa.

'What do you reckon, a quick twenty lengths then get our nails done?' Sheena said, going straight to the pool's edge and sliding gracefully into the water.

Emma laughed. 'Not sure I've got it in me after that workout,' she said, joining Sheena in the water. 'You're amazing, you know that? I don't know where you get your energy.'

'High on life, babe,' Sheena said, striking out and powering through the water.

Twenty minutes later, with even Sheena claiming

exhaustion, the women hauled themselves out of the pool, showered again and dried off briskly, before putting on cosy complimentary robes and entering the spa's beauty zone. Soon they were seated side by side in the manicure studio where two technicians administered gel nails. Then, feeling relaxed and groomed, they'd padded back towards the pool, grabbed a pair of sunbeds, and ordered delicious tropical mocktails and nibbles.

Emma studies her brand-new fingernails. 'Not sure what Ryan will think about my Tangerine Dream nails. He's funny about things like that, prefers me more natural-looking.'

Sheena makes a face. 'Never mind what *he* thinks! If you like them, that's all that matters. Anyway, they look fab with a tan.'

Emma scoffs. 'What tan? I've hardly changed colour. Not like Ryan and Callie, they've only got to look at the sun to go bronze.'

'Emma, stop it. You do that too often,' Sheena says, sternly.

Emma is taken aback. 'What? What do you mean?'

'Putting yourself down. I don't think you know you're doing it. I can tell it's second nature.' Sheena sits up straighter and meets Emma's eyes. 'Well, newsflash, you're bloody gorgeous – same as me, ha! – deal with it.'

'Well, I wouldn't say gorge—'

'See, there you go again.'

Sheena has touched a nerve and clearly has more emotional intelligence than Emma has given her credit for. She hesitates. 'I'm just not particularly confident these days,' she says, lowering her voice. 'And I hate the way I've changed...' she trails off, aware that it would be all too easy to spill family secrets to a sympathetic stranger.

'Is this because of Ryan? Because if it is, all marriages hit a blip sometimes. It's how you handle them that counts.'

'What makes you say that? Ryan and I are fine... I mean, we're not perfect or anything – who is? – but we're happy enough. He's a fantastic dad to Callie.'

Sheena looks unimpressed. 'Yeah, but is he a good husband to you? I mean, I know we were all a bit drunk the other night, but he's quite a flirty Bertie your Ryan.'

Emma feels her cheeks flush and her pulse quicken. At once, her mind returns to the image of a woman's face: long auburn hair framing an ivory complexion, full red lips parted in a sensual smile. Flustered, she shuts the thought down and refocuses on Sheena.

Had Ryan come onto Sheena when he thought no one was watching? She pictures them dancing together, Sheena's arms entwined around his neck. If Ryan *had* flirted with her, it was surely because he'd been given the green light—

'Sorry, I wasn't suggesting that Ryan cheats or anything,' Sheena says, inspecting her electric blue nails. 'Me and my big mouth.'

'No, you're right. Ryan *is* a flirt, and there's nothing he loves more than female attention. And he gets it, in spades,' Emma adds tartly, 'especially with a bit of encouragement. What can I say? He's good-looking and confident... women always hit on him. It's something I've learned to live with.'

Sheena reaches for Emma's hand and gives it a little squeeze. 'Look, Emma, I can tell you're getting upset. It's none of my business what goes on with you two – hey, we've only known each other ten minutes – but you don't need to worry about me, okay? I love my husband. I'm mad about the daft sod, actually. This might be TMI, but I fancy him like you wouldn't believe, and he's perfect for me in every way. He's kind, funny, great with the kids. Oh, and did I mention he earns a shedload of money?' She cackles and rolls her eyes. 'Jack tells everyone he's an accountant, but he owns the company. He's got about sixty people working for him at the moment.' She shakes her head. 'Sorry, I talk too much, it's my biggest fault.'

'Don't apologise, it's good to chat,' Emma says, relieved the subject has shifted away from her marriage.

'Yeah, well, I'm even worse since I lost a close friend. We used to tell each other everything, we could talk all night... about any old nonsense and end up laughing our heads off, you know?'

'Sorry to hear you lost someone close,' Emma says, meaning it. 'Was she poorly?'

Sheena hesitates. 'Kind of... oof, I'm welling up here. I need to change the subject. I shouldn't have mentioned her.' She clears her throat. 'Anyway, you don't need to worry about me around your husband. I'm a woman's woman and it's *you* I want to hang out with.'

'Bless you, Sheena, and thanks for bringing me here today. I've had a lovely time, although you shouldn't have paid for both of us. I'll get Ryan to pay you back.' Emma sighs. 'I suppose we'd better head back soon. Goodness knows what our husbands have been up to while we've been sitting here, putting the world to rights.'

Sheena grins. 'I'm sure they coped. Hey, before we go, let's get a few pics for Insta.' She picks up her mobile, strikes a flattering pose, arching her back and pouting. 'I love a selfie, me,' she says, laughing at herself. 'Come on, one of us together, don't leave me looking like Billy No-Mates.'

Reluctantly, Emma poses cheek to cheek with Sheena.

'You look fab,' Sheena says, tapping the screen to blow up the image. 'Shall I take a couple more of you?'

'No thanks. I'm not really into social media,' Emma admits. 'I've got an Instagram account but I can't remember the last time I looked at it, let alone posted anything.'

'It's not everyone's cup of tea,' Sheena says, scrolling. She raises her eyebrows. 'What's your surname? We can follow each other and stay in touch when we get back.'

'It's Burrows. You'll find me at Emem underscore Burrows. That's what my parents call me.'

'Emem – ahh, that's sweet. Thanks!' Sheena slides her phone back into her bag.

CHAPTER ELEVEN

Holding Callie's hand as he walks up the path to Jack and Sheena's villa, Ryan can hear a child wailing. Cringing inwardly, he rings the bell.

'Mate,' Jack says, opening the door wearing an expression of controlled patience.

'Hey, have I come at a bad time?'

'No, no. Come in.' Jack steps aside and lowers his voice. 'Leo's having a bit of a meltdown, he can be clingy with Sheena, and he doesn't like surprises. He'll be fine in a minute. Still raining?'

'It is. Fancy a walk down to the sea though? It's not like it's cold and some fresh air might do us all good,' Ryan suggests tactfully.

Fifteen minutes later, Ryan, Jack and all three children are straggling along the beach path.

'Why are we *here*?' Leo moans. 'It's raining.'

Jack lays a hand on his son's shoulder and gently propels

him forward. 'Mate, we're having an adventure. Come on, you'll enjoy it when we get there.'

'I *won't*,' Leo says, stamping along, his face like thunder.

'Look!' Callie cries as they near the shoreline. 'What are the black bits, Daddy?'

'Seaweed, Cal,' Ryan says, inhaling the sulphurous smell and taking in the frill of debris that has washed up overnight. 'Must have been a storm out at sea – not that I heard anything.' He laughs without humour. 'A couple of beers and I'm out cold these days, must be getting old.'

Jack nods. 'I thought I heard a distant rumble of thunder, but it wasn't that close. Sheena and I ended up having quite a late one...' Jack trails off, his lascivious smirk leaving Ryan in no doubt as to why he'd been late getting to sleep.

There's a lull in the conversation as the two men fall in step. They watch the children run and play ahead, calling to each other, squatting to pick up shells and pebbles at the water's edge. The sea resembles churned-up dishwater and the waves roll in fast and high, a far cry from the turquoise millpond they are used to.

Jack nods thoughtfully. 'Yeah, that's the thing about Sheena,' he says. 'She's always up for it.'

Astonished by Jack's candour, Ryan gives an awkward little shrug. 'Well, then... you're a lucky man,' he says eventually, thinking, *but why the fuck are you telling me?*

'Only, the thing is, people get the wrong idea about Sheena, you know?'

Ryan frowns. 'Not sure that I do.'

'Just because she's chatty and friendly – and obviously incredibly beautiful – they think she's fair game. You'd be amazed by how many blokes come onto her and assume she's flirting with them. Luckily for me, she's a one-man woman.' Jack grins. 'Hey, looks like the bar's open despite the rain. Cheeky beer?'

'Sure, why not,' Ryan says, keen to get off the subject of Sheena.

What exactly is Jack driving at? Because from where he's standing, it sounds an awful lot like Jack is warning him off. Which is ridiculous. Yes, *of course* he fancies Sheena, despite doing his best to convince Emma that the opposite is true. What red-blooded male wouldn't?

Had Jack picked up on something at the party? Certainly, he hadn't been around during the ten or so minutes he'd been alone with Sheena. The smell of her perfume alone had driven him wild that night, let alone what she was wearing. She knew it, too, getting all glammed up in that short lace dress she'd changed into after checking on the kids. She'd mumbled some bullshit about feeling frumpy in shorts compared to Emma and the old lady from next door. As if. The woman would look amazing in a grain sack.

He'd taken a risk that night by holding her in his arms and slow dancing with her. He'd felt the tension in her taut body at first, but after a few minutes, she'd relaxed, kind of melted into him. He'd made her laugh, too – some lame joke he couldn't remember now – and he'd looked into her open mouth, seen those slightly uneven teeth, which only made her hotter in his view: more real and attainable. He'd almost kissed her. And he could tell she was willing him to, but thank God he hadn't acted on impulse because moments later, Emma came charging out, her face hot and blotchy, her voice high-pitched as she pulled the plug on the whole evening. He'd made a fist of looking more drunk than he felt, just in case she'd seen anything... and he'd just about got away with it. Maybe.

'You're miles away, Ryan. You okay?' Jack asks, staring in a way that irritates him. 'Kids! Come on, who wants a Coke and a bag of crisps?' he yells, shepherding them up the beach towards Juan's Café.

Callie runs to Ryan's side, catching him off guard by throwing her arms around him. 'This is for you, Daddy,' she says, giving him a perfect pale grey shell. 'It's magic.'

A jolt of shame hits him. What the hell is he doing even *thinking* about another man's wife? He's already on probation and they've barely recovered from the last time.

One more slip – so much as a flirtation – and Emma could walk. And for good this time. And then he would lose her. Lose everything: his wife, his daughter, his home. Unthinkable.

The rain has stopped and the sun is a flash of silver behind the clouds. Just as Emma predicted before she and Sheena set off for their spa day. A shudder washes over him out of nowhere. He needs to get a grip, step up and be the man his family deserves.

He glances at Jack, who is now focused solely on his sons. As any good father should be.

Ryan raises Callie onto his shoulders. 'Thank you for my magic shell, sweet pea. I love it and I love you,' he says while she squeals in mock protest.

CHAPTER TWELVE

THEN

Emma lies rigid and sleepless, her ears cocked for the sound of a taxi. She reaches for her mobile phone on the nightstand: it's 2.10am.

Where the hell is Ryan? The pubs have been closed for hours, and even the clubs on the strip in Maidstone town centre close by midnight on Thursdays. The day before, he'd warned her he'd be going out with people from work. That he and several of the team were celebrating the completion of a major project; one that had netted the company its biggest profit to date. A complex basement renovation at a villa in Tunbridge Wells that had included a subterranean swimming pool, hot tub, and gym for an eye-watering budget. As project manager, Ryan had worked tirelessly with the architect and the construction team to deliver the herculean conversion on budget and on time, give or take.

Which was why Emma had encouraged him to go out with the team and get a taxi home from town so he could enjoy a drink or three. To let his hair down – despite the fact that *her* day had been spent mopping up toddler snot and vomit thanks to a combination of a chesty cold and a stomach bug Callie had picked up from a friend's little one. Poor kid. She'd been so brave, hardly grizzling, even after she'd covered herself and Emma in sick shortly after lunch.

Emma stiffens at the distinctive ticking sound of an approaching diesel engine. Thank God, Ryan is home safe. Another half an hour and she would have been tempted to trawl local websites for traffic news or reported accidents. She turns to the wall, scrunches her eyes tight shut, unwilling to get into a conversation about where – and with whom – he has been until this hour.

To Emma's immense relief, the storm in Callie's gut has becalmed overnight, leaving her with just a sniffle, and she wakes up demanding Coco Pops and the small seedless grapes she's partial to.

When Ryan appears, freshly showered and wearing a crisp coral work shirt, Emma is sitting at the kitchen table supervising Callie's breakfast. The TV burbles in the background, its volume on low.

'Hello, my gorgeous girls,' Ryan says, opening the fridge and removing a carton of orange juice. He pours some into a glass. 'Haven't got time for breakfast, I'll have something at my desk.'

Emma watches him gulp the juice in one go. 'Did you have a good night?' she asks, keeping her voice even. 'Only you were pretty late. I woke up around two and you weren't home by then.'

Ryan groans. 'Yeah, sorry. Think I got home shortly after that, glad I didn't wake you.' He shakes his head. 'You can blame Pete Robson. He must feel like crap this morning.'

Emma raises her eyebrows. 'Why? What happened?'

'Oh my God, Em, it would be quite amusing if it wasn't so pathetic. So, poor old Robbo, who by now is at the thin end of an ugly divorce, wanted to celebrate in that club on Fluke Street – you know, the really tacky one, with all the animal prints and fake birds and whatnot where the hen parties go.'

Emma's eyes widen. 'You went there?' She slices a few more grapes and hands them to Callie. 'So, what happened?'

Ryan puts a hand to his forehead and groans again. 'Don't ask. Suffice to say, he was on a mission. He started talking to a couple of girls – well, three to be exact – I mean, the rest of us were mortified, but he's been having a rough time lately and he was enjoying himself... oh, and then the shots arrived. Something vile that you set fire to—'

'Really?' Emma says. 'You seem incredibly together for someone who was drinking Flaming Sambucas until all hours.'

Ryan rolls his eyes. 'If only it had ended there. Next thing, we're out in the cold, tearing round looking for a kebab shop; can't remember the last time I did that. Anyway, we found this dodgy place on Tile Street – they were trying to close up, but in the end they agreed to serve us. So, then we're sitting in the little shelter thing in the town square, freezing our nuts off and eating kebabs like saddos on a Saturday night stag. Suddenly it's gone one o'clock. Of course, by then, all the cabs have vanished for the night. Eventually, we found one poor sod who agreed to take us all on a round trip, which took forever and cost an arm and a leg.' Ryan holds his hands up. 'Not looking for sympathy or anything, but I feel rubbish. Thank God it's Friday and I can knock off at five and get home to my girls. Please tell me we're not doing anything tonight.'

Emma smiles. 'We're not doing anything tonight. Now go... get yourself a bacon sandwich on the way in.'

'Now you mention it, that's exactly what I need.' Ryan pecks Emma's cheek before dropping a kiss on the top of Callie's head. He pauses. 'She seems fine this morning. Must have been a twenty-four hour thing,' he says, almost as an afterthought. 'Okay, must run. Love you both.'

'I love you,' Emma says, noticing how sweet Ryan's breath is, considering the skinful and late-night kebab session.

An hour later, leaving Callie and her favourite teddy snuggled on the kitchen sofa in front of one of her cartoons, Emma jogs upstairs to the laundry basket and gathers up a wash.

There, crumpled but otherwise clean and fragrant, is the shirt Ryan had gone out in the day before. She brings it to her face and inhales, surprised by the light powdery scent around the collar. She examines it carefully, looking for spills of alcohol or chilli sauce – and finds neither.

Ryan had been full of beans this morning, feeding her so much detail about his night out with the guys in the office. Considering its adventures, the shirt has proved remarkably resilient.

A pang of unease grips Emma's heart as she walks downstairs, the laundry balled up in her arms. Had the evening really played out that way? Or had it been an elaborate cover story for something else? And if it had, what was Ryan hiding from her?

She dumps the washing beside the machine and takes a breath.

If Ryan says he's been on the lash with Robbo and the others from work, that's exactly where he's been. Why on earth would he lie to me? No way would he cheat and betray me and Callie. Would he?

CHAPTER THIRTEEN

Emma's body language tells Ryan she is not convinced.

Well, no wonder. He can hear himself, talking too much, piling on the detail, and he knows it, but can't seem to stop.

On and on. All that guff about Robbo chatting up random women; the group of men trawling the streets, ravenous for a late-night kebab...

Some of it was real, of course. Yes, several of the team *had* gone out to celebrate the end of the Tunbridge Wells project; the job that had guaranteed to put end-of-year bonuses in all their pockets.

But they hadn't gone to that godforsaken nightclub on Fluke Street – Ryan wouldn't be seen dead in the place – he'd only said it because he knew it closed later than most of the bars in Maidstone.

In reality, they'd gone somewhere far less exotic. To The George, just off the high street, a traditional boozer that had remained virtually untouched since the nineties. They'd sat upstairs where they'd pushed two tables together and ordered food from the Thursday night specials menu, along with three bottles of Merlot and some of that smelly real ale that a couple of the guys are into. The pub had played nineties rock anthems through a sound system that had seen better days, proven by the ear-shredding distortion of some of the guitar solos.

At the start of the evening, there had been seven of them: Ryan and Robbo (that much was true, as was the poor guy's grisly divorce); along with both senior partners Raj and Henry; Paul, head of client services; and the two girls, Sue, the practice manager, who was fifty-five if she was a day, and Amber, the new girl.

He hadn't known Amber was going to be there; it had simply never occurred to him that she'd *want* to hang out with the older crowd, not to mention that she'd only been on placement for a few weeks and her involvement in the project had been zero.

Regardless, Amber had tagged along and somehow ended up sitting opposite Ryan, her wide green eyes fixed on his, while others in the group made polite overtures to include her in their conversations.

He didn't normally go for redheads – their accompanying pale skin was too doll-like and fragile for his tastes – but Amber was different. Delicate and robust at the same time. Feminine to the point of old-fashioned, she often wore spriggy blouses with piecrust collars and pearl buttons, while on her lower half, hip skimming combat trousers and thick-soled boots gave her a modern androgynous edge. Her hair, breast length and usually swept artfully over one shoulder, could be poker straight one day and a riot of curls the next. But it was Amber's full lips that held Ryan's attention and quickened his heartbeat whenever he had cause to interact with her, which was not often.

She'd freshened up her lipstick for the pub, highlighting her perfect cupid's bow, and he could smell her youthful floral perfume from across the table. He wondered if his male colleagues fancied her as much as he did.

There, he'd admitted it. At least to himself. And it was clearly mutual, or why else had she sat opposite him, completely ignoring everyone else's attempts at conversation?

By nine o'clock, people began to drift off. Raj first, closely followed by Henry and Sue, who lived five minutes apart and shared a taxi home. Reduced to a foursome, they'd jettisoned the second table and clustered together, before ordering another bottle of wine. That too soon vanished, leaving them debating whether to order yet another or call it a night.

Ryan looks at Emma, notices the shadows under her eyes, her greasy hair raked up into a claw, as she tenderly encourages Callie to eat a little more; *to get strong again, after being poorly, sweet pea*, she reasons.

Shame hits him like a slap and, for a moment, he can't breathe and almost chokes on the orange juice he's swigging.

Why the fuck hadn't he walked away with Paul and Robbo just before ten? No harm done at that stage; he'd barely even flirted with Amber, at least, not so his colleagues would have noticed.

Ryan wishes to God he'd left when the others did; wishes he hadn't drunk that final glass of Merlot alone with Amber in the pub. He wishes he'd seen her into a cab, slammed the door, and waved her off – rather than jumping in beside her, the two of them bound for her flat by the river.

Sweat is beading under his arms and collar and he is desperate to get out of the house before he gives himself away. Instead, he makes some crass, dismissive remark about Callie's stomach bug being a twenty-four hour thing, then he kisses his wife and daughter goodbye and leaves for the office with his heart racing in his chest.

When he arrives, reception is unmanned – *where the hell is Amber?* Somewhere a phone is ringing and being ignored as everyone waits for someone else to take the call.

Henry's office door opens and his shiny bald pate appears. 'No Amber this morning?' he mumbles, echoing Ryan's thoughts.

Sue emerges from the tiny kitchen, holding a mug of instant coffee. 'On her way. She sent me a text saying she's running twenty minutes late.'

Henry rolls his eyes. 'Probably hungover: these twenty somethings... can't keep the pace.' He sighs. 'Can somebody *please* answer the phone?'

'I'll get it,' Ryan says, snatching up the nearest handset.

After completing the call, he makes a beeline for the kitchen and finds Robbo wolfing down a bacon sandwich, the lower half of his face smeared with grease.

Robbo raises sandy brows. 'All right? Did you stay long after me and Paul left?' He takes another bite, spilling a dollop of ketchup down his shirt. 'Oh for fuck's sake—'

'Wait, I'll wet a cloth... here, dab it with this,' Ryan says, grateful for the diversion.

'Well? Did you and Amber stay for another drink?' Robbo asks, having removed the worst of the stain. He lowers his voice. 'Dude, it is *soo* fucking obvious that she fancies you; she didn't even look at anyone else all evening.'

Ryan gives him a withering look. 'Gross. I'm nearly twice her age – we all are. God knows what she was doing there last night. So no, Robbo, I did *not* have another drink. I was right behind you, as it goes, although it took ages to find a cab.'

Robbo narrows his eyes. 'If you say so. But *I* wouldn't kick her out of bed—'

'Which is why you're sleeping on your brother's sofa, while *I* am a happily married man with a beautiful four-year-old daughter.' Ryan turns away and flicks the kettle on, determined not to say another word on the subject.

It's noon when Amber's email pings into Ryan's inbox and it annoys him that he feels a frisson of excitement, despite knowing he has already made the biggest mistake of his life. With a tightness in his chest, he opens it.

```
Hi.   Can   we   talk?   Lunch   at   Pret,
1.00? xx
```

He minimises his inbox and glances across the open-plan area to where Amber sits guarding reception. He's managed to avoid her all morning and even now, she has her back to him and he's able to study her for a second, noting her hair is pinned into a messy bun. He gasps as a flashback crashes into his mind; of him grabbing a handful of that long red hair and yanking her head back. They'd been gentle at first, hesitant, then rough and urgent, devouring each other's bodies like savages starved of human contact—

'Got a second, Ry?' Paul's voice. 'Only I've just had a call from Mrs Bonner in Larkfield chasing sign-off on her kitchen extension.'

Ryan jumps, grateful that Amber's email is not on his screen and being overlooked by his colleague.

'Already on my list. I'm just waiting for a call from buildings regs. Can you leave it with me until after lunch?'

'Sure.' Paul's smile is benign. 'Good night, wasn't it? We should go out as a team more often,' he raises his eyebrows, 'although perhaps find somewhere a bit less... last century.'

Relieved when Paul strides away without further comment, Ryan replies to Amber's email:

`Okay, see you inside at 1.00`

He types, then returns to the proposal he should be writing.

Amber is there before him, sitting near the door. She's still wearing her coat, her handbag clutched awkwardly in one hand, while the other grips a cardboard cup containing something frothy. *Ready to run*, he thinks grimly, the knot in his stomach growing tighter.

He attempts a smile. 'Hi. Do you want a sandwich to go with that... or a cake?' Ryan says, noticing the bags under her eyes and the miserable set of her lipstick-free mouth.

When she declines, he goes up to the counter, waits a few moments to be served, then takes his latte back to the table and sits down opposite her.

'So...' He takes a sip of coffee and burns his tongue. 'How are you?'

Amber emits a dry, mirthless laugh. 'Ooh, I don't know. I've been better, I guess.'

Ryan puffs out his cheeks. 'I'm sure. Look, Amber, about last night. You're a smart, lovely – gorgeous, in fact – woman, but you know I'm married, right? And last night... last night was fun and everything, but it shouldn't have happened, and it can never happen again.'

'Tell it like it is, why don't you?' she says in a small voice. Then she smiles. 'Only joking. Yeah, I know that, obvs. I just... I suppose I wanted to speak to you today, to tell you I'm not that person. Not some shallow homewrecking little bitch. Last night was a first for me and completely out of character.'

Ryan raises his hands. 'I never thought that about you for a second. It's not your fault. We were both drunk... and up for it.

But it was wrong on every level. So do you think we can draw a line under last night? Be friends, perhaps?'

'Of course. Yes, I'd like that. Hey, maybe I will have that cake, after all,' she says, her tone brightening.

Ryan had limped through Friday afternoon with a nagging headache and an aching desire to get home to his wife and daughter, which resulted in him tapping on Henry's door to announce he was leaving early as his daughter was unwell.

'Sorry to hear that,' Henry said. 'I hear norovirus is doing the rounds – try not to bring it back with you on Monday, old chap,' he said kindly.

Released, Ryan had gone straight to the florist a few doors down from work, where he'd bought a hand tied posy of autumn blooms and a candle that smelled of clean laundry, before driving straight home.

'Hey, Daddy's home early,' Emma says, a smile lighting her face as Ryan enters the kitchen. She eyes the flowers. 'Are they an apology?'

Ryan nods and places them on the marble topped island before reaching down to hug Callie. 'Hello, stinker. Are you better now?' He turns back to Emma. 'Busted. I'm sorry, Em. I should never have gone out last night; not when you'd spent all day looking after this one.' He ruffles his daughter's hair. 'It was selfish of me to go out drinking.'

'Mmm,' Emma says, her expression unreadable as she eyes the flowers and the scented candle. 'Thankfully, Callie's completely over her nasty stomach bug, there's no sign of me getting it, and we've got the whole weekend free.'

Ryan sags with relief and feels like he could actually burst into tears. 'My favourite kind of weekend,' he manages, keeping it together.

CHAPTER FOURTEEN

Ryan murmurs his congratulations, his voice lost in the chorus of well wishes.

Amber's eyes shine with emotion. 'Thanks, everyone, for this brilliant opportunity. Believe me, I'll be putting my degree to good use and I won't let you down. Honestly, I'm so, so grateful,' she gushes, her cheeks turning pink.

There's the muffled pop of a cork followed by Paul and Sue hastily filling paper cups with Prosecco. 'Grab a drink, guys,' Paul says, reaching for a second bottle. 'Here's to Amber. Well done, we're all thrilled to be working with you,' he says, passing out drinks.

Ryan stands at the back and regards Amber with barely concealed horror. That the object of his grubby little secret had been a temporary fixture had made working with her bearable. Just. Now, that shred of comfort has gone.

He glances around the office, marvelling at how even the senior partners, Raj and Henry, have gathered around Amber, like indulgent aunties crushing on a newborn.

They all bloody fancy her, Ryan thinks cynically.

Robbo swaggers up, doing that stupid annoying thing he does, like he's holding a pistol in each hand. 'Any more of that fizz?' he says.

Ryan shakes his head. 'I doubt it. Frankly I'd rather go home and get a proper drink,' he says caustically.

'No, come to the pub. It's Friday night and it's been a while since we had a drink and a chat, mate.' Robbo swallows the last of his fizz. 'Great news though, about Amber staying on.' He lowers his voice, his expression lascivious. 'She certainly brightens the place up.' He lets out a low whistle. 'Makes a change to have some eye-candy around here, that's what I say.'

'Do you, Robbo? *Do* you say that? Only, from what I hear, that kind of talk can land people in a lot of trouble.' Ryan's shoulders droop, he closes his eyes. 'Sorry, that was uncalled for. I'm just tired, and honestly,' he glances around, conscious of eavesdroppers, 'I'm surprised. I mean, I know the practice is thriving, but I'm amazed we're taking on interns.' He takes a sip of Prosecco, grimaces. 'Oof, this stuff is bad enough when it's chilled. Come on, let's go get a proper drink.'

Robbo's face lights up. 'That's the spirit, mate,' he says, good-naturedly.

'Just give me a minute to text my wife.' Ryan returns to his desk and messages Emma. He wonders fleetingly if Amber will be in the pub later, then shuts the thought down. After signing off and closing his laptop, he grabs his coat from the communal hanging space and finds Robbo. 'Ready, mate?'

'I was born ready,' Robbo says, his grin shark-like.

The Black Swan is heaving; an even split of office workers enjoying a Friday night livener before heading home, and locals glammed up for a night out. The air is thick with cheap aftershave, expensive perfume, and stale alcohol. The jukebox plays The Dandy Warhols' 'Bohemian Like You', causing Robbo to jerk his way to the polished bar with its shiny jewel-coloured optics and Generation Z staff. With a ripple of satisfaction, Ryan picks up on the appreciative glances he gets from a group of women sitting nearby. Birthday cards litter the tabletop and one of the women is sporting a saucer-sized badge bearing the words *Oh shit, I'm* 40.

He cringes as Robbo pauses and leans into the group. 'Happy Birthday, gorgeous – you're catching up with *him*,' he says, pointing towards Ryan as he guffaws at his own joke.

'Give me strength,' Ryan murmurs under his breath, adding, 'actually, Robbo, I'm forty *next* year,' before conceding to his friend's humour with a dry laugh. 'You really are something, aren't you? Honestly, your confidence astounds me.'

Robbo makes a face. 'You're just jealous, mate.'

'Am I? Why's that?' Ryan signals to one of the barmaids, marvelling that she can see properly through the density of her fake lashes.

'Because, Ryan my friend, *you* may be the fit, good-looking one, but women are attracted to *my* dazzling wit and personality,' Robbo says without a shred of irony. 'Hey, did I tell you I got my decree absolute last week?'

'You didn't. Congratulations, we should drink to that; what can I get you?'

Two rounds of expensive Belgium beer and several toasts *to freedom* later, there's a lull in the conversation as Sue, Paul and Amber enter the pub, shiny-eyed and flushed from the evening chill.

Standing beneath a row of downlighters, her hair frizzed by the damp weather, Amber looks ethereal; a Pre-Raphaelite goddess wrapped in street clothes, Ryan thinks with a pang of desire that catches him off guard. She sees him then, her expression becoming stiff and self-conscious. She looks away.

'Hey, look who's here,' Robbo says, getting up and gesturing to the newcomers, who wave in recognition and relief to see a friendly face. 'You took your time,' he says, attempting to kiss first Sue and then Amber on the cheek, despite both shrinking back and looking uncomfortable.

Then pleasantries are swapped and extra chairs dragged to where Ryan and Robbo have been sitting quietly for the last forty-five minutes.

Still glowing with pride, Amber looks around the group. 'My round,' she says, fumbling in her handbag and drawing out her purse. 'Go on, let me – I'm celebrating.'

'I'll give you a hand,' Paul says, noting everyone's order then following Amber to the bar.

Something about the way he looks at her, his fingertips grazing the small of her back unsettles Ryan. *He's besotted, sycophantic twat*, he thinks, wondering why it irritates him so much.

'Ah, bless her. Amber shouldn't be paying, she's only a kid,' Robbo says, inclining his head.

Sue raises one eyebrow. 'Patronising, much? Actually, Pete, she's twenty-three and her parents are loaded, so please, let her buy us all a drink, will you?'

Ryan stiffens. 'You seem to know a lot about her, Sue.' The words are out of his mouth before he can stop himself.

'We've chatted, yes,' Sue answers, her tone prim. 'It's okay to have friends of all ages, you know?'

'I never suggested otherwise,' Ryan says, feeling suddenly older than his thirty-nine years.

Amber returns, laden with drinks. 'So, I got lager for Ryan and Pete,' she says, 'and the rest of us are sticking with Prosecco.' She smiles and throws a grateful glance towards Paul, who is dutifully carrying an ice bucket and three champagne flutes, while Pete scrabbles to make room on the table.

There's another toast, this time of the thank-God-it's-Friday variety, followed by a laboured description of the pub that Amber, Paul and Sue have just come from, before the conversation stalls and Ryan finds himself staring into Amber's eyes.

Feeling an odd blend of fear and attraction, he pockets his phone, excuses himself and heads to the men's room. On his return, he pauses before reaching the others, takes out his mobile with the intention of texting Emma and is surprised to find he already has a message from her. His heart sinks. Surely he's not in trouble yet, it's still early.

He reads the message:

> Don't rush back. Mel's round here after a massive row with Oliver. We're on wine and chocolate! Love you xxx

Cringing at the thought of the histrionics going on at home, and relieved that he's gained permission for a night out, Ryan pockets his phone and returns to the group, catching Amber's eye as he goes.

He wakes with a start, queasy and shivering. Wondering if he's about to throw up, Ryan levers himself into a sitting position and pulls the duvet around him. The unfamiliar room comes into focus as his eyes adjust. Beside him, a woman sleeps deeply, a tangle of long hair half covering her face, her pale limbs peeking from the duvet.

Shit. This cannot be happening. Mortified, he gapes at Amber, willing her not to wake up, his thoughts racing.

What time is it? Where is his phone? And where are his clothes, for Christ's sake?

He stiffens as Amber sighs and turns away from him. Close. He cannot wake her; he needs to extract himself as quickly and silently as possible.

Getting up, he stumbles into a dark mound on the bedroom floor: his clothes. Jesus, that's something. He scoops them up, softly closes the bedroom door behind him and dresses in the stark modern hallway, trembling more from adrenalin and self-loathing than from cold.

Now to find his phone. Where the hell—?

He recalls Amber going through the motions of making them both coffee 'to sober up'. Neither of them had touched a drop, of course... ahh, but his phone... yes, there it is, beside the kettle, discarded right after he'd put it on silent mode.

He checks the time: 03.20. Fuck!

There are four missed calls from Emma and three WhatsApp messages.

With his chest thudding painfully, Ryan checks his coat pocket for his wallet and keys, then lets himself out of Amber's flat and steals down two flights of stairs, holding his breath until he reaches the street.

An involuntary moan escapes him as a bilious blend of shame and relief washes over his quivering body. He looks up and down the deserted street. The damp mid-October chill and the soft burbling of the nearby river is oddly reviving, and it helps to clear his head.

How the hell is he going to get home at this hour? Most days, Ryan drives to the office, but as post-work drinks have recently become a thing, he's started taking the train on Fridays, just in case. Well, even if he had his car, he is in no fit state to drive anyway, given he'd begun the evening with at least four pints before joining Amber in a bottle of sparkling wine.

Clearly at 3.30am, no trains are running, no black cabs will be trawling the streets, which leaves only one solution.

Hands shaking, Ryan scrolls to the Uber app on his phone and fumbles his way through the process, praying that Emma will be fast asleep by the time he gets home.

CHAPTER FIFTEEN

NOW

Driving along the coastal road, just a few minutes from Cala Savannah, Sheena's eyes are fixed ahead. 'Emma, are you absolutely sure about having the boys for a couple of hours this evening?'

Emma smiles, still in a state of post-spa bliss. 'Of course. We had an agreement; you and Jack were kind enough to have Callie while Ryan and I went out, and now it's our turn to give you two a break.'

She gazes at the late afternoon haze from the car window, relieved that the morning's wind and rain has turned to sunshine and blue skies once more.

Sheena chews her lip. 'It's just that, Leo can be a bit...' She searches for the right word. 'Challenging. He's not an easy kid, never has been. God, that sounds awful, and I feel like a bad mother for admitting it, but he and his brother are chalk and cheese.' She puffs out her cheeks. 'The thing is, Leo has... issues, and he can act up sometimes.'

Emma feels a twinge of unease: what exactly is Sheena getting at? 'Look, if you're worried that Ryan and I will be out of our depth—'

'You know what? *Of course* you two can handle Leo, he's just sensitive, that's all.' Spotting the sign for Santa Martina, Sheena slows to a crawl, indicates, and enters the development. She smiles gamely. 'I'll give the boys their tea before I walk them round, then Jack and I will have a couple of drinks in the village and head straight back, okay?'

'When are Mummy and Daddy coming back? Have they gone home to England?' Leo asks, tears welling in his round blue eyes.

Emma kneels in front of him, places her hands on his narrow little shoulders. 'Leo, listen to me,' she says gently. 'You're a smart boy; you know that your mum and dad would *never* go home without you and Lucas.' She dabs a tear from his cheek. 'Anyway, their car's still on the drive and they'd need it if they were going far, wouldn't they?'

Leo nods, reluctantly. 'I suppose so,' he says, his bottom lip trembling.

'Good boy. Now why don't you and I watch a lovely film together, eh?' Emma suggests.

She'd thought Sheena was exaggerating, but Leo has been tearful and anxious from the moment his parents walked out of the door. Lucas on the other hand had casually waved goodbye and instantly demanded that Callie show him all her toys.

Her heart contracts at the sight of the two of them playing 'families' with a motley selection of human and animal figurines.

'Come on, let's choose a DVD from the sideboard,' Emma says, leading Leo by the hand.

The front door opens and Ryan reappears holding pizza boxes. He eyes Leo warily. 'Everything all right?'

'Yep, all good, thanks. Leo and I are about to choose a film. Do you want to join us?'

Ryan nods. 'Sure, I'll just get some plates for these. I got an extra pizza in case the kids fancy a couple of slices... I know they've eaten already, but—'

'Me, please, Daddy,' Callie says, abandoning her game with Lucas and following Ryan into the kitchen. 'Why is Leo such a baby?' she says next, her voice high and clear. 'He's older than Lucas and me.'

Emma flashes Ryan a desperate look. 'Callie, stop it, that's not kind. Leo's not a baby; he's just a bit worried.' She turns to Leo. 'But you're fine now, aren't you, love?'

Callie rolls her eyes. 'Look, he's crying *again*. What's the matter now?'

'She has a point,' Ryan hisses unhelpfully. He raises his voice. 'Callie, that's enough. Here, have some pizza and take a slice to Lucas, will you?'

Leo stops sniffling and folds his arms. 'Don't I get any?'

'Of course. I'm doing you a special plate right now.' Emma forces a smile. 'Have you decided on a film yet?'

'Not interested,' Leo snaps, taking his plate from Emma without a word of thanks.

Ryan shakes his head. 'You shouldn't pander to him; it'll only make him worse. Christ, I hope they're not making a night of it,' he says, his voice low.

Emma glares at him. 'For goodness' sake! Not in front of the kids.'

Finally, all three children are relaxed, settled, and engrossed in *Harry Potter and the Goblet of Fire*, thanks to the villa's old-fashioned DVD player and its generous film selection.

Emma catches Ryan's eye and they sneak off to the

kitchen. 'Sheena's right; Leo *is* hard work,' she whispers, removing a bottle of white wine from the fridge and pouring two glasses.

Ryan glances at the children, relieved that the film has their rapt attention. 'At least they're all fine now. Shall we take our drinks outside?'

'Sure, why not? It'll be dark soon; I'll grab some matches and tea lights, make it cosy.'

Even in the fading light, the air is mild and warm. After dropping candles into jars and lighting them, Emma carries her wine to the end of their garden and gazes out at the flat, inky sea beyond. 'I love it here,' she says quietly, watching the sun slip from the sky.

Ryan steals up behind her, one arm encircling her waist. 'I do, too,' he says. 'Can't believe we're going home in three days. Not that it's been perfect, what with Callie's iPad landing in the pool and that disgusting dead rat in her room.' He takes a sip of wine. 'Which reminds me, after my rainy beach walk today with Jack and the kids, I knocked for John and Max.' He pauses and steers Emma to the table.

'So, how were they?' Emma asks once she and Ryan are seated.

'Okay, I guess. I only spoke to Max. To be honest, I was on a mission. I wanted to know whether they've ever had a problem with rats around here.'

'And?'

Ryan purses his lips. 'She admitted to having seen them by the bins a few times, but never near the houses.'

Emma sighs. 'I guess we were just unlucky then. Did you tell her about *mousey?*'

'No, I didn't want to get into it. I'm surprised Max didn't ask, though. I mean, it's a pretty random subject to launch into.' He frowns. 'Which, on reflection, makes me think that they *have* had an issue with vermin and Max was playing it down so as not to alarm us.'

Emma shudders as she pictures the possibility of dozens of furry little bodies with worm-like tails skittering in the scrub beyond the garden wall. 'Let's talk about something else, shall we?'

'Okay. Did you enjoy your spa visit today?'

'I did, thanks. More than I expected.' Emma runs an index finger around the rim of her glass. 'I wasn't sure about Sheena at first, but she's sweet. I got the impression she's a bit lonely. She told me today that a close friend of hers recently died; must be awful to lose someone so young.'

'That's sad, wonder what happened.'

Emma gives a little shrug. 'I didn't want to pry; poor Sheena got quite choked up.'

There's a lull in the conversation while Emma recalls Sheena's comments about Ryan being a flirt. She decides to say nothing on the subject, aware that it will almost certainly sour their relaxed mood.

'Cheers, love,' Emma says instead, raising her glass and drinking the last of her wine.

It's just turned nine o'clock when the doorbell rings. Emma gets to her feet. 'That'll be Jack and Sheena. Now remember: the kids were fine – even Leo – and *everyone* had a great time,' she says, pasting on a smile before answering the door.

CHAPTER SIXTEEN

Leaving Ryan to supervise Callie's breakfast, Emma takes her morning coffee out to the pool terrace, glad of a few moments to herself.

When she and Ryan had first booked the holiday at the travel agents, seventeen nights had seemed like an absurdly long break, to the point Emma had worried they'd be bored and restless. Yet somehow it has flashed by in a blink.

She checks the time on her phone. It's 08.50am. The thought of boarding a plane in around sixty hours and returning to the same old routine of housework, the school run, and working in the salon three days a week, fills her with dread.

Not that Cala Savannah would win any prizes for excitement, glamour, or luxury, but for spending gentle, quality time together and for reconnecting as a family, it has been the perfect backdrop.

'Mummy!'

Emma turns to see Callie, brown as a berry, already dressed for action in her swimsuit and flip-flops. Reaching out, she pulls Callie down to the sunbed she's sitting on. 'Hey, sweet pea. Where's Daddy?'

'Toilet,' Callie says bluntly.

'Cal, is there anything you'd like to do today? Only we're flying home the day after tomorrow.'

Callie pauses while she discards her flip-flops then she nods. 'Yep. I'd like to play in the pool with Lucas. Did I tell you he's my new best friend? I'm going to see him in England; we're having a sleepover.'

Emma suppresses a smile. 'Oh, you are, are you? We'll have to see about that. Sometimes holiday friends stay in touch, but sometimes it's not possible. Lucas and his family live about an hour away from us in Beckenham.'

Callie cups Emma's face in her small hands. 'Lucky we've got two cars then, Mummy. Simples.'

Emma's laughter is warm and heartfelt. She strokes her daughter's hair. 'Bless you, you're so funny.'

Indignant, Callie frowns and crosses her arms, then she wanders to the pool's edge and runs a hand through the water before returning to Emma and sitting down beside her.

'Mummy, can I go and knock for Lucas?' she asks, shielding her eyes from the sun's glare.

'Darling, it's a bit early. I'm sure Lucas and Leo will come out soon.' Emma moves in for a cuddle. 'Can't we just sit here together and enjoy the peace?'

It's another twenty minutes before Ryan surfaces, striding towards them, his brow furrowed, tension visible in his face.

Emma studies him. 'Are you okay? Please tell me you haven't been stuck in the bathroom all this time?'

'What? Oh, no, I made the mistake of opening my laptop and checking my work emails and got sucked into something, that's all.'

'Anything you want to talk about?' Emma says, hoping the answer is no. Her heart sinks. For goodness' sake, they've not even left yet and already Ryan seems to have lapsed into work mode.

'No, honestly. It can wait until next week.' He turns to Callie. 'Hey, stinker, thought you'd be in the pool by now, what's up?'

'Nothing, she's fine,' Emma says. 'I've just been hearing how Lucas is Callie's best friend and how they're getting together for a sleepover.'

Ryan grunts. 'I doubt that somehow. They live too far away, Cal. Never mind, you've got loads of friends at home.'

Behind them, a door slams. Emma turns and watches as the family next door head towards them before swerving the pool terrace and peeling off to the beach path.

Callie is on her feet. 'There they are!' She calls out to Lucas, her expression morphing from joy and excitement to confusion and disappointment in a nano-second as the whole family marches past without so much as a wave.

Callie's brow furrows. 'Where are they going?'

'Beach, I guess,' Ryan replies, glancing at Emma.

'I'm sure they'll be back later; maybe you can swim with Lucas this afternoon,' Emma says, doing her best to mollify her daughter.

'Or maybe we can catch them up and all go to the beach together,' Callie suggests.

Ryan snatches her small body into his arms and hugs her tight. 'Sometimes it's nicer when it's just us,' he says, meeting Emma's eyes over Callie's head.

Around noon, after a chilled morning spent chatting, sunbathing, and hogging the pool to themselves, the Burrows are again jarred by the sight of their neighbours, sandy and damp-haired, plodding past on their way back to the villa.

This time, Callie is up and running towards Lucas before either Emma or Ryan can intervene.

'Lucas, wait!' Callie shouts, charging at him.

Emma's heart melts as their tanned little bodies clash and their arms go around each other in a hug. Then she's gaping in horror as Sheena, with a fake sickly smile on her face, whispers something to Lucas before dragging him away.

Ryan's face darkens. 'What's that about?' He gets up and makes a move towards them.

Emma strides after him. Whatever has happened? They'd parted on great terms last night: Jack and Sheena, flushed with wine, beaming with gratitude, thrilled to have had a break from the kids and some much-needed time alone together.

Ryan, three steps ahead, blocks the family's path. 'Hi. How was the beach this morning?' he asks pleasantly, despite the hostile undercurrent flowing from Jack and Sheena.

'Mate, excuse us, *please*,' Jack says, his tone laced with attitude.

Ryan glowers. 'Is there a problem?'

Jack squares his shoulders and puts a protective arm around Leo. 'Yeah, I'm afraid there is. Quite a *big* problem.'

Emma's pulse quickens. 'Sheena, what's happened?' she says, appealing to feminine reason.

But Sheena is having none of it. 'I need to get the boys inside,' she hisses, not meeting Emma's eyes. 'I don't want Leo upset again.'

She strides ahead, propelling both boys in front of her, while Callie shrinks back, her little face puckered by hurt and confusion.

Emma starts after her. 'Sheena, wait!'

'I'll speak to you later,' Sheena calls over her shoulder, as she herds Lucas and Leo indoors.

Emma looks to Ryan, still body-blocking Jack's path; the

words *squaring up* spring to mind. She has to stop whatever this is from coming to blows.

'Ryan, Jack, please, can we talk about this?'

Ryan's eyes are fixed on Jack's, his chin jutting out.

'Yeah, if you like. We can talk.' Jack's tone is unpleasant, snarky. 'As long as you keep your kid away from my two.'

Ryan's eyes bulge. 'I'm *sorry*? What the fuck—'

Emma throws Ryan a warning look. 'Stop it. You're not helping, Ryan. Jack, what do you mean?'

'Leo was in bits last night when we got him home and he told us *everything*,' Jack sneers. 'How he was bullied and belittled by *your* daughter making fun of him while the two of you stood back and said nothing.'

Stunned, Emma shakes her head. 'That's not true. That's not what happened at all,' she says, her mind flashing back to the night before.

'So, what? My son's a liar now, is he, as well as a cry-baby and a freak?'

Emma can see Ryan is ready to blow a gasket. She tugs at his arm. 'Ry, can you take Callie inside, please? I'd like to talk to Jack... try and sort things out.'

To her amazement and relief, Ryan steps back, then cursing under his breath, he leads Callie towards their villa.

Emma takes a deep breath. 'Right. Can we just sit down for a minute, sort this out properly, because I think I know what you're referring to and it wasn't quite like that.'

Jack raises his hands in submission. 'Okay.'

They sit on plastic chairs, facing the pool, eyes averted from each other.

Emma steels herself. 'Look, I'm sorry to say that Callie *did* call Leo a baby. But it was a question, not a taunt. She also asked why he was crying – although she didn't put it together and call him a cry-baby. As for her calling Leo a freak, I'm a hundred per cent certain she's never even heard the word, let alone used it. Jack, it wasn't nice that Callie called your son a baby but believe me, she was put in her place for it at the time. That's not bullying, it's just kids being kids.'

Jack looks unconvinced. 'Well, according to Leo, you all laughed at him, then you and Ryan left the children in front of the TV and got drunk in the back garden.'

Emma shakes her head. *God, what a troubled little boy, why on earth would Leo say such a thing?*

'It sounds awful when you say it like that,' Emma says, keeping her tone neutral, 'but honestly, Jack, nobody was laughing – well apart from Lucas and Callie giggling at each other's antics like they do. And as for Ryan and I getting drunk? We had one glass of wine each; surely you could tell we weren't drunk when you came to collect the boys?'

Jack nods slowly, considers Emma's side of the story. 'Okay. Perhaps Leo was being oversensitive, but you can see how it looks, surely? He's not an easy child but he doesn't make stuff up – not that Sheena and I know of... which is why I didn't want them all playing together today.'

Emma is suffused with relief at Jack's softening stance. 'I understand and I'm gutted that Leo's feelings were hurt. I'll get Callie to apologise to him and hopefully they can hug it out. Now can we please put this behind us? We're leaving the day after tomorrow and I'd like to part on good terms.'

Jack throws up his hands. 'Okay. Maybe we can all grab a drink together before you leave?'

'I hope so,' Emma says.

CHAPTER SEVENTEEN

Callie is spooked. 'Why is everybody cross and why can't I play with Lucas?' she asks. But Ryan isn't listening; he paces the floor, anxious for Emma's return.

He doesn't have long to wait.

'So? What the hell was all that about?' Ryan snarls after Callie has been despatched to her room to give them privacy. 'You know, Jack's lucky I didn't deck him, the pompous—'

'Which is why I suggested that you go indoors. I could see you getting wound up and it doesn't help anybody – you know that.' Emma sighs and puts a hand to her forehead. 'Anyway, it's okay, I've sorted it,' she adds before relaying every word of her conversation with Jack.

'So, let me get this straight. Leo is a lying little shit and now you want Callie to apologise for something she didn't do?' Ryan says.

'Sort of. It would certainly defuse things – and she was quite mean to him, remember?'

Ryan simmers. They shouldn't be having this conversation. Just who are these people? One minute they are attaching themselves, desperate to hang out, taking spa trips together and watching each other's kids, then the next, ghosting them because their weird older child has been telling porkies? Suddenly the thought of returning home to normality could not be more appealing.

He rakes back his hair; his forehead is beaded with sweat. 'Okay, Callie can say she's sorry, but then I don't want anything more to do with them. I mean it. I'd lay money on Leo having dumped Callie's iPad in the pool.' He laughs bitterly. 'I'm glad we're leaving soon; I've had enough of this place and the bloody neighbours. It's like living in a soap opera. Going on holiday is meant to be relaxing, an escape from drama.'

Emma shrugs. 'We'll never know about Callie's iPad, will we? As for this latest spat, we need to get past it and not let it colour the memory of a lovely holiday.'

'You're right, of course; we need to kiss and make up – though not literally,' Ryan says an hour later once he has cooled down and the three of them have eaten lunch in the garden. 'Tell you what, I'll go next door with Callie. It'll give me chance to patch things up with Jack.'

Emma raises her eyebrows. 'Okay, if you're sure. The last thing we need is another argument.'

Ryan laughs softly. 'Are you implying I'm hot-headed?'

It is Sheena who opens the door, her expression wary, no sign of her easy sunny smile today.

Ryan clears his throat. 'Sheena, hi. Listen, Emma has filled me in and we understand why you're upset. Clearly there's been a misunderstanding somewhere. Nevertheless, we're all very sorry that Leo's feelings were hurt and Callie would like to apologise to him personally. Isn't that right, Cal?'

She nods, her thumb going briefly to her mouth as she reverts to toddlerhood.

Sheena's face softens. 'Come in. Both boys are in the garden.'

Ryan leads his daughter through the living room and out to the patio, where Lucas is running a plastic truck along the tabletop, and Leo is reading a book with a dragon on the cover. There is no sign of Jack.

'Jack's taking a shower,' Sheena says, as if reading Ryan's thoughts.

'Hi, Callie,' Lucas says. 'Do you want to play builders with me?'

Sheena catches Ryan's eye. 'Maybe later, Lucas.' She eyes Leo, who hangs back staring fixedly at his book. 'Leo, come here, please, Callie wants to speak to you.'

It's a relief when Leo steps forward and Callie gently apologises. Ryan's heart swells with pride as she puts out a hand for Leo to shake.

'Good, all friends again?' Ryan asks. 'And on that note, we'll leave you to it.'

'Cheers, Ryan. And well done, Callie. You did a kind thing,' Sheena says, as she shows them to the door.

'Good girl, I'm proud of you,' Ryan says as he ushers his daughter inside, where Max's unmistakeable whisky and cigarettes voice pipes from the kitchen.

His heart sinks. *What now?*

'Ahh, and here they are,' Max purrs. 'Hello, you two. I just popped round to say that I'm having a little soiree this evening from seven thirty. Just a few old friends and some peeps from the village. Naturally, you're invited and I shall be asking Jack and Sheena as well; they're such a super couple.

It's been a real joy having glamorous young people here this summer.'

Ryan looks to Emma, willing her to invent a reason why they won't be at Max's party but instead she is nodding and smiling gamely.

'Thanks, Max,' Ryan says, 'but we're eating out this evening, aren't we, Emma?'

'Then come afterwards,' Max says, running a hand over Ryan's forearm. 'I insist.'

Ryan shakes his head in annoyance. 'God, that woman's overbearing,' he says after Max has left. '"*I insist*",' he mimics, 'who the hell does she think she is?'

Emma's face falls. 'I thought you liked John and Max. They're just being friendly and polite, so they won't disturb us with their music later.'

'Yeah, obviously. But the thought of having to make small talk *again*, with people we'll never see again, is so tedious.'

'Stop being a curmudgeon,' Emma says, 'you're way too young. I think we should take a leaf out of Max and John's book: get dressed up and have a few drinks. Come on, what harm can it do?'

Ryan concedes defeat. 'All right, if that's what you want,' he says. 'We'll pop round for an hour after dinner. Do you fancy eating at the Italian restaurant in the village?'

'Sounds good.' Emma nods.

CHAPTER EIGHTEEN

Max floats into view, her Moorish jewellery jangling as she moves. She leans in and air-kisses Emma and Ryan, her perfume a heady blend of rose and jasmine. 'Ah, the beautiful people are here,' she croons. 'What can I get you all to drink? John is on bar duty, so just name your poison.'

'Thanks, Max. You look lovely,' Emma says, taking Callie's hand and steering her towards the makeshift bar: a long trestle table loaded with an impressive array of beer, wine and spirits, as well as a selection of soft drinks.

Frowning, Ryan looks around at the well-dressed crowd. 'I'd hardly call this a few friends,' he says. 'There must be thirty or forty people here.'

Cars line the development's private road and Ibiza-style dance music pipes from an unseen speaker. Stained-glass lanterns peep from the lush foliage and thick cream candles in jars surround the pool deck, ready to light after dark.

'Place is a bloody death trap,' Ryan mutters, shaking his head.

Emma laughs. 'Please cheer up, will you, Ry? It's a party for goodness' sake. I can't believe how quickly it all came together; we were only out for a couple of hours. Max certainly knows how to throw a bash.'

Callie's eyes shine. 'It looks so pretty. Can I have a Coke, please?' she says as they approach the bar and are greeted by John.

'Just a beer for me,' Ryan says primly.

Emma beams. 'Well, *I'm* going to have a glass of local sparkling wine,' she says. 'Tomorrow is our last full day and I'm going out on a high.'

'Or a hangover,' Ryan mutters under his breath.

'Yay! That's the spirit, you go for it.'

Emma turns to see Sheena, glamorous in white jeans and a ruffled scarlet shirt, her long hair loose and tousled.

'Wow, you look gorgeous. No Jack?' Emma says, aware that Ryan is staring, transfixed by Sheena's appearance.

Sheena wrinkles her nose. 'He's at home with the boys. I might swap with him later.' She lowers her voice. 'Or I might not. To be honest, he's got a bit of a cob on and isn't feeling sociable.'

'Well, I'm glad *you're* here,' Emma says warmly. 'And listen, I'm so sorry that we upset Leo. It was completely unintentional – Callie hasn't got a mean bone in her body.'

'I know. Things got blown out of all proportion,' Sheena says. She turns to John. 'Hiya. I think I'll join Emma in a glass of cava, please, John.'

'Right you are, ladies.' John fills two glasses. 'Bottoms up.'

Stepping back to allow others near the bar, Emma surveys the guests, waving to a silver-haired couple in their fifties whom she recognises. 'Ryan, look, isn't that Colin and Arturas, who we met on our second night here?'

'It is. And I see they've still got that gormless lump with

them,' Ryan says, his voice low as he eyes a stoop-shouldered young man hovering beside the two of them.

Sheena giggles. 'Oh my God, Ryan, you don't mince your words, do you? Poor kid looks like a fish out of water.'

'That's Teddy, Colin's nephew,' Emma whispers. 'I can remember being that age, when having to hang out with anyone over thirty was utter torture.'

'Hello, hello, we meet again.' Colin trills, stepping to the beat as he walks. 'You remember my husband, Arturas, and my nephew, Teddy? So, how's your holiday been? I must say you're looking disgustingly well and relaxed.'

Emma glances at Ryan, willing him to be civil. 'It's been really lovely, thanks, Colin. We hope to come back next year, don't we, Ryan?'

'Maybe,' Ryan says. 'Colin, Arturas, this is Sheena. She and her family arrived a few days after us. They're staying in the villa next door.'

'And aren't *you* fabulous,' Arturas says, studying Sheena with approval. 'Right, Emma, time to mingle; come and meet the gang...'

As dusk falls, Emma finds herself swept into a whirl of small talk as English, Spanish and Dutch friends of John and Max's are wheeled out for introductions. For a heart stopping minute, she loses sight of Ryan and Callie until, peering into the crowd, she spots her daughter, still clutching Ryan's hand and giggling at something Teddy is saying. She flinches as someone pinches her waist from behind.

'Gotcha!' Sheena says, her face flushed and happy. She takes Emma's empty glass from her and swaps it for a full one. 'Thought you might need another glass of fizz. Cheers.'

Emma clinks her glass against Sheena's. 'Good call, thanks. Hey, it must be great to have a holiday home somewhere hot and romantic,' she says, watching Max hold court over a group of bronzed prosperous-looking expats.

Sheena gives Emma a knowing look. 'Oh, I'm working on it, trust me.'

'Really? What, you and Jack are buying a house in the sun?'

'One day soon, I hope. Thing is, property's *always* a good investment and Jack certainly knows his way around the tax system.' Sheena takes a sip of cava.

Emma feels a stab of envy. 'Well, all I can say is, lucky you.'

Sheena laughs, her eyes glinting. 'Oh, it probably won't happen. We're *soo* bloody busy and disorganised.'

Unsure how to answer, Emma sips her drink and looks around. By now, a handful of people are dancing on the tiled terrace, perilously close to the swimming pool. She watches Max weave her way into the centre of the group, her tanned arms swaying above her head. The younger guests step aside, giving her room to express herself, cheering with approval as she struts and twirls.

'Look at her go.' Sheena sighs. 'Hope I'm like that at her age.'

'Ryan and I have said the same.' Emma catches Sheena's hand. 'Come on, let's have a dance; might even drag Ryan up.'

Still holding Sheena's hand, Emma walks towards the pool but is hit by a sudden wave of vertigo. 'Wow, I need to slow down a bit.' She dumps her glass, already two thirds empty, and continues drifting towards the dancers, a growing queasiness slowing her progress.

She tightens her grip on Sheena's hand. 'Actually, I don't feel well. Seriously, I feel so weird... Sheena, can you get Ryan for me?' Emma says, panic setting in.

Alarmed, Sheena calls out to Ryan, who is there in an instant, his face a mask of concern.

'What's happened?' he asks, steadying Emma with a supporting arm as her legs begin to buckle beneath her.

'Take me home? Please... I don't feel right... I think I might be sick. Callie? Where's Callie?' Emma says, her words slurred, her tongue thick and fuzzy in her mouth.

'I'll get her for you,' Sheena says, finding Callie at once.

'Shit, I knew you were drinking too fast,' Ryan says, his tone accusing. 'We already had wine with dinner earlier. Bloody hell, Emma, you're such a lightweight.' He turns to Callie. 'Come on, sweetheart, let's call it a night. Mummy's feeling a bit poorly.'

'I'm sorry, I didn't mean to...' Emma tries, but the words won't form properly and she's aware of Ryan beside her, half dragging, half carrying her into the villa and up the stairs. Then she's on the bed, floating on its softness, closing her eyes against the stark overhead light, too numb to co-operate as Ryan removes her sandals and sundress, his voice receding, then silent as a dense blackness claims her.

The pain in Emma's skull is rhythmic, insistent. She tries to sit up, aware of someone pulling at her arms. Dear God, this is surely the worse hangover she's ever had in her entire life. She tries to swallow, but her mouth feels full of cotton wool and her stomach roils.

The dragging sensation continues. 'Emma, please. Wake up! You have to help.' Ryan's voice breaks through the fog, his fingers digging into her shoulders, a sob catching in his throat as he begs her to wake up. *To please. Just. Fucking. Wake up!*

As the room shimmers into semi-focus Emma sits up, ignoring the sickness that threatens as Ryan begins to whimper nonsensically.

The words don't make sense; something about Callie. He's saying her name over and over. That she is not in her bed. That he has looked and looked for her: downstairs, in the garden, by the pool. Where *is* she? Please, God, where is Callie?

And it's almost a physical blow, a punch to her solar plexus, when Emma gets it, when she finally understands.

Callie is missing.

CHAPTER NINETEEN

THEN

> I'm pregnant. Need to see you. Tomorrow.

Sitting inside the bubble of his car, Ryan stares dumbly at the words on his phone. Words that mean nothing and everything. Words that make him want to smash his mobile up, reverse off the driveway, out of the warm, comfortable haven that is Wisteria Close, and keep going.

He deletes the text, pockets his mobile, and strides up the path. Before he can insert his key, Emma opens the front door and he's greeted by the warm spicy scent of Christmas baking.

'Daddy!' Callie cries, hurling herself at him. 'Are you on holiday now? And do you know, it's only one more sleep until Father Christmas comes?' Fizzing with excitement, she continues to chatter while Ryan sheds his jacket and shoes in the hallway. He sweeps his daughter up into his arms.

Emma looks on, amused. 'Come on, sweet pea. Let Daddy get through the door.' Her eyes brim with love and happiness as she reaches for him. 'Why don't you put something comfy on, then come down and we'll open a bottle of wine. Callie's already eaten and our dinner will be another twenty minutes.'

Ryan turns away, finding it hard to speak because of the lump in his throat. 'Mind if I take a quick shower?' he manages before heading up the stairs.

Once inside the bathroom, he locks the door and sets the shower running. Then he sits on the closed toilet seat and messages Amber.

> Jesus. Are you sure? Is it mine? Can't meet tomorrow, it's Christmas Eve. Will be in touch soon.

He's about to hit send, then adds two kisses as an afterthought. No point in winding Amber up and stressing her out even more. No wonder she'd messaged him umpteen times already this week.

He'd ignored her on WhatsApp after telling her it was over between them. Which part of *I love my wife and daughter*, and *this has to stop* didn't she understand?

He'd said it to her face, too, weeks earlier – he'd even sent an email from the office on company time – so it should have been pretty bloody clear. Still the messages kept coming.

He'd seen her, mooning around the office, whey-faced and miserable. Well, no wonder...

The room has grown steamy around him. He breathes deeply, imagines Amber's desperation *if* she really is pregnant and *if* the baby is his, because God knows who else she is sleeping with.

He checks himself. Chances are, there is nobody else in the frame. The way she looks at him, the fierce intensity in her eyes when they're in bed together – he can tell she's in love with him, or that she *thinks* she is.

Ryan's temples throb and his hands shake. Now he needs to pull off an Oscar-winning performance to give his family the Christmas they deserve. He will deal with Amber later.

He undresses, discards his clothes in the corner of the room and steps into the shower.

Emma is waiting for him in the kitchen where the smell of shepherd's pie mingles with the scent of Christmas baking. On the dining table, tea lights flicker in festive jars, while two glasses of Shiraz have already been poured to breathe.

'This looks lovely. Where's Callie?' Ryan asks, doing his best to ignore the guilt weighing on him, his default setting these days.

'In the sitting room, watching a Christmas film on the Disney channel. Honestly, I'm glad of the peace.'

She removes the shepherd's pie from the oven. Even in his freaked-out state, Ryan salivates at the sight of the bubbling cheese topping. She takes out a second dish containing spring greens and broccoli spears, then serves up two generous portions and carries their plates to the table.

'My favourite and the perfect way to kick off Christmas. Cheers, love.' Ryan raises his glass and drinks deeply, trying to steady his nerves.

Dinner is hearty and delicious; the room is cosy and festive. In the next room, their daughter watches TV while Emma chats happily about her day: the baking she accomplished, the drinks invitation they've had from a neighbour, the last-minute gift she bought for Callie in town. Normal gentle domestic conversation about a life most people would kill for.

A life that he now risks losing, thanks to his own utter stupidity and fecklessness. A life that he must now do everything in his power to protect.

Christmas Eve dawns dank and misty.

'But I want it to snow like on TV,' Callie says, staring glumly from the kitchen window.

Emma scoffs. 'We'd all like a Disney-style Christmas, sweet pea.' She hands Ryan a cup of freshly brewed coffee and winks at him. 'Maybe it *will* snow tomorrow, but even if it doesn't, it'll still be exciting. Granny and Granddad are coming for dinner and they're bound to bring you lots of presents.'

Ryan's chest constricts at the thought of his in-laws descending. Even now, after all their years together, Emma's parents, Geoff and Deirdre, can still wither him with a single look – and that's when he's on his best behaviour. How is he supposed to look them both in the eye now?

Sweat prickles under his arms as he drinks his coffee. He pushes aside the bacon sandwich Emma has thoughtfully made for him: soft white bread, crispy bacon, lashings of ketchup. Just how he likes it and a rare treat because it is Christmas Eve. His stomach curdles.

'Sorry, Em, I'm not very hungry this morning,' he says, the need to escape suddenly urgent. He gets up. 'I'm popping out for an hour,' he announces, knowing Emma will assume he's going out for a last-minute gift for her.

The sweet smile she gives him confirms this. He pecks her on the cheek, then goes upstairs to dress.

Without a single plan in his head, Ryan drives for half an hour, ending up in some godforsaken rural village on the Kent/East Sussex border. Usually, he'd enjoy the change of scene: the charming blend of wonky Tudor cottages and weather-boarded houses almost hidden within established ivy-clad gardens. Normally, he'd admire the tiny cobbled high streets, lined with Victorian terraces festooned with Christmas lights, looking for all the world like the set of a Dickens novel. Such a contrast to the Burrows' modern noughties-built detached house, identical to whole streets of others on the safe suburban estate he calls home.

Today it doesn't matter where he is – at home or in the office, town or country, city or suburbs – because the guilt he feels has formed a prison of his own making and he is locked in without a key.

Cursing aloud, he pulls over in a lay-by, gets out his mobile phone and calls Amber. This can be sorted. *Everything* can be sorted, he thinks, desperately trying to convince himself.

When his call goes to voicemail, Ryan feels relief and disappointment in equal measure. Well at least he tried to make contact and on Christmas Eve, too. Amber will see his missed call, which will surely mollify her until they can speak properly after the holidays.

A new thought occurs to him: Emma believes he is out buying a last-minute gift for her. In which case, he had better return with something.

He turns the car around, goes to Maidstone town centre, where he parks in the multistorey, and walks briskly into a street lined with jewellery shops and boutiques. Apart from a few other desperate-looking men, pedestrians are thin on the ground and the shops are already gearing up for their Boxing Day sales. Spotting a jewellery store he recognises, Ryan enters and begins perusing the glass cabinets, dazzled by the array of glittering gems.

Clueless and overwhelmed, he's about to leave when a young woman with poker straight hair and a flick of teal eyeliner offers to help.

'I need a gift for my wife,' Ryan mumbles, feeling like a total cliché.

Fifteen minutes later, thanks to the surprising skills of the salesgirl, Ryan exits the store, several hundred pounds poorer and clutching a gift bag.

CHAPTER TWENTY

'Damn, I *knew* I'd forgotten something.'

Emma blots her damp hands on her apron and regards the organised chaos around her, relieved to have broken the back of the Christmas lunch food prep a day early.

She runs a mental checklist of all the vegetables she has peeled and chopped, as well as the pigs in blankets, two types of stuffing and the organic turkey that are all chilling in the fridge. She's remembered the cranberry sauce and a choice of two creamy desserts, in addition to her home-made Christmas cake and mince pies. There's a tin of Quality Street and some after-dinner mints, not to mention an exhaustive supply of still and sparkling wine. And yet, for all the expense and excess, she has managed to forget something.

She looks across at Ryan, snuggled up beside Callie on the kitchen sofa, thinking how utterly miserable he looks. Beside him, Callie sits spellbound, watching an animation about a reindeer who has lost his way in the snow on Christmas Eve.

'Sorry to interrupt your film, Ry,' Emma whispers, 'but I need some help.'

'Sure, what's up?' Ryan asks, as though waking from a trance.

'I forgot the red cabbage. Can you believe it? I mean, I even remembered all the spices and the cloudy apple juice to cook it in.'

Ryan looks incredulous. 'Em, we've already got enough food to feed an army. There are only five of us, for God's sake. Forget the red cabbage.'

Emma shakes her head. 'I can't. Firstly, it's traditional; secondly, it's my dad's favourite and I want everything to be perfect.'

'Yeah, well, good luck with that,' Ryan grunts, his face set.

'Well, cheers for the help, Ryan. I've done absolutely everything on my own, so it wouldn't hurt you to pop out for a bloody cabbage!'

Ryan sighs. 'Shame you didn't realise earlier; I could have got one while I was in Maidstone this morning.' He stretches and yawns. 'Okay, I'll be as quick as I can.'

Hearing Ryan start the car, Emma looks to Callie. 'Sorry I shouted and said a bad word.'

'Shush, Mummy, I'm watching this.'

'Well, that's me told. I don't know why I bother sometimes.'

She goes over to the French windows and peers out at the garden, thinking how drab it looks in the fading light.

At a loss for what else she can achieve until Ryan returns, Emma makes herself a cup of tea. Then, standing by the island, sipping the hot strong brew, she hears the faint buzz of a phone. It takes her a moment to realise that the sound is coming from Ryan's mobile.

'That'll be your other granny,' Emma says, wondering absent-mindedly if Ryan's mum and stepfather have snow in the Peak District. Following the sound, she finds Ryan's phone tucked down the side of the sofa cushion and reaches for it, her smile in place ready to greet Linda.

Amber the screen says before the call flips over to Ryan's voicemail. Emma stares at the mute phone: doesn't Ryan have a colleague called Amber? She glances at the time, wondering why anyone from the office needs him at three fifteen on Christmas Eve. She's about to set the phone down when it vibrates in her hand and the WhatsApp icon appears. She scrolls to the message. There, beside the words *we need to talk urgently* is a profile photo of an attractive red-haired woman. Emma's heartbeat quickens as she taps the screen to expand the photo. The woman's gaze is direct and unflinching, her full red lips curved into a seductive smile. *Sultry* is the word that comes to mind.

Holding her breath, Emma attempts to scroll back through the conversation, but there are no other comments. Is that because there simply are none, or because previous messages have been deleted?

Hearing the distinctive sound of Ryan's car as he mounts the drive, Emma shoves the phone back into the space where she found it, questions filling her mind.

'God, I thought she'd never fall asleep,' Ryan groans, taking a bottle of Prosecco from the fridge, opening it and filling two glasses.

'Bless her, she's so excited.' Emma takes a glass from Ryan. 'Cheers. I've been dreaming about sitting down with a glass of fizz and some nibbles all day. I must have walked five miles just around the kitchen. I hope tomorrow's a success. Daft really, it's only my parents coming round for a roast dinner when all is said and done.'

'You're joking, aren't you? It's a huge pressure.' Ryan's

expression softens. 'Look, I'm sorry, you've done absolutely everything today. Tomorrow will be a different story, just tell me what to do and I'll do it. I've been rubbish today.'

Emma takes a sip of her drink. 'You have been a bit distracted. Is everything okay?'

There's a fleeting sadness in his eyes. 'Work's getting me down, to be honest. I'm just not on top of things and I don't know how to sort it.'

Emma turns away. 'Maybe your bosses need to take on more people, there are only so many hours in a day.' She pauses, remembering. 'Actually, didn't your firm hire somebody recently? I seem to recall you going to somebody's celebration a couple of months ago.'

Ryan hesitates. 'Yes, a trainee. Nice kid, but it will be a while before she can pull her weight and make a difference,' he says, taking a glug of Prosecco.

'Which doesn't help your current workload. What's her name?' Emma says, heat creeping into her cheeks.

'Amber,' Ryan says, avoiding her gaze.

'He's been, Mummy! Father Christmas came in the night and left lots of presents,' Callie shouts, bouncing on Emma's chest.

Ryan groans. 'What time is it?' He reaches for his phone. 'Mmm, nearly six o'clock, nice and early.'

Fighting her way through sleep, Emma sits up, switches on her bedside lamp and attempts to snuggle Callie under the duvet with them, but Callie is having none of it.

'I'm not tired. Quick, get up, get up! It's Christmas!' she cries, tugging at Emma's forearm.

'Okay, we're coming, aren't we, Daddy?' Emma yawns. 'Now go and put your dressing gown and slippers on, please, and we'll go downstairs in a minute.'

'And breathe,' Emma says as Callie skips off to her room. She gets up and reaches for her robe. 'It was always going to happen. Come on, I'll make some tea, then maybe Callie can open one present before breakfast.'

But by nine o'clock, Callie has opened *all* her gifts and the living room is an explosion of discarded wrapping paper and glittery bows, as piles of new toys, games and clothes litter every surface.

'Do you think we overdid it?' Emma asks, watching Callie examine her new things during a moment of peace.

'Maybe. I'm sure we said the same thing last year. No doubt your parents will rock up with a load more stuff for her to chomp through.'

Emma puffs out her cheeks. 'Speaking of which, we'd better get this mess tidied up and ourselves showered and dressed before they get here. I'm going to need your help today.'

Ryan raises his hands. 'Just say the word, I'm all yours. In fact, why don't you go up now while I keep an eye on madam and get all these wrappings into the recycling bin.'

Freshly showered, her hair hanging in damp tendrils, Emma gazes at her reflection in the bathroom mirror. The shadows under her eyes seem darker this morning; a legacy of staying up past midnight to finish wrapping Callie's presents twinned with her early start.

Ryan's mood had morphed from sullen to sweet, improving with every glass of wine they'd drunk and by bedtime he'd been affectionate and amorous.

Emma had fended him off gently. 'I'm shattered, Ry, and no doubt we'll be up early tomorrow.'

Nevertheless, it had felt good to be wanted, and a relief, too, after Ryan had been so remote and miserable all day.

She wipes the steam from the mirror, sets about her usual beauty routine. An image of Amber slides into her mind: alluring, seductive. Young.

Why had a junior colleague been calling a senior staff member on Christmas Eve? It had been on the tip of her tongue to confront Ryan last night, but a part of her didn't want the answer during their perfect cosy family Christmas.

CHAPTER TWENTY-ONE

Emma's parents arrive promptly at noon. All smiles, Ryan wishes them both a merry Christmas and hugs them warmly before hanging up their coats. Both look sparkly and festive; Deirdre in a red sequinned top, echoed by a gash of scarlet lipstick, while Geoff wears a cosy cable-knit sweater with a reindeer motif at its centre.

Ryan stands back to admire his mother-in-law. 'You look lovely, Dee. Reminds me where Emma gets her beauty from,' he says smoothly before turning to Emma's father. 'You're looking well, too, Geoff. We're so chuffed you could come today.'

Callie bowls towards her grandparents, delighted when they feign shock at how much she's grown.

Soon, they are gathered in the kitchen, making the first toast of the day, as Michael Bublé's 'Christmas' plays in the background, swapping small talk about the local traffic and the disappointing lack of snow before Ryan ushers his in-laws into the sitting room.

'I expect Callie would love to show you her presents while Emma and I finish off the magnificent feast she's been preparing,' he says stiffly.

Emma cringes inwardly, noting the flare of her mother's nostrils and something unreadable in her eyes before tottering into the next room.

'Ry, I know you're only being a good host but tone it down a bit, will you?' Emma says once her parents are out of earshot.

'I don't know what you mean,' Ryan says.

Emma giggles. 'Magnificent feast?' She glances at the kitchen clock. 'Right, let's crack on. We've still a bit to do if we're eating at three o'clock.'

Deirdre dabs her mouth delicately with a napkin, then puts her knife and fork together with a satisfied sigh. 'I can honestly say that's the best Christmas dinner I've had in years.'

Emma beams. 'Thanks, Mum. Not quite as good as yours though,' she says loyally.

Ryan gets to his feet. 'It was perfect, Em. Thank you for all your hard work, it was delicious. I'll clear, shall I? Maybe we need a little rest before dessert?'

Having made a valiant effort to eat all her dinner, Callie yawns, her eyelids fluttering.

Emma catches Ryan's eye across the table and nods towards their daughter. '*Somebody* is worn out by all the excitement,' she says softly. 'Why don't you and Dad take her next door and snuggle with her on the sofa while Mum and I finish our drinks?'

'Good idea,' Ryan says, scooping Callie into his arms and carrying her through to the living room with Geoff at his heels.

Deirdre smiles and raises her glass. 'Well done, Emem, that was fantastic. You thought of everything.'

'My pleasure, Mum. Hey, we haven't done presents yet – except for Callie's first thing, of course. We'll let her have a nap and then swap gifts.'

'Good idea.' Deirdre drains her glass. 'Any more of that lovely pink fizz? I could manage a smidge if you'll join me.'

Emma gets up, refills both their glasses. There's a lull in the conversation as something unsaid hangs in the air.

Emma rounds on her mum. 'What? I can hear the cogs whirring.'

'You tell me.' Deirdre shrugs and sips her drink. 'Because something's definitely off with you and Ryan.'

Emma makes a face. 'Mum! Why ever would you say that?'

'I don't know, but there's something...' Deirdre purses her lips, '...and either you don't know or you're not saying.'

'Mother, that's ridiculous,' Emma says, sounding more defensive than she'd intended.

'So, why the performance? Darling, I'm fond of Ryan after all these years but, to be honest, he doesn't normally lift a finger, so why the big charm offensive?' She meets Emma's gaze. 'In my limited experience, men are never more attentive than when they feel guilty. Mark my words, Emma, Ryan's hiding something.'

Unable to meet her mother's eyes, Emma paces to the French windows, but it has grown dark and she can see nothing beyond her own reflection. She inhales sharply as Amber's face seems to look back at her. *For goodness' sake, Emma, get a grip!*

Pasting on a bright smile, she pivots to Deirdre. 'Tell you what, Mum, you join Dad next door while I fill the dishwasher and get the pans in to soak. Then we'll do dessert, followed by presents,' she says, clapping her hands in a show of excitement she does not feel.

Despite her physical exhaustion after a long day spent looking after her family, Emma lays staring at the ceiling. Beside her, Ryan's breath is deep and even. The sleep of the just because, surely, if he had anything to hide – as her mother had so annoyingly suggested – he too would be wide awake.

So why does she feel so unbalanced by nothing more than a random phone call from a work colleague? Why does the very thought of Amber set alarm bells ringing?

She replays the early evening in her mind. After dinner, the whole family had gathered around the twinkling fir tree for another round of present giving. Her parents had spoilt Callie, of course, surprising her with an expensive wooden doll's house and a raft of smaller parcels containing beautifully crafted miniature furniture.

Then the adults had swapped gifts, exclaiming over presents that were thoughtful but predictable. For Emma, a smart new hairdryer with a clutch of styling tools from her mum and dad, and a gorgeous cashmere wrap, and this year's must-have perfume from Ryan. And then, almost as an afterthought, as though he'd forgotten all about it, Ryan had sheepishly produced a ribboned box from an upmarket jewellers.

She'd been genuinely surprised, her heart lifting for a nano-second before her mother's lecture about men being at their most attentive when they are hiding something came back to her.

With the eyes of her family upon her, Emma had faked excitement as she flipped the box open and removed the contents. 'Love, that's so *generous* of you. It's lovely... really gorgeous. Thank you,' she'd said to Ryan, putting her arms around his neck and kissing him.

His reaction had been guarded. 'Do you like it? I wasn't sure...'

She'd been emphatic that she *loved* it but in truth, she couldn't imagine wearing the yellow gold and blue topaz necklace he'd given her with its fussy old-fashioned setting – not to mention the fact that she'd never worn yellow gold in her life, always opting for white gold or platinum.

Was the necklace the result of Ryan's mysterious Christmas Eve dash? He'd been gone for hours and had returned distant and miserable, right up until he'd put Callie to bed. Had he made a fraught attempt at a romantic gesture, only to get it terribly wrong?

From across the landing, a creak of floorboards followed by the sound of the bathroom door opening and closing and her mum clearing her throat, reminds Emma that as much as she loves her parents, it will be an immense relief when they set off for home in the morning.

She turns to Ryan's sleeping form and slips her hand into his, desperate for sleep.

CHAPTER TWENTY-TWO

NOW

'For God's sake, Emma. Your hangover is costing us valuable time.'

Distraught, Ryan hovers behind her while she retches over the toilet bowl. When the nausea abates, she splashes cold water on her face and dives back into the bedroom, dragging shorts and a T-shirt over the underwear she'd slept in.

'Tell me again where you've looked,' Emma says, the tremor in her hands obvious as she laces her trainers.

'*Everywhere.*' Ryan shakes his head. 'Haven't you heard a bloody word I've said? She's gone. Callie's missing.'

A sob bursts from Emma's throat. She breathes deeply, wills herself not to throw up again so that she can think; Ryan is right, they *are* wasting time. She tries to focus. 'You've looked everywhere in the house, yes? And the back garden? What about out the front? She could be sitting by the pool.'

'Emma, I'm ahead of you. I've looked in *all* those places.' Ryan's voice rises in a strangled wail. 'I've looked *everywhere.* Where *is* she?'

Emma's eyes widen. 'Ry, I know where she is. She'll have gone next door to call for Lucas. Come on.'

They run downstairs and out of the front door, stepping over a flower border in their haste to knock on Jack and Sheena's door.

Jack answers, confusion written on his face.

'Is Callie with you?' Ryan demands, his hands balled into fists.

Jack rubs his bearded chin. 'No, mate. What makes you think she's here?'

'Are you sure?' Emma stands on tiptoes, cranes her neck, and peers over Jack's shoulder.

Jack frowns. 'Emma, I'm positive. When did you last see her?' he asks, reasonably.

Ryan gives Emma a withering look. 'When I put her to bed last night, after Emma passed out.'

'Well, she can't be far away.' Jack steps back, calls out to Sheena who appears in an instant, her eyes wide with alarm.

'What's happened?'

'We don't know where Callie is. We thought she might be here with Lucas,' Emma says, her speech thick.

Sheena's face puckers. 'I wish I could tell you that she's here—'

Ryan reaches into his pocket and pulls out his mobile. 'Right, I'm calling the police.'

Sheena raises her hand. 'Wait. Look, I can see you're upset – I would be, too, it's every parent's worst nightmare – but let's have a thorough look for her first, maybe check the beach, you know what a water baby she is.'

Ryan hesitates.

'Sheena's right,' Emma says, 'we don't speak Spanish, so before we set off a whole circus of events, let's look around the development properly then check the beach. Please God, let her just be having a paddle.'

'I'll come, too,' Sheena says. 'Jack, you stay here with the boys. And don't let them out of your sight,' she hisses.

Moments later, they're walking and calling Callie's name, peering into the dark foul-smelling bin shack, before stumbling along the stony beach path through the copse of trees, heads and eyes swivelling as they go.

The beach looks like it always does, which only serves to mock their inner pain and turmoil. They take in a few early birds dotted in groups along the pale sand and the handful of people paddling in the turquoise shallows.

Emma stands for a moment, eyes frantically roaming the groups of holidaymakers, her heart lifting at the sight of a dark-haired little girl around Callie's age – until she turns to the woman beside her and speaks to her in Spanish.

'She's not here,' Ryan says, his voice cracking. 'I know she isn't. Someone's taken her and the sooner we call the police, the quicker she'll be found.' Clutching his mobile, he curses. 'I can't see the screen for the glare. I don't even know how to ring the police here. It won't be nine nine nine like at home.'

'We should speak to John and Max,' Emma says. 'Let's go back to the house and ask them, they'll know what to do.'

With Ryan out in front, the three of them retrace their steps, calling Callie's name, until they emerge onto the development.

'Wait.' Ryan stops walking abruptly, looks down at the phone in his right hand and uses his left to shield the screen. When he raises his head Emma can see the tears in his eyes.

'There's a text from an unknown sender. It says Callie's been taken, that she's okay. But if we involve the police,' he pauses, inhales sharply, 'we'll never see our daughter again.'

Seconds later, another text had arrived. Short and precise, it simply said *await instructions*. Then they'd blindly stumbled back to the villa – thanks to Sheena's gentle but firm persuasion – and once inside, Emma had collapsed on the tiled floor, her legs weak and useless, a Kango hammer drilling in her skull.

Ryan had asked Sheena to leave then, saying they needed to think. To focus. With tears in her eyes, she'd let herself out, promising to return shortly, babbling that if there was anything, *anything* she and Jack could do...

Ryan paces, his expression hollow with fear. 'This can't be happening. I feel like we're stuck in a nightmare because this can't be real. Why would *anybody* snatch Callie? I mean, we're not rich or famous...' He trails off, sits on the edge of the sofa, his head in his hands as a fresh horror dawns. 'If some filthy fucking pervert has got her, I will hunt them down and I will kill them.'

'Don't say that! Don't even think it,' Emma cries, tears coursing down her cheeks as she pictures Callie alone in the dark somewhere, tied up and terrified. She breathes deeply, pushes the image away. 'It won't be anything like that. It'll be about money. Everything's *always* about money.' She staggers to the kitchen, finds a tissue and blows her nose. 'You read the text: *await instructions*. Surely that means whoever's got Callie expects a ransom from us.'

Parched, she boils the kettle and makes two cups of strong instant coffee, places one in front of Ryan and sits down on the other sofa.

'I don't know what to do, Em,' he rasps. 'Every fibre in my body is saying call the police. But what if they're watching us? What if this house is bugged and they can hear every word? We can't take that risk.' He takes a sip of coffee, winces. 'Jesus, Emma, how did this happen? How did they even get in? There are no broken doors or windows, nothing's out of place. We don't even know how long she's been gone.'

Emma shivers despite it being almost thirty degrees outside. 'Look, I'm sorry to ask, but did you lock up properly last night?'

'Of course!' Ryan snaps coldly. 'I locked up, back and front. Not that *you* would know seeing as you were off your face. Emma, how could you have got so drunk? I know you're a lightweight, but Christ—'

Emma shakes her head. 'I don't know. I didn't even drink much. I had one glass of wine with dinner at the restaurant and I was only on my second glass of fizz at the party when everything started to spin. Ry, it was so sudden. Maybe it wasn't just alcohol, perhaps it was sunstroke.'

Ryan shakes his head. 'Unlikely, we've been here over two weeks, you're used to the hot weather by now. Emma, I know this sounds ludicrous, but what if you were drugged? What if all of this was planned?'

Emma's stare is one of incredulity. 'Surely not. Why would anyone—?'

'You said you had two drinks. I was with you when John gave you the first; what was your second?'

Emma frowns, trying to remember. 'Er... I was with Max's friends, Colin and Arturas. They introduced me to a whole bunch of people – no idea who any of them were – and then Sheena gave me another glass of sparkling wine.'

Ryan sits up straighter. 'So you're saying it was Sheena who gave you the last drink you had before you passed out?'

'Yes. But surely you don't think—'

'Oh God,' Ryan groans. 'I'm such a fucking idiot!'

Emma is on her feet. 'What? Ryan, tell me. What do you know... what's going on?'

He chews his lip, a deep flush creeping up from his throat. 'After I helped you into bed to sleep it off, I tucked Callie in, told her I loved her,' he puffs out his cheeks and swipes a hand over his face as his voice breaks, 'then I went back to the party.'

Emma shakes her head in disbelief. 'Sorry, you... you did *what*? You went *back* to the party? Why would you leave us alone in the house when I was clearly very unwell to return to a party you never wanted to go to in the first place?'

Ryan stands, unable to look at her. He prowls the room, checks his phone again and swears under his breath.

'Oh, I get it,' Emma says eventually. 'It was because Sheena invited you, and you thought you'd have some fun with her while *I* was out cold. Wow! After everything we've been through... all the work we've done on our marriage. And to think I actually *liked* Sheena... So she drugged *me* and kept *you* out of the way while someone else kidnapped Callie?' Emma says, putting the pieces together in her head.

'Emma, I swear nothing happened. I was only there for another hour, hour and a half at tops. We just talked, danced a bit, had another drink... that's it.'

Emma laughs bitterly. 'Oh shut up, Ryan. Can you hear yourself? Do you think I give a shit about that now? Because we are done. Over. All that matters now is getting our daughter back and for that, we'll need to work together and put on a united front whether Sheena is involved or not.'

CHAPTER TWENTY-THREE

Ryan's eyes are black with desperation as he paces the living room. 'Give me one good reason why we shouldn't go next door and confront Jack and Sheena this instant. For all we know, they've got Callie locked up in there. God, Emma, we can't just do nothing.'

'We've been through this,' Emma croaks, her throat raw from weeping. 'The second text said *await instructions*. That means that whoever's got Callie will be in touch soon. Until then, we need to sit tight. I hate this as much as you do; *more*, for Christ's sake. I *carried* her, Ryan, she's my only child and right now she could be alone, terrified, and crying for her mummy.'

The image she has conjured is too much. With bile rising in her throat, she crosses to the sink and splashes water on her face, breathing deeply before returning to the sofa.

Ryan shakes his head. 'I knew something was off with them. Too matey too quickly. I wouldn't be surprised if they've been biding their time since they got here. But the question is why?'

'Stop. None of this is helping. We've no reason to think Jack and Sheena are involved in any way.' Emma wipes her eyes with the heel of her hand. 'Sheena looked devastated this morning, genuinely upset. You said yourself, there must have been thirty or forty people at the party last night. Any one of them could have slipped something in my drink – and whoever it was, made sure I wouldn't wake up to Callie being taken.'

'Yes, yes, I know,' Ryan says. 'But apart from the gay couple we've met before, I couldn't recognise a single one of them again, could you?'

Emma shakes her head. 'Maybe if—'

Ryan's phone buzzes in his hand and he silences her with a look. 'God, Em, this is it.' He sucks air into lungs before reading aloud: 'We have your daughter. The price for her return is 100,000 euros. Time and location to be advised. Await instructions.'

Emma grabs the phone from Ryan's hand and reads the message for herself. She shakes her head, her chin wobbling. 'No! I don't like the wording. There's no mention of whether Callie is safe or not. How do we know she's even alive?'

'Exactly what I was thinking,' Ryan whispers. 'What do we do, Emma? What the hell do we do?'

'We ask for proof. Message them back, saying we need to be sure she's okay then they'll get the money.'

Ryan stares back blankly. 'What if we piss them off and they... they hurt her because of us?'

A sob escapes Emma's throat. 'If they plan to hurt her, they'll have done it by now. Ryan, we need to know.'

Trembling, all fingers and thumbs, Ryan taps out a message.

'Oh God, *please* let her be okay,' Emma whimpers when the phone remains ominously silent.

Ryan pockets his mobile. 'We need some fresh air. We have to keep it together, at least until we figure out how to raise 100,000 euros, and fast.'

The midday sun only worsens the throb in Ryan's head.

How is it even possible that everything looks the same, from the vibrant purple hibiscus bushes to the gleaming white render of the villas, set off by the cloudless blue sky. Their very existence has been ripped apart, yet life surges normally and happily all around them.

As he and Emma pass John and Max's property on their way to the beach path, the door opens and Max appears, hauling two black rubbish bags. 'Good morning, you two,' she calls. 'Hope your heads are less sore than ours this morning.'

'Wave, smile and keep going,' Ryan instructs from the corner of his mouth without breaking his stride. 'The last person who needs to know is Radio-Max. If we tell *them* what's going on, we might as well announce it on the six o'clock news.'

Moments later, emerging onto the golden sand, Emma sinks to her knees. 'I don't know what to do. Ryan, tell me what to do.'

He drops down beside her and grips her wrists. 'Em, we have to keep it together. We're going to get her back. No question about it. It'll be a challenge to raise the money, but I've already been doing some mental calculations. Listen to me, we can just about pull the ransom together. We've got £70,000 in our joint savings account and I can draw down a loan of up to twenty grand from Barclays with just one phone call—'

Emma shrugs. 'How?'

'Simple. I've banked there since I was eighteen and they're desperate to give me money. Em, that amount has been on ice since we got planning permission for the extension we never got round to and it's still on file. Only two weeks ago, they rang to chase me on it. Like I said, they're gagging for my business.'

'But that still leaves us short.'

'Actually, it doesn't,' Ryan says. 'Don't forget the exchange rate. It varies all the time, of course, but I reckon we'll need between eighty-six and eighty-eight thousand pounds to hit the mark.' He pauses. 'And if Barclays drag their heels – which they won't – I'll ask Mum for the rest.'

Emma clasps her hands together. 'What! Ryan, you can't. She'll want to know why and we can't involve her, we can't involve anyone, there's too much at stake.'

'Then we'll come up with a plausible reason why we need the money immediately. We'll say we've fallen in love with an apartment out here and we need a lump sum to secure the deal before we fly back. Mum's always fancied a holiday home in the sun.'

'We're meant to be flying home tomorrow evening,' Emma says, her voice small. She takes a deep breath and shudders. 'Ry, what if we raise every penny we can and we *still* don't get Callie back. What if this whole thing is just an elaborate con?'

'Emma, it *is* a con. An outright con. Kidnapping a child for ransom money is exactly that,' Ryan says, exasperated.

'But why us? Why Callie? I mean, there are three children on our villa complex alone and hundreds, possibly thousands in the resort. None of this makes sense.'

'No, it doesn't. But I feel sure that Jack and Sheena are involved, whether she spiked your drink or not.' Ryan gets up, dusts the sand from his shorts and offers Emma his hand. 'Come on, let's go back to the villa.' He pulls her to her feet. 'We need to get on the phone and start moving money around; I'll need my laptop for that. Hurry up, the clock's ticking.'

Emma watches in awe while Ryan phones and negotiates with his bank, flying through their stringent security checks calmly and even managing to sound upbeat.

He's a brilliant liar, she thinks, unnerved. No wonder he'd managed to fool her during his affair with Amber.

Finally, Ryan ends his call and closes his laptop, a

triumphant look beneath the sheen of sweat on his face. 'It's done and unless technology fails us, we should have all the money before noon tomorrow.'

Emma puts her head in her hands. 'I don't care if we have to sell our house and everything we have, I just want her back,' she sobs. 'I want my baby back.'

CHAPTER TWENTY-FOUR

THEN

On Boxing Day, after waving Geoff and Deirdre off, Ryan and Emma cocoon themselves in front of the TV with Callie, watching Christmas films and snacking on leftovers and sweets.

As the credits roll on their third festive movie of the day, Ryan heaves himself off the sofa with a yawn. 'It's exhausting doing nothing. Maybe we should plan something for tomorrow; give us something to aim for.' He pats his midriff and glances at the half empty tin of chocolates on the coffee table. 'A trip to the gym wouldn't go amiss, if I keep this up, I'll be needing a whole new wardrobe by spring.'

Emma laughs. 'Don't exaggerate. It's only for a couple of days and everyone does it, cut yourself some slack. Anyway, we're supposed to be having drinks with the neighbours tomorrow.'

Ryan blinks. 'Are we?'

'Yes, I'm sure I told you. Ruth and Kevin are having a few people round. I suspect they've invited the whole close out of politeness.'

Ryan groans. 'Do we have to? Kevin's such a boring git,

always banging on about his job in IT and as for Ruth she's, like, thirty-five going on sixty.'

'Ouch. That's a bit mean. They're good neighbours, like most people around here.'

'You go, I'll stay here with Callie,' Ryan offers. 'Seriously.'

Emma sighs. 'Callie's coming with us. It's an early thing. The invite said from 3pm, and there'll be other children there. Please come, just for an hour or two.'

Ryan visibly wilts. 'Maybe...'

Emma goes to the window, peers into the gathering dusk. A few houses are in darkness, their owners away for the holidays, while others are ablaze with fairy lights. She focuses on Kevin and Ruth's house, diagonally opposite theirs. Twinkling white lights adorn every tree and shrub, and a white star flashes from their gable. She wonders idly how it got there; had Kevin scaled a high ladder himself, or had he paid someone else to?

She glances back at Ryan, now engrossed in his mobile phone, a scowl darkening his expression. 'We should go,' she says firmly, 'make an effort.'

The following morning, prompted by a glittering frost and a clear blue sky, Emma suggests a family walk ahead of their neighbours' party. Soon all three of them are bundled into padded coats, scarves and beanie hats, striding towards the end of Wisteria Close where a gap between two houses leads them to their local country park.

With a pang of nostalgia, Emma thinks back to the first time she and Ryan had seen their house, when it had just been the two of them. They'd been blown away by the extra space they'd be gaining by swapping their two-bedroom flat in south London by buying *further out*. At the time, a four-bedroomed detached house with a garden and garage seemed the height of luxury, and the existence of a thirty-acre green space, just a few hundred metres from their front door, had clinched the deal. They'd even discussed getting a dog but eighteen months later, Callie's arrival had been disruption enough for both of them, and the idea of Emma taking on another commitment while Ryan worked long hours in the office had soon lost its appeal.

'Remember when we talked about getting a puppy?' Emma says after Callie has stopped to pet three dogs in quick succession.

Ryan smiles. 'I do but you've got enough on your plate now you're at the salon three days a week. Maybe one day though.' He gazes wistfully ahead, his thoughts elsewhere.

Emma tucks her arm into his. 'Ry, what is it? What's troubling you? And don't say nothing because I can tell something's off,' she says gently while Callie skips ahead, singing to herself.

Ryan pauses, then wheels around to face her. 'You know I love you and Callie more than anything, don't you?'

Emma searches his eyes. 'I'm sensing a but here.'

'No, there's no but.' Ryan shakes his head. 'But sometimes I think our lives are so small and *safe*. And I wonder what it would be like if we just sold up and took off somewhere – to live like church mice for a while, in a place where nobody knows us.'

'That sounds like running away to me, but from what? I thought we were happy here. I thought *you* were happy. Most people would kill for what we have: each other; a healthy, beautiful daughter; three out of four parents still with us; a lovely house; enough money. Surely, it's greedy to ask for more.'

Ryan laughs bitterly. 'Not *more*, Em. *Different*. Less, even. So that I don't have to sell my soul for nine hours a day to rich arseholes who think having an orangery bigger than their next-door neighbour's is the be-all... honestly, I get so tired.'

'Maybe all you really need is a holiday,' Emma says,

realising they have circled back to where they started and are only a few minutes from home.

She gathers Callie in, looks across at Ryan's profile, noticing the miserable set of his mouth and the haunted look in his eyes. Something has happened, something he isn't telling her, and the change in him is marked. And it's not even recent. He's been acting weird, detached and evasive for months. Specifically, since the night he'd gone out with his work colleagues to celebrate a lucrative contract. A few weeks later, it had happened again: a casual after-work Friday night drinking spree, when he'd been out until four in the morning, telling her the next day that he'd needed to look after Pete Robson who was so drunk no taxi would take him unescorted. Emma swallows the lump forming at the base of her throat. Amber had been there on both occasions. That much she knew after Ryan had casually dropped her into the conversation.

She consciously slows her breathing. The urge to dig deeper is almost overwhelming – until she catches sight of Callie's happy carefree face and is silenced by the thought of ruining their peaceful family Christmas.

'Come on,' Emma says eventually, 'let's go home. We can have a bite to eat and relax before the party this afternoon.'

At two fifteen, leaving Callie under Ryan's supervision, Emma goes upstairs to freshen up for the party. The simple act of showering and changing into a short sweater dress worn with Lurex tights and long black boots lifts her mood.

'You look pretty, Mummy,' Callie says, running in and jumping on the bed while Emma sits at her dressing table applying mascara.

'Thank you, Cal. I'll just finish my make-up then we'll get you changed into something lovely and sparkly, okay?'

Callie nods, leaps off the bed and runs off to her own room.

Emma listens. There's no evidence of Ryan getting ready to go out; no sound of water running in the other bathroom, neither has he come in to change his clothes. With a pang of unease, she leans over the landing banister.

'Ry? Callie's up here with me if you need to get ready,' she calls out, hoping she comes across as helpful rather than bossy.

Ryan appears at the bottom of the stairs. 'Yeah, about that,' he says, walking up and pausing at the top. He puts a hand to his forehead. 'I'm sorry, Em, but I'm afraid I'm not going. I've just had an email from Raj and he's asked me to meet him in the office for a couple of hours.'

Emma's eyes widen. 'Oh no, you're joking. But you're on holiday and the practice is closed, for God's sake. What's so important that it can't wait until New Year?'

'He wants to talk about a new project. Says it's very lucrative and that the client wants to hit the ground running in January.'

'Is there something you're not telling me? I know you're hiding something and—'

'Emma, please. Get off my case. I've already said I'm under huge pressure at work. It will all sort itself, trust me. Now, you go with Callie, have a great time and I'll see you later.' Ryan, brushes past her, muttering that he needs to make himself look presentable.

CHAPTER TWENTY-FIVE

The texts from Amber had restarted on Boxing Day afternoon, while Ryan lazed on the sofa with Emma and Callie, watching *Home Alone* 2 and eating Quality Street. The first message was mournful but polite. Ryan almost felt sorry for her.

> Sorry I missed your call on Christmas Eve, hope you're having good hols – please call again. xx

An hour later, two more messages arrived in quick succession, civil but impatient.

> Need to speak to you urgently, please get in touch. x

Followed by:

> Ring me asap!!

Ryan deleted all three messages while Emma looked out of the window and wittered on about the neighbours opposite.

Then he turned his phone off and slid it into his pocket, fuming inwardly.

How dare Amber keep hassling him like this? It was beginning to feel a lot like stalking. He'd said he'd get in touch after Christmas and he'd meant it. And she knew the score. He had never hidden the fact that he was married with a small child and from the get-go, *she'd* done all the running.

Well, what a flake she'd turned out to be! Spoilt, too, and used to getting her own way: a private education, a smart modern flat overlooking the river that she'd bought with assistance from the Bank of Mum and Dad, and a job she'd charmed her way into – one that she was woefully under qualified for, in his opinion. She was beautiful, middle-class, overindulged by her parents, and as a result, petulant. Well, he was not at home to it. Not today, not ever.

And whether Amber was pregnant or not – and even then, it didn't necessarily make *him* the father – she needed to learn a few life lessons, patience being one of them.

So, he'd left his phone switched off overnight, waiting until Emma was in the bathroom before turning it on the next morning.

He gaped at the screen as three more messages bounced before his eyes, feeling sick to his stomach as he read Amber's increasingly desperate demands.

> Don't ignore me. Am carrying your child FFS.

But it was the next message that froze Ryan's blood in his veins and made his heart thump painfully in his chest.

> I know where you live. Get in touch or I'll be
> forced to turn up at your house.

And just for good measure, a final chilling threat:

Am not bluffing, Ryan – fucking call me. NOW.

Ryan wants to curl up in a ball and cry. He wants to throw up. He wants to smash something with his fists. How dare Amber do this to him? He'd treated her like a grown-up and been straight with her all along. What did she expect? That he'd dump his family without a backward glance, run to her side and they'd stroll off into the sunset together? Why couldn't she see their office fling for what it so obviously was?

He catches his breath. What has he done?

If Emma finds out about Amber, that he has slept with her, let alone that she claims to be pregnant with his child, it will kill her. God alone knows what he'll do about the whole sorry mess longer term, but right now he has one priority: get Amber back in her box to keep her away from his family.

He's quiet at breakfast, impatient with Callie when she rattles on and on about some shitty plastic toy she's seen on TV. She's just had a ton of new stuff, for Christ's sake. How can his little girl be so materialistic at such a tender age?

It's a relief when Emma suggests wrapping up warm and going for a walk. But even outside in their local country park, with blue sky overhead and ice-cold air in his lungs, he feels suffocated.

Because Emma is watchful. Something has set her antenna twitching and she keeps asking him what's wrong. He tells her that work's bringing him down, that he's under pressure, and that he dreams of escaping the rat race – getting away somewhere, just the three of them, and starting again. And oddly, even though it's an excuse as to why he's so bloody miserable, as the words come out of his mouth, it sounds more and more appealing...

He breathes deeply. Slow down. All this could blow over. He'll talk to Amber, kindly, respectfully. Appeal to her sense of sisterhood. Why would she want to ruin the innocent lives of his wife and child, who've done absolutely nothing to her? Because it's Ryan's guess that if push comes to shove, Amber won't want that at all.

Back at the house, their faces pink from the cold, they head into the kitchen where Emma throws a snack together while Ryan makes mugs of tea for the two of them and pours juice for Callie. Then together they sit up at the kitchen island and graze on leftovers with the TV on in the background.

'Em, I'll clear these bits and watch Callie while you get ready for the party,' Ryan says as they are finishing up. 'And take your time.'

'Thanks,' Emma says, 'if you're sure.'

Ryan smiles. 'Of course. I just need to check my emails, then I'll follow you up and change my shirt or something.'

As promised, Ryan tidies round and loads the dishwasher, switches the TV to a kids' channel to occupy Callie, and opens his laptop. Then he emails Amber, apologises for not being in touch sooner, and asks her to meet him at the pub near their office at four o'clock.

CHAPTER TWENTY-SIX

It's a few minutes past four when Ryan enters the Black Swan. He looks around, wonders if the pub is closed for the holidays given the stark overhead lighting and the lack of music – and for that matter, customers.

Satisfied that Amber hasn't arrived before him, he heads back towards the entrance, intercepting her in the small lobby area between the street door and the main bar.

Their eyes lock for a second as Ryan is rendered speechless by her beauty.

Amber's smile is wry. 'Leaving already?'

'Hi. Yes, it's completely dead in there; I thought we could go somewhere else?' Ryan says, recovering.

She purses her lips, ponders for moment. 'Tell you what, why don't we get out of town and find a country pub with a real fire.'

Ryan's heart sinks. This isn't going to be easy. She's already acting like they're on a date: dressed to the nines in a close-fitting jersey dress visible beneath her open coat, and tan suede over-the-knee boots. She looks chic, expensive, and sexy as hell.

Her suggestion to find a quiet country pub with a cosy fireplace only reinforces his theory.

'I don't have much time,' Ryan says curtly. 'And obviously I'm driving, so I won't be drinking.'

Amber raises her eyebrows and laughs. 'Neither will I, obvs. Or have you forgotten?'

Ryan opens the door and ushers her into the street. 'Come on, I'm parked round the back,' he says, ignoring her inference.

'I've not been in your car before,' Amber says, settling back with a sigh.

Ryan glances in the rear-view mirror where Callie's booster seat mocks him silently.

And you never will again. 'It does its job,' he says, pulling smoothly out of the car park and joining the traffic. 'There's a decent boozer on the M20 at junction eight. We can be there in ten minutes. The food's not bad, if you're hungry?'

Amber smiles and crosses one long boot over the other. 'Maybe, my appetite's all over the place because of the baby.'

Ryan cringes. Amber is sitting in Emma's seat, crowing about the baby, and it feels all wrong. Sweat prickles under his armpits and his temples begin to throb.

Neither of them says much until they arrive at The Pear Tree. At least the car park is busy, which alludes to there being a few punters inside.

'What would you like to drink?' Ryan asks once they've settled at a table tucked inside an alcove and close enough to the fireplace to benefit from its warmth.

Standing at the bar waiting to be served, Ryan notices that most of the patrons are in couples or family groups. He pictures Emma, chatting with the neighbours at Ruth and Kevin's get-together; imagines Callie playing with some of the local kids, and a lump fills his throat. *What the hell is he doing here?*

When it's his turn, he orders two Diet Cokes but changes his mind at the last minute.

'Actually, make that a single gin and tonic and a Diet Coke,' he tells the barman, hoping to steady his nerves.

Then there's nowhere to hide, nothing else for it but to return to Amber with the drinks and hear her out.

'You were ages,' she says, her tone peevish. 'So, are we talking or what?'

'Yes, obviously, that's why I'm here. And by the way, I don't appreciate being threatened.'

Ryan sips his drink, feels the comforting familiar burn in his throat. 'So, let's talk about your news. What makes you think you're pregnant?'

Her expression sours. 'I'm very well, thanks for asking. Oh, hang on, you didn't. And FYI, I don't *think* I'm pregnant. I *know*. I've taken two tests: one at home, and one at my GP's surgery. Both were positive. I mean, it's not ideal and I certainly didn't plan—'

'Not *ideal*? It's a fucking disaster. How could you let this happen?' Ryan says through gritted teeth. 'Are you absolutely sure that it's mine?'

Amber's eyes widen. '*It*, as you so charmingly put it, is our child. And yes, of course I'm bloody sure. Are you implying that I sleep around? And before you ask, I also know how far gone I am, and I can link it back to the Friday night we celebrated my new job.'

She takes a sip of cola and grimaces. 'God, I'm going to miss alcohol.'

Ryan's head spins. 'You're not serious? You don't mean to tell me you're actually having this kid?'

'Duh?' She makes a face and waggles her head, reminding him how immature she is. 'Absolutely! God, Ryan, it goes without saying.'

His heart is pounding now. He gulps his drink then adjusts his expression to one he hopes is less hostile. 'Amber, I'm sorry, but it's a bit of a shock as you can imagine. For one thing, you told me the first night we... got together, that you were on the pill.'

'I am, but occasionally I forget to take it, or I get it mixed up with my antidepressants.'

Oh God.

'I wasn't aware you took them,' Ryan says evenly.

'It's not the kind of thing one advertises at work, is it?' She smiles. 'Anyway, I'm so much better than I used to be—'

Bombs are going off in Ryan's head.

'And apart from your lack of enthusiasm – which I assume is temporary while you get your head around things – I'm thrilled about the baby.'

Ryan nods slowly. 'Amber, surely you can see that this isn't the right time. You've just got yourself a great new job, and you're young and beautiful with everything ahead of you. Why would you ruin a great opportunity – not to mention your fabulous figure – with a kid?'

She leans in and rests her hand on his arm. 'Because it feels so right. You and me, a little one of our own.'

'Amber, there is no *you and me*,' Ryan says, panic rising in his chest. 'Look, you're a lovely young woman – beautiful, clever and above all *kind*. Which is why I know you won't want to hurt my family. Because whatever mistakes you and I have made, my wife and my little girl have done nothing wrong. So please, think carefully about whether you have the baby or not.'

He can see the conviction ebbing out of her as her spine softens and tears well in her eyes. Her hand shakes as she raises her glass to her lips.

'I know,' she whispers eventually, 'things aren't perfect, but I love you, Ryan, and I know we could be really happy together.'

'And in another life, we might have been, but I'm married and I can't leave my family,' Ryan says, attempting to sound regretful. God in heaven, at this point, he'll say anything to keep this neurotic woman from destroying his entire life.

Hope blooms in her eyes. 'So you love me, too? I knew it... I could tell when we were in bed together. I've never felt such a strong connection with anyone before.'

'Amber, it doesn't matter what we *feel*. We have to do the right thing for everyone. Now is not the time to have a child.' He pauses, steels himself for what he is about to say. 'I think you should consider a termination – they're quick and painless these days. I'll come with you and I'll pay for it, obviously. Then after that, we can be friends, but nothing more.'

Tears spring into Amber's eyes and roll down her cheeks. Embarrassed, Ryan looks around and hopes nobody is watching them.

'Come on, don't cry,' he says, squeezing her shoulder awkwardly and getting to his feet. 'Let's go for a little drive, then I'll take you home. We can talk some more on the way.'

CHAPTER TWENTY-SEVEN

NOW

In Callie's room, Emma flings open the wardrobe and chest of drawers and starts stuffing the contents into a holdall.

Confused, Ryan hesitates in the doorway. 'Em, what are you doing?'

'I'm packing Callie's things. We need to be ready, so the moment we get her back we can fly straight home,' Emma says, her speech muffled by sobs. 'I can't just sit and wait. I can't bear it—'

Ryan reaches for her and pins her arms to her sides. 'I know, I feel exactly the same. But we're going to get her back. I promise.' He holds Emma at arm's length. 'Em, look at me. Callie has been kidnapped for *money*. If they hurt her, we won't pay and that's all they care about, so we *know* she'll be all right. We've got to keep it together, keep the phone charged and wait for instructions,' Ryan says, parroting the last text. He tugs gently at Emma's arm. 'Come on, downstairs. I'm going to make us both some tea and toast, then we're going to speak to Jack and Sheena, calmly and quietly, so we can gauge their reactions and see if they let anything slip.'

Sheena ushers them inside; she looks as though she's been crying. 'Hey, come in. I was just about to knock to see if you'd heard anything.'

'Yeah, another text arrived,' Ryan says. 'This time demanding a ransom. But we still don't know where Callie is or how we'll get her home.'

Sheena's hands fly to her mouth. 'Oh my God. Okay, well at least you know what this is about now. Are you going to... I mean, can you *afford* to pay what they want?'

'Not really,' Emma says quietly, 'but our daughter's life is hanging in the balance, so obviously we'll move heaven and earth to get her back.'

Sheena tilts her head. 'Listen, whatever you need, Jack's always got money in the business. What you're going through is beyond heartbreaking and I can't begin to imagine how you're coping.' She turns towards Jack as he comes in from the garden, his flip-flops slapping the tiles as he approaches.

'Sheena's right,' he says. 'If you need money, it's yours. We can sort the rest at home once this nightmare is over.'

'Thank you, I appreciate it,' Ryan says. 'But we've got the money.'

Sheena's eyebrows shoot up. 'Oh, well that's good... isn't it? Come and sit down.'

She glances towards the garden where her sons are playing happily in the afternoon sun. 'Lucas asked me where Callie is today; he said he wants to play with her.' Her voice catches and she looks away to hide the tears welling. She takes a deep breath then offers everyone a drink.

'Thanks, but we've just had something,' Ryan says. 'Look, sorry to ask, but have either of you seen or heard anything odd in the last couple of days?'

Sheena shrugs. 'Like what? Obviously Max and John had a

houseful last night, but all their friends are so lovely – and wealthy, too – so I can't believe there's any connection there.'

Emma lifts her chin. 'Anything's possible though, isn't it?'

'We think Emma might have been drugged last night,' Ryan says, coolly. 'And actually, Sheena, it was *you* who gave Emma the drink that knocked her out.'

'*Me?*' Sheena gapes.

Jack is on his feet. 'Whoa, now hold on a minute. What are you saying? That my wife drugged Emma and we're involved in some way?' He shakes his head. 'That's fucking outrageous – I just offered to lend you the ransom, for Christ's sake.'

'Weird though, isn't it?' Ryan replies. 'One minute, we're all there chatting and laughing as a family; the next, Emma's taken ill after a couple of drinks and only a few hours later, our daughter is snatched. And meanwhile, *you*, Jack, are nowhere to be seen.'

'We also know,' Emma adds quietly, a slight tremor to her voice, 'that Sheena stayed at the party and insisted Ryan join her after putting me and Callie to bed.' She meets Sheena's gaze. 'Now why would you do that, Sheena?'

Jack curls his lip. 'What, so now you're implying that Sheena and Ryan had some secret assignation?' He laughs bitterly. 'You've both got a fucking nerve. Emma, I trust my wife, shame you can't say the same about Ryan, although it comes as no surprise to me; I've seen the way he looks at Sheena. It's disgusting.'

Sheena flushes and puts a hand to her forehead. 'I know you don't mean any of this and that it's grief and anxiety talking. Emma, nothing happened between me and Ryan, I just wanted a wingman for the evening; I didn't know anyone else. We were just having a laugh and a dance.'

'She's right,' Ryan mumbles. 'Nothing happened between Sheena and I, but it does mean that Callie was basically alone, given Emma was out cold. Obviously, I'll regret going back to the party for the rest of my life, but all we care about now is getting our daughter back.'

Sheena raises a hand. 'I understand. But if you think we were connected in any way, you're wrong.' She turns to Jack and squares her shoulders. 'Get the kids in. We're leaving. Tonight. I don't care if we have to sleep at the airport. It's devastating that Callie's missing but the fact we're under suspicion is outrageous.' She turns to Ryan and Emma. 'Now, can you go please, we need to pack.'

Ryan checks the battery on his mobile: it's at eighty-seven per cent. 'Please, *please*, get in touch,' he begs, staring at the screen and willing a message to appear.

'It's been hours. Why haven't we heard from them?' Emma says, jumping up and pacing the living room for the umpteenth time.

Hunched on the sofa, Ryan rolls his shoulders. 'Maybe they're waiting until after dark?'

'Why? What's that got to do with anything?'

'It means we'll be even more scared and desperate. Perhaps someone is playing with us and extorting a shedload of money is secondary.'

'But why? Ryan, we're just tourists. We don't know a single person on this whole godforsaken island,' Emma snaps. 'Oh, this is unbearable, I can't take it... we don't even know if Callie is—'

'Emma, stop it. She's fine,' Ryan warns. 'She'll be scared and she'll be missing us, but don't even think about her being hurt, or worse. They want money, that's all, and they'll get it. But we've got to be patient.'

'Do you think we should ask John and Max for help?' Emma

asks. 'They live here, they know people. They've got connections.'

'Which is exactly why we can't say anything. If we tell them what's happened, we risk them going straight to the police because, obviously, they'll be upset and desperate to help. No. At this stage, the less people who know, the better.'

Emma collapses onto the sofa. 'But what if the kidnapper is one of their friends? We don't know anything about that crowd. We don't even know what time she was taken. I still can't believe you didn't look in on her when you came home late after being out with Sheena.'

'I was a bit drunk and very tired, Emma. I'm sorry. Don't you think I feel bad enough and that I regret everything about last night? You've no idea how much I hate myself for leaving the two of you alone.'

The sound of car doors slamming and a commotion outside prompts Ryan to open the front door. He peers out. 'Shit. Jack and Sheena weren't joking about leaving tonight,' he says, his expression grim. He watches, tongue-tied and helpless. Neither Jack nor Sheena acknowledge him as they march in and out of the house next door, filling the car boot before finally buckling the kids into the back seat and reversing off the drive.

Ryan shuts the door and leans heavily against it. 'Fuck, Emma, they're not just leaving, they're *running* because they're involved, I know they are.' His voice breaks with emotion. 'And I can't believe we let them get away.'

CHAPTER TWENTY-EIGHT

THEN

Ryan pushes his plate aside, unable to finish the lasagne Emma has lovingly cooked from scratch for him. He takes a mouthful of red wine, reaches for the bottle, and pretends to study the label.

'I've got to go to sodding Bristol,' he says, his tone flat.

Emma frowns. 'Bristol? What for?'

'Henry has asked me to go with him. He's interested in pitching for the conversion of a dilapidated former care home into a boutique spa hotel.'

'Wow. That sounds ambitious. Bristol though... surely, you've got enough work on in Kent and Sussex alone without going that far afield.'

Ryan puffs out his cheeks. 'Between you and me, the prospect of opening a regional office out west has been on the table for months. Henry was brought up in Somerset; he's got a soft spot for that part of the country.'

How easily the lies come to him these days, Ryan muses, topping up their glasses.

'You'll be telling me we're moving there next,' Emma says, picking up both their plates and carrying them to the draining board.

Ryan's smile is wry. 'Would that be so bad?'

'I don't know. I've never been there.' Emma frowns. 'So, when are you going?'

'The day after tomorrow. We'll stay in some god-awful corporate hotel overnight and drive back Friday morning. I'll be back by lunchtime, and we can start the weekend early.'

Ryan gets up, walks over to where Emma stands at the sink and encircles her waist from behind. 'Thank you for dinner, Em. Delicious as always.' He lifts her hair and kisses the nape of her neck. 'Now, you go and sit down and find something for us to watch on TV while I clean up.'

When Emma turns to him, her expression is one he can't quite read. 'Thanks,' she says eventually, leaving him alone with the clearing up and his thoughts.

On Thursday morning, Ryan prepares to leave home an hour earlier than usual.

'Henry's stiffed me with the driving. I just hope the traffic's not too grim,' he explains smoothly, wondering whether Emma is being particularly watchful or whether he is imagining it.

Sipping coffee at the kitchen table, brows furrowed, she seems pensive. She looks up at him, pulls her dressing gown tighter around her body. 'Where exactly are you going again?'

Ryan falters for a nanosecond. 'Actually, I don't have the address, but I'm told it's about three miles from Bristol City Centre. Henry knows exactly where we're going of course.' He pats himself down. 'Right. Keys... wallet.' He glances at the small holdall he's packed.

Emma follows his gaze. 'Don't you need your briefcase for the meeting?'

Ryan shakes his head. 'Not this time. Henry's got the presentation on his laptop. He's leading, of course.'

'Of course,' Emma echoes. 'Well, drive carefully, won't you? Text and let me know you got there safely.'

'I will. I'll give you a call this evening to say goodnight.'

'Okay.' Emma looks across to where Callie sits toying with her breakfast cereal and watching cartoons. 'Daddy's going, sweet pea.'

Callie turns and waves, both hands winking like stars.

'Bye bye, my angel, you be good for Mummy,' Ryan says, kissing her.

Callie's grin is impish. 'No, *you* be good, Daddy!' she says sweetly, causing a knot to form in his chest.

Then he crushes Emma to him. 'I'll be back before you know it,' he whispers, releasing her and heading to the front door.

Ryan drives out of Wisteria Close and beyond the prying eyes of the neighbours before he pulls over and reaches for his mobile.

> On my way. See you in twenty mins.

He texts Amber, adding a kiss.

But the traffic is lighter than usual, and after only fifteen minutes, he's pulling into the car park belonging to her building. He closes his eyes, breathes deeply, trying to quell the nausea churning in his stomach.

Now that the termination's going ahead, now that it's *really happening*, he feels like a total shit. Because today a young woman – a girl who believes she's in love with him – will get rid of her baby, a child she claims to want, and one who exists solely because he couldn't keep it in his pants. His mouth waters perilously and for one horrible moment, he thinks he might actually have to lean out of the car and throw up. He lowers the window, gulps the cold January air, and waits for the feeling to pass.

He needs to keep it together. To be the strong one. Because the chances are, Amber will be a mess, a churning sea of tears, angst and regret.

With a pang of shame, he recalls nipping out of the office and grabbing a coffee with her on their second day back at work after New Year.

'Look, of course I'm happy to go to the clinic with you,' he'd said, his tone soft with what he hoped sounded like empathy, 'but wouldn't you prefer to go with your mum, or even a female friend?'

She'd fixed him with a cold stare. 'You don't listen, do you? I've told you before, my parents live abroad. Anyway, I'm not involving them in this shitshow until it's all over.'

'Of course. I understand,' Ryan had nodded. 'Please don't worry. I'll be there. I'll pick you up at your flat, take you to the... thing, the clinic, then wait with you while you sleep it off at home. I'll stay overnight if you want me to.'

Her eyes had filled with tears at that. 'Oh, Ryan, would you? Thank you. Yes! Of course I want you to. I *need* you to stay with me.' She'd smiled then; a saccharin smile that chilled his bones. 'And you expect me to believe that you don't love me...?' She'd said, trailing off with a little shake of her head.

Ryan shudders, closes the car window, and texts Amber to say he's downstairs.

Pale and silent, Amber turns her face away from him as they flash along the country lanes. Today her clothes are baggy and shapeless, even her copper hair looks dull and limp, and it occurs to Ryan that he's never seen her this way before.

By the time they check into the small private clinic just outside Tunbridge Wells, Amber is visibly shaking, and it takes huge personal resolve for Ryan not to dump her in the lobby and drive off at high speed.

A nurse old enough to be Amber's mum leads them into a clean but stark little room with pistachio walls and a trio of botanical prints above the bed.

'Can you undress for me, lovely?' the nurse asks kindly. 'Just pop the gown on and I'll be back with the doctor in a minute.' She indicates the plastic bag on the bed which contains a spriggy hospital gown, then bustles out, leaving Ryan and Amber alone together.

'I don't think I can do this,' Amber says softly, sinking onto the edge of the bed.

Moved by her obvious sadness and fragility, Ryan sits down beside her.

'Amber, you can. We've talked it all through. Having a baby right now isn't right for either of us – and we both know it.' He gives her hand a gentle squeeze. 'Just think, in a few hours, you'll be back in your own bed, and I'll stay with you while you sleep.' He forces a smile. 'Hey, I'll even treat you to my dreadful cooking if you can face something to eat. Come on, you'll be fine.'

Amber turns her wide green eyes on him. 'Will I, though? Do you *really* think I'll get past this?'

Ryan nods. 'I know you will, and you'll be back to your old self in no time,' he says, tearing the wrapping from the gown and handing it to her.

CHAPTER TWENTY-NINE

NOW

It's after sunset when the text Ryan and Emma have been desperate for finally arrives. They gasp at the sight of Callie, pale and blank-eyed, clutching a teddy bear that doesn't belong to her. The background, which has been digitally blurred, offers no clue as to either the location or the type of environment she's being held in.

At the sight of her daughter looking lost and vulnerable, tears flow down Emma's cheeks. 'God, Ryan, look at her little face. Where *is* she? Is this all we're getting? How do we know it wasn't taken hours ago, and since then they've—'

'Emma, stop. You're not helping.' Frowning, Ryan studies the photo. 'Look, that isn't the expression Callie makes when she's scared or in pain; she looks more cross and fed up than anything. And that mark on her face?' – he taps the screen with his index finger – 'That looks like dirt to me, not a bruise.' He narrows his eyes. 'What else do you notice?'

Emma shakes her head, wipes away a tear that has splashed onto Ryan's phone.

'They haven't restrained her.' Ryan says, a note of hope in his voice. 'No gag, nothing binding her wrists... I think she's okay. Em, judging by this, whoever's got her, is treating her well; not that I wouldn't kill the bastards if I could get my hands on them,' he adds darkly.

Emma takes a ragged breath and blots her tears with a tissue. 'Do you really think so? Is that your gut instinct?'

'Yes.' Ryan puts an arm around Emma's shoulders.

She sniffs. 'But why haven't they asked for the money yet? All we know is that they want 100,000 euros. We've no idea where and when it's meant to happen and the longer it goes on—'

'Maybe they're giving us time to get the cash together. Think about it, only someone who's filthy rich could rock up at a foreign bank and draw out that sort of money. If they've been watching us, they'll know we're not wealthy.'

Emma throws up her hands. 'So what does that mean? That they're professional kidnappers experienced in extorting money?'

Ryan studies his daughter's image again. 'I don't know. But look at the teddy bear. I've seen the same one in the gift shops around here, and in Mahon, too.'

He taps the screen to expand the shot and passes the phone back to Emma. 'See? Look at his little matador trousers and waistcoat – typical tourist junk that you can get anywhere.' He sighs heavily. 'Unfortunately, it doesn't tell us anything.'

'Maybe they gave her the teddy to comfort her because, deep down, they're decent people with children of their own, and they're just poor.' Emma speaks slowly, thinking aloud.

Ryan scoffs. 'Jack and Sheena seem like decent people. And they've got kids.'

Emma shakes her head. 'It's not them, I know it isn't. They were so spooked that they took off. Anyway, from what I hear, they're loaded – why on earth would they need the ransom?'

'We only know what they've told us about their

circumstances. Let's face it, Em, we haven't a bloody clue, have we?' Ryan walks over to where his laptop is charging on the kitchen worktop. 'Come on. Let's do some digging online – see if we can find anything that confirms they are who they say.'

Standing beside Ryan, gazing at his laptop screen, Emma is aware of the tremor in her legs. Black dots dance in her peripheral vision and a queasy hotness suddenly engulfs her. Neither of them has eaten more than a few mouthfuls of toast all day, existing only on tea, coffee, and adrenalin.

She breathes deeply, which only increases the dizziness. 'Ry, if I don't sit down, I'll faint.' she whispers, gripping the worktop for support.

'I'm a bit light-headed myself,' Ryan says. 'As little as we feel like eating, we need to keep our strength up so we can stay focused. We also need to get a few hours' sleep at some point, so we can function properly tomorrow and keep our wits about us while we deal with the bank and the kidnappers.'

Emma shuffles to the fridge, her legs shaking. It comes as no surprise to find they are out of food, having planned to eat out this evening before setting off for home tomorrow. 'We'll have to go into the village,' she murmurs weakly.

'Okay, I'll drive us – you're in no fit state to walk. You can sit in the car while I grab us a takeaway,' Ryan says, reaching for his car keys.

The first few mouthfuls of Chinese food stick in Emma's throat, almost to the point of making her gag. But she manages to eat a small portion and instantly feels more alert.

Ryan's response is much the same. 'Right,' he says, rinsing his hands after they've finished the food and consigned the cartons to the bin. 'Let's get to work – starting with what little we *do* know about Jack and Sheena.'

'Okay, so Jack and Sheena's surname is Havers,' Emma says, remembering. 'I'm clear about that because it was on Sheena's debit card when we went for our spa day, and the reason it stuck is because my favourite teacher at school was called Miss Havers.'

Ryan's fingers fly over the keys with surprising speed. 'Right. And where do they live? Beckenham, isn't it?'

'Yes, I overheard Leo telling Callie they lived there when Lucas invited her for a sleepover.'

Ryan squints at the screen. 'Mmm. Nothing that looks like it might be connected. What about social media? You'd think a good-looking couple like them would be all over it like a rash.'

Emma's eyes widen. 'Yes, of course! Sheena's a fan of Instagram. She even followed me and I meant to follow her back, but I forgot all about it.'

Ryan clicks his fingers. 'Quick, get your phone. Jesus, Em, you could have mentioned it sooner.'

Emma retrieves her mobile from the coffee table and scrolls to Instagram. She grimaces. 'It's so long since I posted or even looked at it, it's asking for my password.'

Ryan rolls his eyes. 'Well, go on then...!'

'I can't remember... I think it's—'

'For fuck's sake, Emma. *Please.* It's important.'

And then the answer bounces into her head. Sweetpea2017, she types, remembering that her password is her pet name for Callie, followed by the year of her birth.

'Okay, I'm in,' she says, discovering she has five new followers since the last time she checked in months ago. Three are from men in America; one is from a customer at the salon and the latest is from Sheena. She taps the 'follow' button, then goes to Sheena's profile, astonished to find she has over two thousand followers. Surely Sheena doesn't know all these people? She checks her recent posts, her heart racing.

'Well?' Ryan leans in as Emma scrolls through dozens of photographs, the most recent depicting scenes of a good-looking family enjoying a glorious holiday in the sunshine.

'These were all taken here. Look, that's Sheena and me on our spa day.' Emma stops scrolling and gasps, unable to quite believe her eyes.

'What?!' Ryan grabs the phone from her. 'Oh my God,' he whispers, staring at the screen in horror. 'I knew it,' he says, finding his voice, his eyes blackening with rage.

There, as plain as the blue sky overhead, is a montage of photographs featuring Callie with Lucas and Leo, looking for all the world like the third child of the family: Callie perched on a sunbed, flanked by Lucas and Leo, all three children's hair wet from swimming and grinning goofily; Callie and Lucas hugging, eyes scrunched shut in a sweet moment of affection; Callie and Leo at the side of the pool, their skinny legs dangling in the water. Happy, exuberant photographs of three young children who could be siblings or best friends, having fun on a carefree family holiday.

Sheena's post is loaded with hashtags in what Emma assumes is the standard format: #FamilyFun #Holidays #Menorca #SantaMartina #CalaSavannah.

Ignoring the pounding in her ears, Emma scrolls to the likes and comments. 'Hundreds of people have liked these photos,' Emma says, glancing at Ryan, whose face has paled beneath his suntan and is now a sickly yellow.

'How fucking dare they use our daughter as click bate?' he says, his hands balled into fists. 'God alone knows who has seen this. The stupid cow has even named our exact location.' He shakes his head. 'This stinks. Either Jack and Sheena are directly involved in Callie's disappearance and this whole trip has been a set up from the start, or they're stupid and naïve enough to have accidentally advertised Callie to any random weirdo out there. Either way, they're responsible for her going missing. No wonder they took off when they did.'

'I can't believe Sheena did that,' Emma murmurs, her hand covering her mouth. She gazes in utter horror as she scrolls through the posts again and again, her chest growing tighter.

'Yeah, well, she did. And hundreds of people have seen our little girl, practically naked—'

'Don't,' Emma silences him. 'Just stop. Ry, I talked to Sheena. A lot. She's very open and friendly. I honestly don't think she did this maliciously. None of the photos are in any way dodgy-looking; they're just sweet, spontaneous snaps of kids having fun at the pool. That said, I agree with you. Whether directly or accidentally, it looks like Jack and Sheena have played a part in Callie going missing.' She inhales sharply and closes the app. 'The question is, what are we going to do about it?'

CHAPTER THIRTY

THEN

Emma could tell Ryan had lied to her. Everything about the words he'd used and the way he'd spoken to her that evening screamed of deceit. From the way he couldn't look her in the eye, to his lack of appetite – Ryan leaving home-made lasagne on his plate was unheard of – to the way he'd chased her out of the kitchen and insisted on doing all the clearing up himself.

And the more she thinks about it, the more convinced she is. Because wherever Ryan is today, whatever he is up to, pitching for a contract in Bristol with one of the firm's partners is not it.

Taylor, one of the senior stylists, interrupts her thoughts. 'You okay, Emma?'

Emma smiles. 'Yeah, fine. Sorry, Taylor, I was miles away. I hate it when the salon's this quiet, gives me too much time to think.'

'Bloody boring, an' all. Typical mid-January,' Taylor concedes glumly. She leans over the counter and peers at the reception computer. 'What time's my next client due?'

Emma checks the appointment software. 'Mrs Cope's due at eleven o'clock for her roots.'

'Best get ready then,' Taylor says, glancing at the wall clock above the desk.

'Actually, Taylor, can you cover for me, please? Just for a couple of minutes, I need to ring Callie's school,' Emma says.

'Yeah, of course,' Taylor answers, releasing Emma from her post.

Emma thanks her, goes out to the back room and retrieves her handbag from her locker. Then she takes her mobile into the staff loo and dials the landline for Ryan's work.

After four or five rings, a male voice answers, announcing himself as *Pete Robson speaking*.

'Hello? Is Henry there, please? This is Joyce, his cleaner,' Emma blurts, thinking on her feet, although God alone knows whether Henry even *has* a cleaner, let alone why she would be bothering him at the office.

'He is. Bear with me while I put you through, our receptionist is away today and I'm not familiar with this phone system,' Pete says, sounding flustered.

So, Henry is *not* on his way to Bristol and Amber has the day off. Doing what exactly? And with whom?

'Er... I'll call back in a minute, s-sorry,' Emma stammers, ending the call before Pete Robson can reply.

There's a light tap on the door, followed by Taylor's voice asking if she will be long.

'Coming,' Emma says, quickly washing her hands before she fakes a smile so bright it borders on manic.

Keep it together, be professional. My marriage is nobody's business but mine and Ryan's...

'Thanks. Sorry about that, Taylor,' Emma says.

Taylor inclines her head. 'Aww, your little one's not poorly, is she? It's horrible when they're ill.'

'No, Callie's fine. It was about her after-school club,' Emma says. *Now I'm telling lies, too; how infectious they are,* she thinks, returning to her desk.

It's nine fifteen when Ryan finally calls and she's not heard a peep from him all day, despite messaging him three times.

'Where are you?' Emma asks coldly.

'What?' *Hesitation, thinking space.* 'I'm at the hotel. It's basic, but clean enough. I've just finished dinner in the restaurant. That was pretty basic, too. Never mind. I'll be home by lunchtime tomorrow.'

'So, how did it go?'

'It went well, although there's at least one local firm in the frame already, so we'll see,' Ryan says.

'Right. Why are you whispering?'

'Whispering? I'm not. I probably sound a bit hoarse from talking too much during the presentation. And I'm very tired. Think I'll watch a bit of TV to unwind, then go straight to sleep.'

And then she hears it. A woman's voice. Calling Ryan's name. Twice.

'Who else is there?' Emma asks, her palms prickling with sweat, her mouth desert dry.

'Mmm? Nobody. I've got the TV on. How's Callie?' Ryan says, changing the subject abruptly.

'Fine. She's fast asleep.'

'You should join her, Em, get an early night while you've got the place to yourself.' He yawns loudly. 'See you tomorrow. Should be with you about midday, depending on the traffic. Love you. Night.'

'Goodnight,' Emma says, ending the call without the usual string of endearments.

Bombs are going off in Emma's head. For months, there have been clues and red flags. A slow but consistent accumulation of evidence that Ryan is sleeping with someone else. Her heartbeat accelerates as she pictures herself, acting out some dramatic and cathartic gesture – like running amok in Ryan's wardrobe with a pair of kitchen scissors, or dumping his stuff on the front lawn for the neighbours to enjoy the spectacle – but ever the voice of reason, she holds back, determined to hear the truth, or at least Ryan's version of it.

Breaking her own rule about never drinking alone, Emma goes to the fridge and pours white wine into a large glass. Then she goes up to bed via Callie's room, where the sight of her sleeping contentedly, surrounded by her favourite soft toys, brings tears to her eyes. She fights the urge to scoop Callie up in her arms, tiptoes away to her own room, and closes the door behind her.

How can Ryan do this to Callie, never mind to *her*? He adores his daughter. And until recently, Emma had thought she and Ryan adored each other.

Well, hold that thought. Because perhaps she is being fanciful – paranoid, even – and maybe all her suspicions can be explained away.

She imagines confronting Ryan. Pictures him holding her tight to his chest, kissing the top of her head, and telling her she's being ridiculous – as if he could even *look* at another woman – right before he offers her some other completely plausible explanation for his recent odd behaviour. Reasons for the random nights out with people from work; his brooding, distant mood all through Christmas and New Year; and the unexplained (and to date unacknowledged) phone call from Amber on Christmas Eve, as well as justification for his mysterious and impromptu half day at the office the day after Boxing Day.

And now this. The oldest cliché in the book; the overnight work trip, which, in itself was perfectly reasonable. Except that she'd caught him out in at least one lie. Certainly, Ryan had not gone to Bristol with Henry because according to Pete Robson, Henry was in the office and able to receive calls. For that matter, had Ryan gone to Bristol at all? Pete had let slip that their receptionist was absent. A coincidence? Or had Ryan taken Amber away, to wine, dine and seduce her far from home?

Emma shudders as she imagines them in bed together in some soulless corporate hotel room, or worse, making love by the glow of a roaring fire in a cosy Cotswolds love nest.

Feeling utterly powerless, she undresses, puts on her dressing gown and huddles under the duvet. Then she gulps a third of the wine in one go. Its numbing effect is instant, warming, and pleasant to the point she's almost tempted to creep downstairs, grab the bottle from the fridge and drink the rest.

'For God's sake, Emma, get a grip,' she whispers, taking a deep breath and settling back against the pillows. She reaches for the TV remote control and surfs the channels for something comforting and familiar but it's a futile exercise and after a few minutes, she switches off.

Lying in the dark, with only the sounds of the night for company – the hoot of an owl, the yowling of two cats vying for territory, and the wuthering of the wind against her window – as the minutes turn to hours, Emma knows she will not sleep tonight.

CHAPTER THIRTY-ONE

NOW

On waking, there's a blissful drifting sensation before Emma remembers that Callie is missing, her world has imploded, and her sanity is hanging by a gossamer thread.

With a surge of vertigo, she sits up, still partially dressed in yesterday's clothes. Ryan lies beside her, also wearing the same shorts and T-shirt he's had on for the last twenty-four hours; she shakes him roughly.

'Ryan, wake up. We've been asleep. God knows how, but we must have dropped off.'

Ryan hauls himself into a standing position and reaches for his phone. 'Shit. Still nothing.'

And it starts all over again: the physical pain in Emma's chest, the nausea that comes in waves, and worst of all the gnawing emptiness that now occupies the space where only this time yesterday her heart, lungs and stomach had happily co-existed.

'Why haven't we heard from them?' she whispers, raising the blind and letting the light flood in.

Ryan shakes his head, despair etched into his face, which appears to have aged ten years overnight. 'Maybe to taunt us.

Make us more desperate, so that once they get in touch, we'll do anything to get her back.'

Wearily, they stagger downstairs, go through the motions of making coffee and taking it out to the garden but are soon driven indoors by the low buzz of cheerful conversation coming from John and Max's terrace.

'If we can hear them, they can hear us,' Ryan hisses, closing the sliding doors for privacy. Then he opens his laptop, logs in to their joint bank account, and angles the screen towards Emma.

'Look, Em. Check the balance. It worked. All the money's there – and a little over,' he says, a degree of relief washing over him. 'Question is, what are the kidnappers expecting? I mean, even *I* know that we can't just drive into town, walk up to the counter of a high street bank, and ask for 100,000 euros in cash. There are rules, currency laws.'

Emma folds her arms and hugs herself. 'So, what then? What do we do?'

'We wait. We wait for instructions and do whatever they say. What choice have we got?'

Emma's eyes fill with tears. 'We should be going home today. All three of us. We're still booked on the six thirty-five flight out of Mahon this evening.'

Ryan shrugs. 'We can't think about that now. It's obvious that we're going nowhere. Tell you what though, we're meant to check out of this place by noon at the latest. Em, where should we go?'

'A hotel? I don't care; we'll sleep in the car... whatever it takes—'

The sound of the doorbell makes them both jump.

Ryan slams his laptop shut. 'Who the hell is that?'

Emma puts a finger to her lips. 'No idea,' she mouths.

It rings again, this time an insistent jingling.

Ryan rubs at his scalp in annoyance. 'Shit. Must be the old

bag next door,' he whispers. 'Please, Em, get rid of her. We don't want her sticking her nose in.'

Emma nods mutely, composes herself and goes to the front door, while Ryan eavesdrops, tucked just inside the living room.

'Well, hello! How *are* you all?' Max drawls. 'Now, if I'm not mistaken, today's your last day here, isn't it?' she says, pressing on without waiting for an answer.

Emma tries to speak, but nothing comes to her. Instead, she stands gaping at Max, aware of the ludicrousness of the situation.

'All packed?' Max asks, seemingly unaware of Emma's misery.

'Almost. What... what can I do for you, Max?' Emma says eventually.

Max beams. 'Well, I couldn't let you leave without giving you a bottle of our gorgeous local gin. It's made nearby in Mahon – you simply must take a bottle home.' She proffers an attractive bottle. 'A little something to remember us by.'

She pauses, her expression quizzical. 'Emma, are you all right, my dear? You're looking a little peaky, to say the least. Where's that's dashing husband of yours? And little Callie? I missed her at the pool yesterday – I've grown so fond of seeing her splashing around and having fun. She's such a joy to watch.'

Emma's gasp for air and the buckling of her knees at the mention of Callie are entirely involuntary. A high-pitched sound escapes her, not a word but a yelp.

Max steps closer. 'Emma? What's the matter? What's happened, you look quite—'

'Max, I can't bear it.' Emma sobs, unable to stem the tears spilling down her cheeks.

Max's eyes bulge. 'Oh God. Here, let me help,' she says, backing Emma into the hallway and taking her arm firmly to steady her. She jumps at the sight of Ryan lurking inside. 'Ryan? What's going on?'

'Christ, that's all we need,' Ryan mutters. He shakes his head at Emma, who is now leaning against a wall for support. 'You'd better come in, Max,' he adds. 'It's bad news, I'm afraid. Someone's taken Callie.'

The colour has drained from Max's face and her eyes are round with shock. 'Are you absolutely sure? She couldn't have, say, gone for a walk to the beach or to the shops and lost her bearings?'

'We've searched thoroughly around the beach and the development. As far as we know, she was taken from her own bed on the night of your party. Max, it's definitely an abduction; we've already heard from the kidnappers.'

'Dear God in heaven,' Max whispers, her hand flying to her mouth. 'But why... why didn't you tell John and me? Surely we can help.'

'How, exactly? By inviting the kidnappers round for drinks?' Ryan says tartly. 'Look, these people aren't messing around. They've got our daughter and they want a hundred grand. That's it, that's what we're dealing with, okay?'

'Ryan, calm down,' Emma warns. 'Max only wants to help.'

Max waves away her concern. 'It's fine. I understand.' She massages her temples for a few seconds. 'You poor, poor things. What you're going through is unimaginable. I'm so, so sorry. You've spoken to the police, I take it. What do they say?'

Ryan closes his eyes, shakes his head slowly. 'No, we haven't. It's been made clear to us that if we involve the police, we'll never see Callie again.'

Emma nods. The older woman's complexion has turned an

odd shade of putty. 'It's true. We can't go to the police in case they're watching us.'

Max releases a long shuddering sigh. 'I thought it had all stopped,' she says, her eyes fixed on the tiled floor.

'All *what*?' Ryan is on high alert. 'You thought all *what* had stopped?'

Max hesitates before meeting his gaze. 'It's happened before: a spate of abductions. But the gang responsible are in jail. At least they *were*.'

'What gang? Max, tell us. What do you know about this?' Ryan demands.

Max backs towards the sofa and perches on its edge. 'Please, both of you, sit down while I tell you what little I know.'

Gone is the flirtatious manner, the affected drawl. Now, the words coming out of Max's mouth are imparted softly, sincerely, with compassion and sadness.

'About eight years ago, during the course of one summer, three British children disappeared. Three little ones, from three separate families and all about Callie's age. They were there one minute, gone the next. The parents were contacted, a ransom demanded, but then nothing. Silence. As far as I'm aware, those children were never seen again, although it's possible they were found later of course,' she pauses, 'but that would be news to me.'

Emma shakes her head. 'No, that can't be right. That didn't happen.'

Ryan gets to his feet. 'Max, I'm sorry, but I can't sit here and listen to this alarmist drivel. If three kids had been abducted in Menorca, it would have been all over the world media.'

Max arches an eyebrow. 'You would think, wouldn't you? But there was an enforced media blackout led by the Spanish government.' She shrugs. 'Understandable really. Menorca's whole economy runs on tourism. Eventually the gang responsible were caught and the whole thing was hushed up.'

'But if that's the case, how do *you* know all this stuff?' Ryan says.

'Oh, I know a lot of things. John and I...' Max pauses, searches for the right words, '...are well connected. We know a lot of people on this island, and one of our closest friends is a retired police officer. He was very senior in the Met where he ran a major incident team for seven years. He told us what was happening; it's somewhat of an open secret among local expats.'

Sweat beads on Ryan's forehead; he pushes back his hair. 'But you said the gang are behind bars. You said they were caught.'

'And they were. But there may be other contacts, other *cells*. Who knows what world these monsters inhabit, and what they're capable of.'

Seething, Ryan turns away. 'Right, well now you've terrified the shit out of us even more, can you just go? We're expecting a message from whoever's got her.'

Max gets to her feet. 'I'm so sorry. I didn't mean to frighten you or make things worse. I suggest you speak to our friend Graham Kennedy. He may be able to advise you off the record, and without involving the Policía Nacional.'

Emma throws Ryan a desperate look. 'What do you think? Surely if he's retired and from the UK, it can't hurt, can it? Depending on how much he knows about this gang, he might be able to lead us to Callie. I can't stand the waiting, the not knowing.'

Ryan shakes his head. 'We can't take that risk. Max, please, can you give us some time alone to think about it? And in the meantime, *please* do not tell your friend. Don't tell anybody. Your silence could literally mean life or death.'

'I understand.' Max mournfully eyes the bottle of gin she's set down on the coffee table. 'You might need a nip of that for your nerves. Tell me to mind my own business, but presumably you're due to leave here today?'

Emma puffs out her cheeks. 'Yes, we'll throw everything in the car and find somewhere nearby.'

'There's no need,' Max says gently. 'I know the owners; they're decent people. Nobody is due here for at least another week. I'll get in touch with them, say you've both been hit by a virus and that you need to stay a few more days.' She gives a sad little shake of her head. 'Please, if there's anything I can do, however small or foolish it may seem to you... well, good luck. I'll see myself out.'

It's Emma who breaks the stunned silence left in Max's wake.

'Do you think we should speak to the retired cop? Ryan, we need help with this. The longer we do nothing—'

Ryan buries his head in his hands. 'I don't know. It's bad enough that Max knows. Christ, Em, she's not exactly discreet, is she? How do we know she's not on the phone to the police right now, or gossiping to her mates in the village? The more people who know, the more dangerous the situation becomes. *No police* means *no fucking police*, okay?' He eyes his phone with disgust just as a text alert sounds.

He snatches it up and stares at the screen. 'God, Emma. It's them. This is what we've been waiting for.'

CHAPTER THIRTY-TWO

Emma's eyes are wide and frantic. 'For God's sake, Ryan, just tell me what it says. Is Callie okay? When are we getting her back?'

Ryan rereads the text, his Adam's apple bobbing visibly. He angles himself to Emma and reads aloud: 'Transfer 100,000 euros by 16.00 hours today to ensure handover at midnight. Drive to Monte Toro, turn off 2.5 kilometres before sanctuary of La Virgen at the summit. Find the stone folly that looks like a bridge and wait. Parents must come alone. No police, no third party. Account details to follow for immediate deposit.'

There's a beat of silence while they digest the information they've been given.

'At least now we know what we're dealing with,' Ryan says, 'although Christ knows how we'll find a pile of fucking rocks on a mountain in the dark.'

'How do we know they'll even show up once we've transferred the money? What if they've no intention of giving Callie back to us?' Emma says.

'Em, we can't think like that, we've got to do as they say. What choice do we have?'

'But those other children... Max said—'

'Forget Max. She has too much time on her hands. I'm not interested in the rumours and hearsay of a load of gossiping pensioners. Come on, let's go for a walk. We can think it through while we get some fresh air. We'll grab a coffee on the beach and maybe by then we'll have the account details for the transfer.'

At Juan's Café, sitting under a rattan canopy sipping *café con leche* surrounded by smiling holidaymakers, Emma feels as though she's having an out of body experience.

How have their lives derailed so badly and in such a short space of time? She glances at Ryan, his face pinched with anxiety, still gripping his mobile phone like a talisman.

As if reading her thoughts, he looks up, drains his cup and gets to his feet. 'Let's go. I can't stand the sight of all these happy people.'

Sharpened by caffeine, they march back to the villa, slide open the garden door, and let the sun stream in.

Ryan glances at his phone. 'Nothing yet,' he says, taking his laptop from the kitchen counter and carrying it to the sofa.

'What are you doing?' Emma asks, sitting down beside him.

'Searching for news stories about children going missing in Menorca,' Ryan says, his hands flying over the keys.

'But Max said the whole thing got hushed up. What did she call it?'

'A media blackout was the expression she used. In which case, how could she possibly know the truth about what really happened? Perhaps the children were safely reunited with their parents and it ended well.' There's a note of hope in his voice.

Emma watches his long, tanned fingers roaming the keyboard, clicking link after link. Eventually he stops, before slamming the lid down in frustration.

'Nothing. Fucking nada.' He gets up and paces back and forth.

'Which means one of two things,' Emma says quietly. 'Either everything Max said is true: the children were abducted, and the story got hushed up; *or* it's just local gossip, an apocryphal story that never really happened.'

'Yeah, well, my money's on the latter,' Ryan mutters. 'The alternative doesn't bear thinking about.'

'We'll never know, will we? Unless,' Emma pauses and glances at Ryan, 'we speak to Max's retired cop friend. I'm sure he'd give us an honest account of what happened that summer.'

Ryan scowls. 'I thought we were handling this ourselves? We've talked about this. What if they're watching us? The wording in the last message said *no third party* – that means anybody, anyone at all. Emma, we have to do as they say. Do you understand?'

'Yes,' she says meekly before heading upstairs for a shower in an attempt to clear her head.

It's almost ten thirty when the text arrives.

'This is it; we're on,' Ryan says, reading the message through to the end. 'Okay, this one is all figures. Sort code and account number, I'm guessing, plus the name of some corporate sounding company.' He purses his lips. 'Who the hell are AMCO International?'

'They sound like a proper company,' Emma says.

'Yeah, they do. Clever bastards must have created a shell so the bank doesn't get spooked and the transaction goes smoothly. Emma, look up AMCO International online.'

'Nothing. I can't find anything that looks as though it's connected,' Emma says after a few minutes of scouring the internet.

Ryan sighs. 'Okay, we're wasting time. I'll call the bank now, stick to the story about buying an apartment over here and then contact the currency broker I've cued up to make the transfer for us.'

Emma's eyebrows shoot up. 'Wow. That was dynamic of you. When did you do that?'

'While you were showering, earlier,' Ryan says. 'It's a global firm in Canary Wharf and they don't come cheap. The thing is, Em, they guarantee a same day service which is critical for us, so we'll worry about fees and so on when this nightmare comes to an end.'

'Assuming it does end,' Emma says under her breath.

She can hear Ryan on the phone to the currency broker in London, laying it on with a trowel about how he'll lose the property he's buying if the money arrives later than three thirty that afternoon. And she hates herself for even thinking it, however fleetingly, but it crosses Emma's mind that a tiny part of Ryan is actually enjoying the drama and the pressure.

She recalls at least two occasions when her mother had described Ryan as a hot-head – and goodness knows she's seen enough outbursts of temper over the years – and now, suddenly, his pent-up drive and energy have an outlet. Somewhere to go; a genuine life or death emergency that requires a steely focus and a mental agility that he's never needed more.

'Yes!' Ryan says, punching the air in triumph shortly after two o'clock. 'We did it, Em! I have an e-receipt in my inbox: those bastards have got our money.'

Emma cringes and wonders how Ryan can possibly be so pleased with himself when they've been fleeced for every penny they have and more, and are still no closer to getting their daughter back.

CHAPTER THIRTY-THREE

THEN

On the night of Ryan's so-called business trip, restful sleep eludes Emma. Instead, she dozes fitfully, only to patch in and out of nightmares in which she is a struggling single parent living in poverty, while Ryan thrives in his glamorous new life with Amber.

The following morning, mired by a queasy, jittery anxiety she can't shake off, Emma staggers blindly through walking Callie to her reception class at the local infants' school first thing, then mechanically going about her usual household chores until it is time to collect her.

The previous evening, during their stilted phone call, Ryan had said he'd be back by midday, but it's three forty in the afternoon when he finally walks through the front door, pale and dishevelled.

Callie, not long home from school, throws her arms around him as he lingers by the front door and dumps his overnight bag, shoes, and jacket.

'Have you been good for Mummy?' Ryan asks, scooping her up in his arms and kissing her cheeks.

Emma hangs back and searches his face, a knot of dread in

the pit of her stomach. He looks terrible. She says as much, adding, 'And you're late. I thought you said you'd be back at midday.'

Ryan rubs his stubbly chin. 'There was an accident on the M4. You should have seen the carnage... boy, am I glad to be home.' He heaves a long rattling sigh and it's obvious he means it.

'Want a drink?' Emma asks, sidestepping him by heading back to the kitchen when he leans in to hug her. She picks up an unfamiliar smell; something stale and desperate.

Ryan nods. 'Please. A cup of tea would go down well. While you do that, I'll just nip upstairs.'

All day Emma has vacillated between wanting to confront him; to have it out with him – whatever *it* is – but now, the thought of a big blow up on a Friday evening in front of their daughter is unthinkable. Because whatever is going on with Ryan, she needs to pick her moment so that if her worst fears are confirmed, she can protect Callie from the immediate fallout.

Ryan returns five minutes later, wearing an ancient pair of jeans and a faded sweater that is one of Emma's favourites. He picks up the freshly made mug of tea, blows on it, and takes a sip. 'Thanks. Hey, don't I get a kiss? I missed you.'

Emma stiffens when Ryan lightly brushes her lips as she pictures him kissing Amber. But any coolness on her part either goes unnoticed or is ignored. Smiling, Ryan crosses to the sofa and sits down heavily next to Callie, who is playing with her tablet.

A heavy sigh escapes him. 'Uh, am I glad *that's* over. I suspect it was a waste of time and petrol, to be honest.'

To be honest. Emma recalls reading somewhere that people often use the phrase when they are about to lie.

'Really? Why do you say that?'

Ryan purses his lips. 'It was obvious from the outset that the contract will go to a local firm and we were only there to make up the numbers and provide an alternative quote. Never mind. C'est la vie.'

He turns to Callie. 'What have you got there, sweet pea?' He pulls her onto his lap while she explains her game to him in considerable detail.

Emma's heart softens. Whatever else Ryan is or is not, he is a brilliant father and Callie adores him. She inhales sharply, suddenly overwhelmed by an intense feeling of fear. Tears spring into her eyes and she turns away. Even if Ryan *is* cheating on her, splitting up and wrecking their daughter's home life is not an option.

And yet, she has to know.

She *has* to know. And if Ryan *is* seeing someone else, she needs to shut it down, before it's too late and before Amber becomes bigger than both of them.

She smiles brightly. 'Hey, why don't we go out for dinner tomorrow night, just the two of us? When was the last time we got dressed up on a Saturday night?'

'Where are we going to get a babysitter at such short notice?'

Emma opens the bits and bobs drawer, where she fishes beneath the takeaway menus and mini-cab flyers for a card she's recently saved. 'Funny you should ask that. I saw Meghan across the road the other day and she practically begged me to give her some work. She's sixteen now and very sensible for her age. She's had cards printed and everything. Ah. Got it,' she says, waving Meghan's card.

'Great idea. Give her a call and see if she's free.'

The distinctive aromas of lemongrass, ginger and sweet chilli scent the air, making Emma and Ryan salivate as they study the menu.

'We were lucky to get in,' Ryan mutters, glancing at Emma before continuing to browse.

Emma agrees. 'Maybe they had a cancellation. I love Thai food, why don't we have it more often?'

A waitress wearing traditional Thai silks takes their order and soon they are tucking into green curry, pad-Thai noodles, and a selection of delicately spiced vegetables. And whether it is the spiciness of the food, or the fact that her nerves are frayed, Emma drinks faster than usual and they are on their second bottle of wine before they've even finished the main course.

'Ryan, I have to talk to you about something,' Emma begins, after the table has been cleared and they've been presented with dessert menus. 'And, love, believe me when I say I'm not looking for an argument, but it's important and I need you to be honest with me.'

Ryan looks wary. 'Ok-ay, fire away.'

Emma takes a deep breath and lowers her voice. 'So, here's the thing. I know that you lied to me. About Bristol, I mean.'

Ryan narrows his eyes. 'Why would I do that?'

Nausea swirls in Emma's stomach, she takes a gulp from her water glass. She hadn't intended to have this conversation tonight, but thanks to the wine and the softly lit intimacy of the restaurant, the words have bubbled out.

'Because I think you're seeing someone else.'

There's a beat of silence before Ryan scoffs. 'Jesus, Em... well, thanks for the faith.'

'Look, I'm not proud of checking up on you, but I rang your office on Thursday morning and asked to speak to Henry. Ryan, the person who answered the phone, was about to put me through to him when he should have been halfway to Bristol with you. But that's only part of it. The other thing – the bit that really scares me – is that Amber wasn't there on Thursday.'

Ryan shakes his head in disbelief. 'So, you put two and two

together and got nine?' He takes a gulp of wine. 'Is that it? Is that the case for the prosecution, or is there something else? Because I can explain both factors and neither have a bloody thing to do with me seeing someone else – which I'm *not* by the way, just so you know.'

'Tell me then, because I have been going insane with worry,' Emma says quietly, hoping Ryan isn't about to lose his temper and create an ugly scene.

'The reason Henry was in the office on Thursday when he was originally due in Bristol, is because his ulcer flared up the night before and he couldn't face a long car journey, so he asked Raj to step in at the last minute. Which was fine; they are equal partners after all.' He dabs his mouth needlessly with a napkin and drops it on the table in a crumpled heap. 'And as for our intern-slash-receptionist not being there, she's been ill with flu. I doubt she'll be in next week either, which is a pain, as we'll all be charging around like headless chickens trying to answer the phones as well as do our jobs.'

Emma feels cautiously encouraged. 'Okay. If that's what happened... it's just... you seem so distant. So *preoccupied*. I've been turning myself inside out for weeks; sick with worry that you've been seeing Amber. I mean, God knows, you've been out with the people from work enough recently, so you've had plenty of opportunity.'

Ryan pushes his chair back and signals to the waitress for the bill. 'Wow, I never had you down as the neurotic jealous type, Emma, and it's not a good look. The drinks after work thing only started because a few of us were trying to support poor old Robbo while his divorce was going through. But if that's how you feel...' He leaves the words hanging in the air like smoke.

'Can we have the bill, please?' Ryan says when the waitress glides over. He waits until she is out of earshot before saying,

'Well, thanks for that, Emma. Thanks for ruining our first night out in ages and what could have been a perfect evening.'

Neither of them say much on the journey home. The friendly taxi driver, proud owner of a broad scouse accent and a sense of humour, makes several inroads at small talk, but Ryan is having none it and after three attempts, the driver gives up and the fifteen-minute journey is played out in silence.

They arrive home to find Meghan sitting in the dark, swigging Coke from a can, and glued to a re-run of *Love Island*.

She jumps to her feet, surprise registering on her young face. 'Hey! You're back early. Did you have a nice time?'

'We had a lovely dinner, thanks, Meghan. How did it go with Callie? Is she in bed?'

Meghan nods. 'Ah, bless her. She's so sweet. We drew mermaids together and then we watched the Disney channel for a bit before I put her to bed.'

'Great. Excuse me, will you?' Ryan grunts, leaving Emma alone with the babysitter.

'Thanks for looking after her,' Emma says. 'Is it okay if I pop round with the cash in the morning? I'll pay you up to ten thirty as that's what we agreed.'

Meghan starts to protest, then shrugs and thanks her. 'Please ask me again, won't you? Callie's lovely, a real sweetie.' She zips up her hoodie and reaches for her phone. 'Na-night then.'

After seeing Meghan to the door, Emma finds Ryan slumped on the kitchen sofa, staring mournfully into a glass of wine. He doesn't look up as she approaches, nor does he offer her a drink.

'I'm sorry,' she says, sitting down beside him. When he doesn't respond, she gets up, takes a glass down from the shelf and pours herself one. 'Ryan, please. Talk to me. Surely you can see where I'm coming from?'

'Not really, no. Look, if you don't trust me, our marriage won't survive, will it?'

'I do. I do trust you. It's just that Amber is so... young and really beautiful, you know?'

'Can't say I'd noticed.' Ryan takes a sip of wine. 'I suppose she's pretty enough, if you like that kind of thing. Anyway, how do you know what Amber looks like?'

'She rang you over Christmas and her photo came up. Ryan, she's gorgeous, she looks like a model.'

Ryan huffs. 'Well, not to me. Em, she was only calling to give me a message; she answers the phone for God's sake, it's her job.' He sighs, gets up, and dumps the last of his wine down the sink. 'Right, I'm going to bed and I suggest you do the same. And, Emma,' he pauses, a pained expression on his face, 'let's not talk about this again, okay?'

CHAPTER THIRTY-FOUR

By Monday morning, Ryan is relieved to be back at work after a weekend spent walking on eggshells.

Emma confronting him at the Thai restaurant on Saturday night – albeit in her calm, circumspect, Emma-ish way – had been a close call. Caught off guard, his response had been tantamount to gaslighting.

Stuck in traffic, inching towards the office, he cringes as he recalls the hurt and confusion in her eyes. Naturally, he wasn't proud of his behaviour – accusing Emma of being jealous and paranoid like that was *not* his finest hour – but surely any sane husband and father caught out in a small (and in the grand scheme of things, harmless) dalliance would have done the same, wouldn't they?

What had happened with Amber was deeply regrettable on every level: poor judgement on his part, too many variables, and more than a whiff of bad luck.

How the hell was he supposed to know that Amber was mentally fragile? That she had a history of depression and anxiety? Certainly, there were no outward signs. Quite the reverse. He'd had her pegged as a super-confident and indulged rich kid. And as for her falling pregnant, well that was just unfortunate, and he'd dealt with *that* hurdle as swiftly as possible.

He's relieved when the traffic opens up ahead. In under five minutes, he'll be at work, secure in the knowledge that Amber will have phoned in and excused herself for the next few days. It was what they'd agreed. Space and time for Amber to lick her wounds in private while he refocused on his workload and his family.

Swinging into the firm's car park and backing into his usual space, Ryan feels a renewed optimism.

One hand jammed in his trouser pocket, the other holding a mug of coffee, Henry rocks on his heels. He lowers his chin, peers over the rim of his glasses and waits for the post-weekend buzz to die down.

'Morning, comrades,' he begins, as all heads swivel in his direction. 'So, some news to kick off the week. I'm afraid we may have lost our latest recruit, certainly in the immediate term. As you may remember, Amber was off sick on Thursday and Friday last week, but it now transpires that she was dealing with a family emergency and I understand the situation worsened over the weekend. As such, Amber expects to be away for at least a fortnight, possibly longer.' He pauses, gives a slight nod. 'Can I ask for you all to be patient and flexible while we recruit a replacement for reception. Sue has kindly offered to stand in today and we have a temp arriving in the morning.'

Henry stops talking and looks around at the sea of faces, his eyes coming to rest on Ryan's, who, to his immense irritation, feels himself flush.

Why is Henry staring at him? What – if anything – does he

know? Surely Amber hasn't told him about their fling and please God, don't let her have mentioned the abortion.

Henry clears his throat. 'I'm sure that like Raj and I, you wish Amber all the best and are keen to see her lovely smiling face about the place soon. Okay, that's it for now. Have a good week, all.'

There are murmurs of assent as Henry goes to his office and people return to their desks. Ryan can see Pete Robson trying to catch his eye, but he ignores him, opens his laptop and studies his inbox.

Undeterred, Pete sidles up to his desk. 'Coffee, mate?' he asks pleasantly. 'I'm making myself one.'

Ryan pretends to be engrossed in the email he's reading. 'Cheers, Robbo, white no sugar,' he says without looking up.

A moment later, Pete returns carrying two piping hot drinks and sets down a mug bearing the words *Genius at Work* on Ryan's desk.

'So, what do you make of that then?' Pete says in a low voice.

'What do I make of what?'

'You know, Amber vanishing off the face of the earth like that.'

'Clearly she *hasn't* vanished if she's been in touch with Henry claiming a family crisis.' Ryan sighs, spinning his chair round to face Robbo. 'And actually, it's none of our business, is it?'

'I just thought, what with... you know, you two being close, etc., you might...' he trails off, bobs his head and grimaces.

'Look, Pete, I don't know what gave you the idea that we're *close*,' Ryan draws air quotes with his fingers, 'but I don't know any more than you as to why Amber's taking time off.'

Pete looks doubtful. 'If you say so, mate,' he says, smirking as he walks away.

The morning passes in a frustrating blur of unreturned calls and unresolved emails. At twelve forty-five, Ryan gets up and grabs his coat from the reception closet.

'I'm just popping out for an hour,' he tells Sue, currently stationed at Amber's desk, fielding visitors and phone calls as well as managing her own workload. He sees her mouth twitch with disapproval.

'In fact, I may be longer,' he adds, just to annoy her. 'My contact at town planning has been engaged all morning, so I might pop into the council offices, try and catch him that way.'

It's a lie, but like Sue or anyone else is likely to check up on him, he muses, striding outside into the cold air where, in his haste to escape, he almost collides with Pete Robson.

'Hello, mate. How's it going?' Pete says, attempting to waylay him.

'Fine. Look, I'm just on my way to get a bite to—'

'Great, mind if I tag along? I've got another thirty minutes yet, so I'll keep you company. You off to the caff?'

Ryan cringes inwardly at the word *caff*, aware he's in no mood for Robbo's unfunny stories or petty office gossip. He's about to make an excuse when he recalls their exchange about Amber.

'Good idea,' Ryan says, changing tack. 'A sausage sandwich might actually hit the spot,' he adds, knowing he is speaking Robbo's language.

As greasy spoons go, Ryan has seen worse; the place is spotless if dated, and it's only the telltale smell of fried food that gives it away.

'Not bad.' Ryan nods, tucking into his sandwich while Robbo slurps from a mug of tea. 'You not eating?'

'Couldn't wait, Ry, mate. I had a bacon roll for elevenses. I'd just been for a brisk walk when I ran into you.' He pats his midriff and mimes horror. 'I put on a few pounds over Christmas. Believe me, the struggle is real.'

'You look good to me, buddy.' Ryan takes another bite, unsure how to steer the conversation round to Amber. Only, he doesn't need to.

'So, what's *really* going with our Amber, then?' Pete says, sounding genuinely concerned. 'I mean, she's only a kid – girls of her age shouldn't have family problems. It's not right.'

Ryan swallows the last of his food and slides his plate to one side. 'True enough. Maybe there's been a death in the family,' he says innocently.

'Nah. Shall I tell you what I think?' Pete says, glancing from side to side.

'Be my guest.'

'I reckon she's got boyfriend trouble. Someone's let her down and she's taken it badly. Wouldn't surprise me if he's married, know what I mean?' Pete raises his mug and eyes Ryan over the rim.

'Really? What makes you say that?' Ryan asks smoothly.

'Oh, you know... I have my sources.' Pete taps the side of his nose, still holding Ryan's gaze.

'Pete, if you've got something to say—'

Pete raises his hands. 'Hey, none of my business. I just hate seeing good people get hurt. There's no need for it.'

'You're obviously trying to make a point,' Ryan says.

'Mate, she told me all about your little fling. I guessed anyway. Sad part is, she thinks she's in love with you and that there's a chance you'll leave your wife. I mean, I tried to tell her otherwise, but these youngsters, they only see and hear what they want to.'

Ryan feels a painful twist in his gut. Shit. He needs to manage this situation and fast, before it's all around the office ready to leak out at the next Christmas party or corporate awayday where spouses and partners are present.

He nods slowly and feigns empathy. 'Poor kid. I had a feeling she'd confide in you, Pete. You're kind and a good listener. She'd have picked up on that, of course. Just as she did with me. I should have seen it coming a mile off, but I just wanted to be supportive, you know? To be a friend to her. And anyway, I admit I was flattered at first – what bloke wouldn't be... she's gorgeous, after all. So, I admit I was a bit flirty at first.'

Ryan sighs, a pained look in his eyes. 'That was before I knew she was delusional. And with a history of mental illness. Medication, counselling, the works. Of course, then I tried to extract myself, but the more I told her I loved my wife and that there was no chance of us getting together, the more fixated she became. Like it was a challenge.'

Pete's eyes widen. 'Are you saying you never—' He lets out a low whistle.

'God, no. Never. I mean, yes, we went out drinking a few times, and she cried on my shoulder more than once, I can tell you.' He pauses. 'But as for sleeping with her. Mate, I'm forty in March, I wouldn't know what to with a girl like that – I'd be scared to death. And anyway, I'd never cheat on Emma.'

He can see Pete weighing up his story, wondering who to believe. 'Pete, be careful, eh? You could be next. You think it's a compliment at first – a girl like that telling you how much she wants you, that she's in love with you. Well, believe me, that sort of obsession is scary shit.'

Pete frowns. 'Right... well, in that case, I'll reserve judgement,' he says cryptically. 'Let's hope a week or two off work calms her down a bit and breaks the cycle, so to speak. Hey, maybe that's the family crisis. Maybe she's had a breakdown.'

'Highly likely.' Ryan glances at his watch. 'We should be

heading back. And, Pete, keep it under your hat. I'm not proud of how I've handled things. I should never have confused her, and now I'm trusting you as a friend not to let rumours escalate. Are we cool?'

Pete fixes Ryan with a shark-like grin. 'We are ice, mate,' he says, getting to his feet.

CHAPTER THIRTY-FIVE

NOW

Brows knitted, Ryan studies the map, zooming in until Monte Toro fills his laptop screen.

'Okay, Em, so here's the thing. Monte Toro isn't just some random hill as we first thought, it's actually the highest point on the island and a well-known tourist destination, which means it will be well signposted.' He closes the link he's viewing and opens another depicting a different route. 'Plus, we've got satnav, so finding this place shouldn't be too much hassle. It will all be okay. In a few hours' time, Callie will be safely back in our arms, I know it.'

Emma stands, blinking at him for a moment. 'No, you don't. You don't know anything. For all we know, Callie might have left the island by now... she could have been put on a boat to God knows where. Ryan, they've already got the money – they can do what the hell they like.' She lets out a guttural wail. 'Oh God, I can't bear it. The waiting is agony.'

What planet is Ryan on? Is he so naïve that he accepts the kidnappers' word as gospel? Or is it because he knows something she doesn't?

All afternoon, Ryan has been wired and anxious but also

energised and with a steely focus. Almost as if he's enjoying the thrill of the chase. Either that, or he's in such deep shock and denial that he is refusing to see how critical the situation really is.

Because the fact that they've been fleeced of 100,000 euros, with absolutely no proof of Callie being returned to them alive and well, sickens Emma to her stomach. Yet here is Ryan, acting as though they're on some glorified treasure hunt.

He reaches out, takes her by the shoulders and faces her head on. 'Em, please. Have a little faith. I know Max spooked you talking about those missing children, but we know she's a drama queen, not to mention completely bloody tactless. And even if it's true, she said it happened years ago.' He rolls his eyes. 'Stupid old cow had no right to say those things.'

'Hey, don't blame Max. She even suggested we speak to her retired policeman friend, so it's obvious she wants to help.'

Ryan scoffs. 'We can do without her kind of help.'

Emma goes into the kitchen, her arms folded across her chest to stem the constant pain that throbs there. 'Do you want some tea?' she asks, putting on water to boil.

'No, thanks.' Ryan continues to stare at his laptop. 'But why *here*; why Monte Toro? Do you think that's where Callie is being held?'

Emma shrugs. 'I don't know. Ryan, I'm so scared, I can't—' she inhales sharply. 'I can't picture her, and I can't *feel* her. All we've had since she was taken is one grainy phone snap of her holding a teddy bear in what looks like someone's house.'

'Which is better than her being held in some filthy concrete bunker,' Ryan says. 'Honestly, Em, I've got a feeling about all this – and it's going to be fine.'

'I hope to God you're right,' Emma says, dropping a teabag into a mug and pouring water over it.

Leaving Ryan to his online research, she carries her cup out to the garden where the sun has lost its ferocity. She takes her phone from her shorts pocket and checks the time: it is six forty, only three minutes later than the last time she'd looked. She's almost winded to note that they should have taken off on a British Airways flight bound for home a few minutes ago.

'We are never going on holiday again,' she says aloud as she starts scrolling through the dozens of adorable photos of Callie: swimming in the pool with her dad, paddling in the sea, or playing with Lucas and Leo on the pool deck and in the communal gardens. Playful, carefree images that are a million miles from her current reality.

Her thoughts turn to Jack and Sheena and the boys. She wonders if they are still on the island, or whether they've taken an earlier flight and are at home in south London by now.

Remembering Sheena's fondness for Instagram, she opens the app, finds her profile, and is about to trawl through her posts but is shocked to find that all the Menorcan photos have vanished. Confused, she refreshes the screen, sure she must have missed something; after all, only yesterday, there had been dozens of happy snaps, including beautiful, achingly sweet photos of Callie playing with Leo and Lucas.

The queasy feeling that never leaves her intensifies. She returns to the living room, mug of tea in one hand, her phone in the other, to find Ryan still engrossed in his laptop.

'They're all gone,' Emma whispers. 'All the photos have disappeared.'

Ryan looks nonplussed. 'What's happened?'

'Sheena's Insta account... all the photos of Callie? Well, they've gone. In fact, not just the ones of Callie, but *all* of them. Every photo from this holiday has disappeared.'

Ryan is on his feet. 'I knew it. She's deleted the whole lot so they can pretend they were never here. Oh my God, Emma. Don't you see? This is practically an admission of guilt. I *knew* they were involved. All over us like a rash one minute, then getting out of dodge only hours after Callie's disappearance the next.'

Emma chews her lip. 'I agree, it is pretty damning. Why else would they delete a whole holiday's worth of photos?'

Ryan checks the time on his mobile: it's six fifty. 'In about five hours, we'll know for sure. And I'm telling you, Emma, if Jack and Sheena are behind all this and they've harmed a single hair on Callie's head, I will kill the pair of them with my bare hands.'

'And spend the rest of your life in jail? What good is that to Callie and me? No, Ryan, you're not going to *kill* anyone. Because as soon as Callie is back with us, we're getting on the first UK flight available and the minute we land, we're going straight to the police. Promise me.'

Ryan buries his head in his hands. 'Yes, of course. It's just...' He rubs at his scalp in frustration. 'I *knew* they were involved and yet we let them drive away. And you know what else? It wouldn't surprise me if they've been chipping away at us all along. Remember how we found Callie's tablet in the pool? That happened right after they arrived.' He shudders. 'And that disgusting dead rat on Callie's bed? I thought it was a bit bloody convenient the way Sheena was lurking around outside the villa within a few minutes of us finding it.'

'I'm starting to think you're right,' Emma says. 'Why though? Ask yourself why a nice, respectable couple with children, who live in leafy Beckenham, would follow us here and abduct our daughter. It doesn't make sense, it really doesn't.'

'Because that's not who they are. They're con artists, Em, don't you see?'

'To think I actually liked Sheena,' Emma says in a small voice.

'Yeah, well – me too, for like, a *day*. Actually, I never liked

Jack, I thought he was a smug, pompous oaf if we're being honest.' Ryan snaps his fingers as another thought occurs to him. 'Em, all communication from the kidnappers has come through my phone, hasn't it? Well, except for the UK travel agent and the car hire company, nobody has this number. *But* the amount of time we spent hanging out together during that first week, it would have been a breeze for Jack or Sheena to pick up my mobile, ring themselves so they could store the number and then delete the call entry.'

Emma shakes her head sadly, recalling her warm, gentle interactions with Sheena; two mums getting to know each other, swapping news and trading confidences.

Ryan is on his feet. 'Right, we need to keep it together, keep our wits about us. I'm going for a shower; it will make me feel more alert. After that, we'll pack all our stuff, load the car, and then make some strong coffee. We've got a long night ahead of us.'

CHAPTER THIRTY-SIX

Rigid and shivering in the passenger seat, Emma stares into the impenetrable darkness. Beside her, Ryan grips the wheel, the tension in his jaw visible by the dash light, reminding her of their drive to Gatwick airport two and a half weeks earlier.

She remembers how they'd whinged about the traffic and moaned about the possibility of missing their flight. Now as they flash along the unlit roads towards Monte Toro, each locked in their own thoughts, Emma makes a silent vow never to sweat the small stuff again.

On the back seat there's a duvet that does not belong to them, lifted from Callie's bed, in addition to two of her favourite plush toys, her softest hoodie and jeans – all chosen to comfort and reassure her that she is safe, and that nothing bad is ever going to happen to her again. Behind Emma's seat, a supermarket bag filled with bottles of water and juice, sweet and savoury snacks, chocolate, and fruit; anything that might tempt Callie to eat a few mouthfuls once the handover has taken place.

The SUV's boot is packed with stuffed holdalls, leaving

them no reason to return to Cala Savannah or the villa ever again.

Emma had waited until Ryan was in the shower to creep next door and say goodbye to Max and John, who, after all, had shown them nothing but friendship since their first day at Santa Martina. She'd felt disappointed to find their car gone and their villa shuttered, admitting to herself that saying goodbye to the older couple wasn't her only reason for seeking them out: it was also to share her story. She'd planned to tell John and Max in detail where and when they were going, so that if the kidnappers decided to murder all three of them near the summit of Monte Toro, *somebody* would know the truth and their bodies would be found, identified, and laid to rest together.

For the umpteenth time that day, tears had sprung into her eyes as she'd imagined her parents' agony and confusion at being contacted by the police, only to learn that their daughter, granddaughter, and son-in-law had been murdered on holiday – victims of an elaborate scam gone wrong.

'We should be there in around twelve minutes,' Ryan says, his voice thick with emotion.

Emma doesn't answer as she hears the car engine change in tone as they gain altitude.

She's read online that Sanctuary of the Virgin of El Toro is beloved by tourists and is a popular wedding venue. 'It's meant to be a happy place,' she tells Ryan. 'People get married there and there's a beautiful statue of Jesus.'

'Well hold that thought. Not that I'm religious, but right now we need all the help we can get.'

'Oh God, I feel sick. I'm going to throw up,' Emma says, putting a hand to her mouth.

'No, you're not. We're both going to keep going. Stay focused on the task in hand and do whatever it takes to get our baby back.'

The road is steep and winding. Overhead, stars sprinkle the indigo sky, silhouetting the peak of Monto Toro as their journey nears its end.

Ryan hunches forward in his seat, peering through the windscreen. 'Okay, we must be close to the turning. The instructions said 2.5 kilometres from the summit and counting down by the satnav, it's got to be here somewhere. Then we're looking for a stone folly shaped like a bridge.'

Slowing to a crawl, he grips the wheel. 'Where the fuck is the turning? There's no track, just rock and scrub.'

'Maybe we missed it?' Emma offers desperately. Then: 'Look, there! It's narrow but it's definitely a track.'

'Yes! Well done, Em.' Ryan turns the wheel sharply, holds the car steady as it rumbles along the pitted surface, throwing dust in its wake. And they're holding their breath, watching, waiting, until the track runs dry and they're facing a small barren clearing; a crop of boulders, pale and smooth beneath the moonlight as it slides from behind a veil of cloud.

'This is it,' Ryan says, 'a pile of rocks shaped like a bridge.'

'Or an altar.' Emma shudders, adrenalin coursing through her, her heart beating fast as a sparrow's wings. 'But there's no one here. Ryan, there's nothing... what do we do now?'

Instinctively, Ryan turns off the ignition and kills the headlights; still the stone folly glows eerily by moonlight. He checks the time on his phone: 11.53. 'We wait, Em,' he says. 'We just wait.'

CHAPTER THIRTY-SEVEN

THEN

Emma regards the mound of discarded clothes on the bed with dismay. This evening, nothing feels right and everything she tries on makes her feel too fat, too frumpy, or just downright dull.

'Em, it's just drinks and dinner with the people from work. I don't know why you're making such heavy weather of it,' Ryan says impatiently. 'You'll look great whatever you wear, you always do.'

'I just want you to be proud of me,' Emma says, eyeing the pile of rejects despondently.

Ryan's tone softens. 'I *am* proud of you, always. Look, what about the lacy fitted dress I like you in?'

'What, the red one? Isn't it a bit tarty?'

Ryan wiggles his eyebrows. 'You say tarty, I say *smokin' hot, baby*,' he says in a ridiculous gangster voice.

Emma relents. 'Okay. Give me a few minutes – at least my make-up and hair are done.'

Fifteen minutes later, after kissing Callie goodnight and hurriedly blurting last-minute instructions to Meghan, the babysitter, Emma and Ryan get in the taxi they've booked and set out for Hawthorn Hall.

'Wow, this is very grand,' Emma says as they purr along the ribbon of gravel that leads to the hall's entrance.

Ryan pays the driver and arranges to meet him in the same place at midnight, then they walk the last few metres, with Emma gripping Ryan's arm as her high heels sink into the shingle. She breathes deeply, trying to calm her nerves.

'Relax,' Ryan says, reading her apprehension. 'You wait, it'll be a fun night, even if the venue looks a bit stuffy.'

'I hope so,' Emma says.

Once inside, they pass through the grand entrance and into the tiled Georgian foyer with its sweeping central staircase, where neoclassical art adorns the walls and a vast chandelier sparkles overhead.

Hovering in reception, Sue smiles and strides forward.

'Hi, good to see you both. Emma, you look lovely – an absolute vision,' she gushes, shaking Emma's hand whilst barely acknowledging Ryan.

Taken aback by the warmth of Sue's welcome, Emma relaxes a little. Perhaps the evening will be fun and enjoyable, after all.

They follow her as she walks briskly in kitten heels. 'Perfect. So now we're all here, except for Paul and his girlfriend, and I've just left word with reception to send them out to the terrace.' She glances over her shoulder. 'We're wringing the last rays out of this glorious spring sunshine. It really lifts the spirits, don't you find, Emma? You'll need that wrap, though – there's still a nip in the air.'

Sue keeps up a running commentary as they pass through

the restaurant area – a grand hall of a room, with taupe velvet swagged curtains framing French windows that open onto a cloistered terrace and the elegant lawned gardens beyond.

'Come and sit by me,' Sue says, steering them both out to a group of tables where the clink of glass and the hubbub of light conversation greets them.

Henry rises in his seat and springs forward, his hand outstretched to shake Ryan's. 'Hello, hello... so glad you could make it.' He turns to Emma. 'Hello, my dear, you look stunning,' he says, leaning in to kiss Emma's cheek.

A ripple of *hellos* echoes around the tables as Emma and Ryan weave their way to a pair of empty seats.

Sue takes a bottle of champagne from an ice bucket and fills two glasses. 'Let's start as we mean to go on, shall we? Cheers,' she says, passing them to Ryan and Emma.

Emma takes a grateful sip, then peers round at Ryan's colleagues and their partners. With a pang of relief, she realises she isn't the only woman who has dressed up. Suddenly, her scarlet lace dress feels entirely appropriate for the evening ahead.

A handsome Indian man in a well-cut ivory jacket leans across. 'Welcome, Emma. I'm Raj and this is my wife, Kate,' he says. 'I don't think we've met before. I'm sure I would have remembered.'

Kate, resplendent in a sapphire silk dress nods and raises her glass. 'Lovely to meet you, Emma. Hey, do you like dancing? I hear a DJ has been booked for later.'

'Er, yes, not that I can remember the last time—'

'Ha! We'll soon remedy that, won't we, Michelle?' Kate turns to a well-groomed woman in her fifties to her other side. 'Emma, this is Michelle; she's married to Henry. Oh, and do you know Pete Robson? That's him on the end.' Kate lowers her voice. 'I don't think he's brought anyone; he's recently *divorced*.'

She mouths the last word as though it is somehow shameful, or worse, contagious.

Emma is saved from having to respond by the arrival of another couple.

'Ah, full house. Paul and his girlfriend are here,' Raj says, getting up to welcome them. Another round of greetings and introductions ensues, chairs are shuffled, and glasses refilled.

A few minutes later, at the distinctive ting of silver against glass and some shushing from those nearest, the buzz of conversation dies away and all eyes fall on the partners, Henry and Raj, who are now on their feet, benign smiles in place.

Henry clears his throat. 'Good evening, everyone, and a huge welcome. This won't take long; Raj and I have no wish to eat into valuable drinking time.' He pauses for a few seconds' polite laughter. 'So, firstly, thank you all for coming tonight and for giving up a precious Friday evening. I know most of you have families you'd rather be with, but nevertheless, we are celebrating.' He looks round at the sea of faces, some already flushed from wine. 'Because tonight marks fifteen years of Sutton & Singh Architects and Project Management, and Raj and I could not be happier or prouder.' Henry gestures towards his partner, who picks up the mantel.

Emma's attention wanes while Raj lists some of the firm's most memorable projects, heaping praise on a few named individuals, Ryan among them, who have been instrumental in their success.

Finally, Henry draws their speech to a close. There's a burst of enthusiastic applause before Sue is on her feet and taking charge as she ushers everyone into the dining room.

Emma catches the look of irritation on Ryan's face.

'Don't know why *she's* being so bloody bossy,' he mutters as they file into the restaurant. 'She's only the office manager.'

Emma glares at him. 'In that case, she's probably organised

most of tonight,' she whispers, puzzled by the apparent chill between them.

The meal consists of three courses, all beautifully presented but made up of safe and predictable options.

Nibbling on smoked salmon terrine, Emma finds herself sitting between Paul's girlfriend, Freya, an attractive but slightly gauche young woman who keeps checking her phone, and Pete Robson – or Robbo, as most of the men call him – who, from the moment they sit down, seems hell-bent on making Emma laugh.

From Ryan's descriptions of him – not to mention tales of Robbo's misadventures on various nights out – Emma had imagined him to be an awkward, even odious person, but she soon realises that his motor-mouth humour, lame puns and awkward gestures are just a ploy to mask his shyness.

Not for the first time, she reflects on Ryan's lack of empathy. She glances across at him, now deep in conversation with Henry, and wonders if he is angling for promotion. With only fifteen staff in the company, other than the two senior partners, there appears to be no hierarchy. It surprises Emma that so few women work at the practice. Sue, the office manager, is one of only three, the others being Grainne, an Irish woman who works in accounts, and the studious looking Nancy, their relatively new receptionist, and presumably, Emma muses, Amber's replacement.

Later, as dinner concludes and the waiting staff begin to clear away, Sue is again tasked with herding the twenty-odd guests into a small intimate function room for the final phase of the evening.

Getting to her feet for the first time in almost two hours, Emma realises she is slightly tipsy – thanks to Pete Robson topping up her glass throughout the meal. She's grateful when he offers her his arm as they walk towards the library with its mahogany-panelled, book-lined walls, and where a DJ has set up at one end of the room, complete with a psychedelic light machine that creates a club vibe.

There's a tangible shift in mood as the younger guests come to life, ordering drinks from the well-stocked bar, and people are forced to shout over the music: a blend of contemporary dance tunes punctuated with the odd rock power-ballad.

Emma tries to sit down, happy to watch others dance, but Pete is having none of it, pulling Emma to her feet and leading her to the centre of the small dance floor where he dips and twirls her, playing to the gallery for comic effect, and making her wheeze with laughter.

'Pete, stop, please,' Emma says, wiping her eyes. 'Seriously, I need a break. Would you mind getting me some fizzy water?'

'Lightweight,' Pete says, flashing Emma a good-natured grin before joining the small queue at the bar.

Emma finds a leather sofa and sits down gratefully, aware of the burning sensation in the soles of her feet.

Sue flops down beside her. 'Oof, I'm too old for this,' she jokes, her face flushed and happy. 'Are you having a nice time, Emma?'

'I'm having a lovely time, thanks, Sue. You must have been planning this party for months.'

Sue nods. 'Well, as long as Raj and Henry are happy. I love my job and I'm so fond of them both. They've been like family to me, especially since my divorce.' She glances to where Pete stands jerking rhythmically at the bar as he waits to be served. 'Look, Emma, just say if Robbo's annoying you – he can be a bit much sometimes.' She grimaces. 'He's kind of... a child.'

Emma laughs. 'Pete's okay. He's been great company and not at all what I expected after some of the things Ryan's told me about him.' She turns her attention to the dance floor where at least a dozen people are throwing shapes loosened by alcohol.

'Excuse me, Sue,' Emma says, going in search of the cloakroom.

Alone in the powder room and enjoying the peace, Emma washes her hands and studies her reflection in a large gilt mirror, relieved she doesn't look as tired as she feels.

She takes her phone from her clutch bag and checks that there are no messages from the babysitter. It's eleven fifteen. In forty-five minutes, she and Ryan will say their goodbyes, find their taxi and head home to their sleeping daughter. She longs to ditch her dress and heels and the relief of knowing she'll soon be falling into bed is palpable.

She starts back towards the party, but as the music and laughter grows louder, she finds herself craving fresh air and solitude, so changes tack, passing silently through the deserted dining room and out onto the terrace, knowing she's unlikely to be missed. Feet throbbing, she limps to a low wall, where she sits, her face turned to the starry sky, enjoying the coolness of the night air.

Her heart sinks when a door rattles behind her; at this stage in the evening, the last thing she wants is to make small talk. She scooches lower and has tucked herself out of sight when she recognises Ryan's voice.

'Well, what is it?' he says, his tone brittle. 'You've been giving me daggers all night. What's going on?'

Emma stiffens. Who is Ryan speaking to so rudely?

'Can you blame me?' hisses a familiar voice she can't quite place.

'Come on then, spit it out if you've got something to say,' Ryan answers, his tone sneering and unpleasant.

There's a pause. Then: 'I've heard from Amber. She's been trying to contact you but you've blocked her, haven't you?'

Emma's hands cover her mouth and she smothers a gasp. She realises that the other voice belongs to Sue. A sudden queasiness washes over her and she shivers in her lace dress.

'Shit,' Ryan says. 'Yes, I blocked her. We had an agreement. No more contact. I thought – I *hoped* – once she left the company, she'd leave me the fuck alone. But no, she keeps messaging me, sending emails. She even tried to ring me at home one evening. The woman's obsessed with me!'

'Yeah, you keep telling yourself that, Ryan. Well, Robbo might be naïve enough to buy all that guff about her having a massive crush on you, but not me. I'm too long in the tooth and I know your MO.' A beat of silence follows. 'She told me everything, Ryan. You were vile to her. You can't use people like that, especially when they're as young and impressionable as Amber. There are consequences.'

'Since when were you two such great mates, anyway? You're practically old enough to be her mother,' Ryan sneers.

'Which is possibly why she talks to me; sees me as older and wiser, perhaps.'

Emma can hear Ryan breathing hard, she pictures him weighing up his response. 'Look, I'm not proud of what happened but it was just a fling, a stupid, meaningless mistake. And I'm sorry if Amber got hurt, but she'll get over it. She's young... shit happens in our twenties.' There's a pleading tone in his voice when he adds, 'For God's sake, Sue. You can see how I'm fixed. I love my family—'

'I made a point of chatting to Emma tonight and she's lovely. And far too good for you,' Sue says tartly. 'Ryan, do the right thing. Get in touch with Amber – check she's okay and bloody apologise for treating her like rubbish, will you?'

'Okay, I will... I'll contact her. But, Sue, please don't say anything to anyone. Especially not Emma. I'll make it up to her, I promise, or die trying,' he says mournfully.

'Oh, stop being dramatic,' Sue snaps.

Emma hears the French doors being opened and banged shut, followed by a yawning silence except for the throb of dance music emanating from the library, and the frantic swooshing of her heartbeat pounding in her ears.

CHAPTER THIRTY-EIGHT

NOW

By twelve minutes past midnight, Ryan's patience has expired. He switches on the car headlights, floodlighting the rock formation and the surrounding patch of scrub.

'Shit. What do we do now?' He bangs the steering wheel with his palm. 'They've got the money, we've followed their instructions to the letter and still there's nobody here.'

'Maybe we're in the wrong place,' Emma says thickly, blowing her nose and wiping away the tears that won't stop falling.

'No, this is the place – exactly as it was described on the text. Something's not right.'

'Oh, you think?' Emma cries. 'God, Ryan. *None* of this is right – how can it be? Our little girl has been taken and we don't know if she's alive or dead.'

Ryan narrows his eyes and listens for the distant purr of a car approaching, but the only sounds are the clicks and whines of the night critters. 'Stay here, I'm getting out,' he says, making no attempt to comfort Emma. 'Maybe they've left a message and hidden it beneath the rocks.'

Emma's fists are balled up in frustration. 'They're not

coming, are they? *Nobody* is coming. Please, Ryan, face facts! We can't do this on our own, we need to go to the police.'

Ignoring her, Ryan steps out of the car and into the beam of light, a cloud of tiny insects fizzing around him as he walks.

'Wait, I'm coming with you,' Emma says, terrified that Ryan, too, will disappear.

The stifling heat of the day has been replaced by a cool wind and she shivers as goosebumps break out all over her body. She reaches for Ryan's hand, but he shakes her off.

'I need to focus,' he whispers, staring ahead into the silvery light. He pauses mid-step. 'What's that?' he says as they near the rock formation, which by now is looking less like a bridge and more like a table. He freezes, his face contorting in horror.

'Oh God, no... no please, please don't let it be—' Emma whimpers, her teeth chattering as they reach a filthy roll of carpet tied at each end with string.

Emma retches and turns away as Ryan, his hands shaking violently, drags the lumpen fabric from its hiding place.

He too is choking back tears, bargaining with God as he tugs hard at the filthy ties until they give way, exposing the contents.

He recoils suddenly, a bubble of hysterical laughter catching in his throat.

'It's nothing, Em. Just a pile of old clothes.'

Emma straightens up, clutching her stomach. 'Are you sure? It's not her...?' she croaks.

'Positive. I swear, when I find these people, Emma, I will kill them for what they're putting us through,' Ryan says, sinking to his knees.

Moments later, they stumble back to the car and Ryan snaps off the headlights, mindful of preserving the battery. He covers his face with his hands. 'I don't know what to do,' he whispers. 'Maybe you're right, maybe it's time to go to the police.'

He reaches for his phone and checks the time – 12.19am – and is startled when a message lands.

For a second, he stares dumbly at the screen. 'It's from them,' he says.

'Change of plan,' he reads aloud. 'Return to Cala Savannah immediately if you want to see your daughter alive. 01.00hrs at Juan's Café. No police. No third party.'

Ryan throws the car into reverse, revving so hard that the wheels spin and a choking cloud of dust flies up as they head back to the main road and hare down the mountain.

With three minutes to spare, they dump the car at the edge of the beach, then stumble across the sand towards Juan's Café, where a neon sign mocks them with its promise of ice-cold drinks.

Emma eyes the neat rows of tables and the stools that line the bar under its cheerful rattan canopy. As with Monte Toro, they are completely alone.

'Fuck! Another wild goose chase!' Ryan screams, throwing up his hands in despair. 'Someone is playing with us and when I find out who it is... What have we done, hmm? What the hell have we done to deserve this?'

Emma sobs, grief and exhaustion felling her to the sand, where she sits hugging her knees. Collapsing beside her, Ryan faces out to sea. He looks at his phone. 1.01am.

'Where is she, Em... where's our baby?' he howls, snot and tears blurring his features.

But Emma doesn't answer, instead she stares fixedly ahead, her eyes trained on the beach path that she and Ryan have used dozens of times during their holiday. Wordlessly, she touches his arm and inclines her head towards the disc of bright light drawing closer.

'Jesus, Em. Someone's coming. By the look of it, they're on foot and carrying a torch. What do we do?'

Emma's eyes are wide; she tries to reply but no words will come as the light draws steadily closer.

Springing to his feet, Ryan lurches forward. 'Who is it? I can't tell if it's one person or several,' he says in a low voice. 'Emma, stay here, keep your eyes peeled and scream your head off if anyone else shows up.'

'Ryan, wait. They could be armed with a gun, or a knife... be careful.'

But Emma is on her feet now, adrenalin flooding every cell of her body; poised to run or scream, whichever is necessary to survive. She gapes in horror and fascination, hypnotised as the torchlight draws closer, bobbing rhythmically with each step taken by the bearer.

Ahead, Ryan breaks into a jog, but he stumbles, his hands going out to break his fall.

Ignoring his comments about waiting by the bar, Emma powers forward as fast as she can, closing the gap between herself and Ryan so that she's only ten or so metres away when he stops in his tracks, his body language wary.

'What are *you* doing here? What the fuck is going on?' she hears him say.

CHAPTER THIRTY-NINE

THEN

Desperate to escape, Emma strides through the hotel as fast as her heels will allow, passing through reception and out onto the gravelled drive. She stares in dismay at the fleet of cars, and tries to remember the model of car she and Ryan had arrived in. Despite her fragile state, the image of a silver Mercedes comes to her.

'You're waiting for Mr and Mrs Burrows?' she asks, bending at the saloon car's window.

'That's right, madam. Going back to Wisteria Close, Eden Hill. Nice evening?'

Emma nods mutely. 'Change of plan, it's just me,' she says firmly, opening a rear door and getting in.

Blinking back tears and shivering from shock, Emma pulls her wrap around her as they speed along the country lanes. She pictures Ryan searching for her just before midnight, imagines him asking people if they've seen her, fuming when neither Emma nor his ride home can be found.

Well, let him fume. Because whatever else happens tonight and during the next few days while Emma scrabbles to pick up the pieces of her shattered life, *nothing* can possibly make Ryan feel as desolate as she feels right now.

Somehow, she holds it together during the twenty-minute journey, even managing a few sentences of small talk with the driver. Finally, feeling like a husk, she arrives home to find Meghan sprawled on the sofa under a throw, watching Netflix.

'Everything okay? Any problems with getting Callie to bed?' Emma whispers, discarding her high heels.

Meghan smiles sleepily and stretches. 'Hey, Emma. All good, thanks. I read to her until she fell asleep; some book about a family of beetles? Anyway, she seemed to like it.' Meghan frowns, looks past Emma. 'Where's Mr Burrows?'

Emma gives a funny little laugh. 'Oh, Ryan and a few others have gone to another party. Honestly, I don't know where he gets his energy because I *cannot wait* to get into bed.'

Meghan stifles a yawn. 'Yeah, me too. I'll leave you to it then, Emma. I'm in all day tomorrow morning if you wanted to, you know—'

'Of course. I'll pop round with the cash straight after breakfast. Thanks a lot, Meghan. Goodnight.'

Emma walks the teenager to the front door, locks up carefully using the top and bottom bolts that cannot be released from outside, then goes into the kitchen and repeats the exercise with the back door. Then she fills a pint glass with water and goes around switching off the lights. Water in one hand, handbag in the other, she tiptoes upstairs, pokes her head around Callie's door, and finds her sleeping.

Her heart stutters at the sight of her daughter dozing peacefully, innocently unaware of the potential misery that lies ahead.

Emma takes a deep breath, goes to her own room, and closes the door. Once inside her en suite bathroom, she discards her party clothes in a crumpled heap and puts on her dressing gown. Then she gets into bed, reaches for her mobile, sees that it is twelve forty-five and that she has a dozen missed calls from Ryan. She calmly sends him a message.

> I heard you talking to Sue, so I know all about Amber. I'm at home with Callie. Please stay away, Ryan. You don't live here anymore. Text me tomorrow to arrange collection of your things.

She rereads the message, almost caves in at its starkness, then steels herself and hits send, putting her phone on silent so as not to get drawn into a back and forth with Ryan. Then she finds a packet of paracetamol in her bedside cabinet, swallows two with water, turns out the light and allows herself to cry.

Emma cries and cries, until her throat hurts and there are no tears left, finally falling asleep as tentative rays of spring sunlight creep through the gap in her curtains.

'Mummy, Mummy, wake up! Daddy's in the garden and he's crying. Come quick!'

Callie's small frame resting squarely on Emma's chest is surprisingly heavy as she fights through sleep. She swallows hard, her mouth dry from last night's wine, her head fuzzy as the painful memories start to flood in.

Emma gently manoeuvres her daughter aside, gets out of bed, and uses the bathroom. Then she pulls on leggings and a hoodie ready to face the music while Callie continues to chatter about Ryan's predicament.

Downstairs, Callie leads Emma by the hand into the kitchen and points to the French windows where Ryan stands slumped against them, like a fly on a windscreen.

'See, Mummy? I told you. Why is Daddy outside?'

'That's a very good question, sweet pea,' Emma says briskly.

For God's sake! How *dare* Ryan play for sympathy in front their daughter. She'd been clear enough in her text to him last night, yet here he is, putting on a show of being the injured party.

'Emma, please let me in, we need to talk,' Ryan wheedles through the glass. He rattles the door handle. 'Come on! This is ridiculous. Whatever you think you heard—'

Emma stands eye to eye with him, thinking how ill and desperate he looks, and wonders where he spent the night. She squares her shoulders. 'Ryan, I don't *think*, I *know*,' she says.

'Mummy, let Daddy in, he might be cold,' Callie says, her chin puckering.

'Thank you, darling. I *am* cold – it's freezing out here,' Ryan lies as the April sunshine caresses the patio.

Emma bends to cuddle Callie, who looks to be on the brink of tears. No way will she speak to Ryan in front of her.

'How about we have some breakfast and then maybe Meghan can take you to the swings?' she suggests brightly, thinking on her feet.

Callie eyes her father and shakes her head. 'I want Daddy.'

'Fine,' Emma says through gritted teeth, realising that yet again, Ryan has manipulated the situation to his advantage.

'Thank you,' Ryan says once Emma has unlocked the door and grudgingly allowed him to enter. He swings Callie round, lifts her pyjama top and blows raspberries on her bare stomach, making her shriek with laughter.

'She's not two,' Emma snaps, irritated by Ryan's behaviour.

'I know. Look, I got your message. Needless to say, I haven't slept a wink. But, Emma, you can't just throw me out when it suits you. Just let me explain—'

'Not in front of Callie,' Emma seethes. 'You are unbelievable, you really are.'

Ryan looks affronted. 'I could say the same – telling me I don't live here anymore when I pay the fucking mortgage!' he mouths over Callie's head.

He goes to the pull-out larder. 'Sweet pea, Mummy's a bit tired and confused this morning. What do you fancy, Cocoa Pops or Weetabix?' he asks innocently, daring Emma to challenge him.

CHAPTER FORTY

NOW

Emma stands beside Ryan, her heart pounding, her breath coming in snatched gasps. Before them, almost within touching distance, two figures dressed in shapeless black clothing; the context is all wrong, but their identities are unmistakeable.

'Where is she?' Ryan asks hoarsely. 'Where's our daughter?'

Max lifts her chin, her face ghoulish by torchlight. 'Wouldn't *you* like to know. Shall we?'

She marches past Ryan and Emma in the direction of Juan's Café. Beside her, John grips her arm with one hand and wields the flashlight with the other.

'What the hell are you doing? Talk to us!' Ryan barks, jostling in front of them and attempting to block their path.

Max's laughter is cold and humourless. 'Speak to us like that again and this conversation is over,' she warns, adding, 'Emma, I'm sorry you've been caught up in all this; it's not about you.'

Emma looks from Ryan to Max. 'What isn't? Max, I don't understand. We're supposed to be meeting the kidnappers. Why are you and John here?'

Ryan's face twists with rage. 'Emma, keep up, will you?

They *are* the kidnappers.' He jabs a finger towards Max. 'And I swear, if you've so much as messed up Callie's hair, I'll—'

'You'll do what, exactly?' John interrupts, his tone even. 'Do I need to remind you who's in charge here?'

There's a beat of stunned silence except for the gentle breath of the waves, as all four of them trudge up the beach towards the moonlit café, its silhouette reinforced by the neon sign.

Emma's mind whirs. 'Will somebody tell me what's going on?' she cries.

'Yes, *do* tell us,' Ryan says, breathing hard as they reach the bar.

Max points to a table where light from the sign pools. 'Sit down, both of you – opposite John and me. I want to see your eyes.'

'Where's Callie? What have you done to her?' Ryan repeats once they are seated.

Max shrugs and makes a face. 'Nothing. We haven't done anything to her. What sort of vile apology of a human being would harm a child?' she says, her words dripping with contempt. 'Oh, that's right. That would be *you*, Ryan.'

A sob catches in Emma's throat. 'Why would you say that?' She sniffs, her thoughts racing.

Max ignores her, closes her eyes briefly. 'I could use a bloody drink,' she says, thrusting an open hand towards John.

He passes Max a hip flask; it glints in the moonlight. 'A snifter to oil the conversation, my love,' he says.

Ryan emits a bark of manic laughter. 'Jesus, you people are out of your minds! This isn't one of your lame expat parties.'

John sighs. 'You see, this is the problem. This is exactly the sort of attitude that has led us to where we find ourselves.'

'Max, John, if you know where Callie is, I am *begging* you, just tell us,' Emma says.

'Oh, they know all right,' Ryan says. 'This whole shitshow is down to them.'

'Ah, but the difference, Ryan, is that *your* daughter is safe and well. While *ours*...' Max looks wistfully up at the sky, just as a cloud slides back from the moon, revealing the gleam of tears in her eyes. She leans closer to Ryan. '...is dead. And all thanks to you.'

Ryan bridles. 'What the hell are you talking about, you mad old woman? You're not making any sense. You've stolen our money, now tell us where Callie is.'

'Ryan, just shut up and listen,' Emma begs, a bilious feeling washing over her.

Max sips from the hip flask and wipes her mouth with her hand. 'You should listen to your wife,' she says, turning her gaze on Emma. 'I'm sorry, Emma. Forgive me, but I'm sure you'll understand once you hear what I have to say.'

Ryan scoffs. 'Spare us the drama!'

'As I was saying, you'll be relieved to know that Callie is fine. We, on the other hand, will never see Amber again.'

Emma stiffens at the mention of Amber's name. 'What do you mean? Max, ignore Ryan and talk to *me*,' she says, ice-cold fingers clutching at her heart.

Ryan falls silent, his bluster replaced by a haunted look. He buries his head in his hands. 'Amber is your daughter?' he says quietly. 'She can't be, you're... you're both too—'

'Old?' Max's face softens. 'Amber was my miracle menopause baby; twelve years younger than her sister and the most beautiful child John and I had ever seen. Almost too perfect for this world.'

'God, Ryan, what did you do?' Emma says, slowly shaking her head as she recalls the suddenness with which Amber had disappeared from their lives.

'Nothing. I don't understand. I haven't a clue what you're

talking about. Of course I didn't kill Amber, why would you say that?' Ryan stammers, panic in his eyes.

Emma reaches across and gropes for Max's hand. 'How did Amber die?' she asks, her voice barely audible.

'Car crash. Drunk as a skunk and spaced out on pills, she blacked out at the wheel and hit a tree.'

Emma flinches at the directness of her words and the hardness in her voice, but Ryan looks vindicated. He gets up, paces a few steps, then sits again.

'Max, John, I'm so sorry to hear that Amber passed away, I had no idea. It must have been devastating for you both, but clearly that's got absolutely nothing to do with me. Just tell us where Callie is and we can put an end to this charade.'

'Keep telling yourself that, Ryan.' Max takes another sip from the hip flask and chokes on the strong-smelling spirit.

Emma composes herself, her hands clutched tightly in her lap as she waits for the coughing to subside. 'Look, I want you to know that I found out about Ryan's affair with Amber. We even split up for a while, but we worked through it and I forgave him.' She lifts her chin, reaches for Ryan's hand and gives it a proprietary squeeze. 'Whatever you think of Ryan, your daughter *knowingly* chose to have an affair with a married man, so it's outrageous of you to blame him for her death. I'm sorry for your loss, but accidents happen.'

'Really, Emma? How touching. But I doubt you know everything,' Max says, an unpleasant smile on her lips. 'Did you know, for instance, that far from being a tawdry one-night stand, they were seeing each other for months?'

'Look, I don't know or care about the details. It doesn't matter to me,' Emma says, her gaze defiant. 'Ryan acted like an idiot and he's regretted it ever since. He got lured into a meaningless affair by a much younger woman. That's it. Big deal.'

'Except that it wasn't like that,' Max sneers. 'Ryan seduced Amber – a naïve young woman who was mentally and emotionally vulnerable – and she fell in love with him. What's more, either Ryan felt the same about her, or he let her *think* he did.' Max cackles softly to herself. 'It doesn't bode well for your future together, does it?'

'All right, you've had your fun,' Ryan says, his eyes black with anger. 'Our marriage has fuck all to do with you. It's clear that you're just twisting the knife and making stuff up to get back at me. And as for Amber being mentally vulnerable, how could I possibly have known that? Do you think it's the kind of thing someone advertises at their place of work? Max, you speak of her as if she was an innocent child, rather than a manipulative little—'

Emma raises her hand. 'Ryan, *stop*. None of it matters now, we can't change the past.'

Max looks suddenly deflated. 'We saw her, you know, shortly before she died. She flew out and stayed with us in March. We hardly recognised her. She was a husk. Depressed, thin, exhausted. She hardly ate a thing, just drank; all afternoon and all evening – said it helped to numb the pain.' She turns her gaze back to Ryan, contempt in her eyes. 'She'd always been so loved, you see. So *cherished*. I don't think Amber could get her head around being dumped like a used Kleenex.'

Ryan rolls his eyes. 'Oh, come on!'

'But then she seemed to rally,' Max continues, ignoring Ryan. 'She said she felt better, that her medication was finally helping, and she wanted to go home and make a fresh start. She even talked about going back to work, which we encouraged of course. Amber was a very bright girl and destined for great things.'

John covers Max's hand with his. 'It was the end of March by then,' he says, his voice gruff. 'We drove Amber to the airport, waved her off at departures and that was it. We had no idea we'd said goodbye for the last time.'

Ryan scrapes his chair back. 'I'm sorry, I really am, but you can't blame me for a car crash. Thousands of people are killed on the roads every year.'

'Oh, I can and I do. The old Amber would *never* have got behind the wheel after drinking – and as for mixing medication with alcohol...You changed her, Ryan – *you* did that.' Max bangs the table with the flat of her hand. 'Now get out of my sight; I can't bear to look at you.'

'As soon as you tell us where Callie is,' Emma says, her tone steely.

Max grunts, takes her mobile phone from her pocket and stabs a few keys. 'It's done. Wait here.' She gets stiffly to her feet and turns to her husband. 'Get one of the boys to pick us up, will you, Johnnie; I haven't the energy to walk back along that blessed beach path.'

Emma eyes them both coldly. 'No. You're not going anywhere until we get our daughter back. I'm sorry for your loss but taking a child from her parents, out of spite and revenge, is outrageous. So is fleecing us of every penny we have, then sending us on a wild goose chase up a bloody mountain in the dead of night. Oh! Not to mention the stunt with the carpet that was made to look like a body. Have you any idea—'

Max laughs nastily. 'Did you like that? It was a last-minute addition and it took some organising, I can tell you.' She curls her lip. 'A little pay back, after Ryan dismissed us so rudely. There I was, bringing you a present and offering the services of our retired policeman friend. There really is no end to your husband's arrogance.'

'You weren't offering help! You were rubbing salt in our wounds,' Ryan says. 'All that rubbish about a spate of abductions.'

Max shrugs. 'What can I say? I've always been creative.'

'My God, you're enjoying this. Ryan's right. You really are quite mad—'

Emma is silenced by a squeal of tyres as an SUV mounts the curb between the road and the beach, twenty or so metres away. And as she watches, her heart pounding, her breath held, a rear door opens and someone unseen lowers Callie to the ground, slamming the car door behind her.

Sobbing, Emma lunges forward, calling her daughter's name as Ryan flies past and covers the gap between them in a few bounds.

'Mummy, Daddy!' Callie cries, running towards them while the SUV makes its escape, and Emma falls to her knees, opens her arms and envelops her child, breathing in her familiar scent, and squeezing her tighter than ever before.

'We've got you, baby,' Ryan says, dropping to the ground and encircling his arms around both of them. 'You're safe now.'

CHAPTER FORTY-ONE

THEN

Emma's eyes blaze. 'That was a shitty thing to do. Now Callie is confused and scared. Well, I hope you're pleased with yourself, pulling a stunt like that!'

Ryan sits up at the kitchen island, clutching the mug of coffee he has made for himself, unable to look at her. 'Of course I'm not. I hate myself. And I couldn't be more ashamed. I've made some awful, terrible mistakes that I'll regret for the rest of my life.'

'Oh, you think? I don't even know who you are anymore. You are not the man I married, Ryan. And you're not Callie's father, either.' Emma rakes back her hair, paces to the French windows and stares out, unseeing.

Determined not to cry, she swallows the huge lump in her throat. 'You've got two hours,' she says, matter-of-factly. 'Two hours until Meghan brings Callie home from the park, and I want you gone by then. I'll tell her you're working away somewhere... that she'll see you in a few weeks. You needn't take everything today, but pack enough so you can manage for a while. It'll take us both a few days to appoint a solicitor and—'

Ryan's eyebrows shoot up. 'Whoa! That's ridiculous, stop

talking like that. Look, I'm not leaving, we're not splitting up and you're not telling Callie anything about me. We can work through this. Together. You're massively overreacting.'

'Oh, don't you dare, Ryan.' Emma laughs bitterly. 'Do not turn this around on me. I'm not the one who's been lying and cheating for months. And with a much younger colleague. What a fucking cliché! You disgust me.'

Ryan's shoulders slump. He seems to be shrinking before her eyes and looks pathetic, still in his going-out shirt from the night before, now grubby and untucked. 'Yes, all right,' he says. 'Believe me, you couldn't hate me any more than I hate myself right now. But, Em, I know we can get past this. Amber meant nothing... the whole thing was just a daft flirtation that got out of hand because she was so needy and obsessive. It wasn't me that—'

Emma shakes her head in disbelief. 'Ha! There you go again. Don't insult my intelligence. Clearly you were flattered and things escalated. And believe it or not, I'm not going to dig for details. The thought of you together makes me feel sick to my stomach.' Emma exhales slowly, trying to slow her heartbeat.

'Emma, I need you to know that nothing much happened with Amber. It was just a couple of drunken fumbles. At no point did I feel anything for her. It's *you* I love, always have and always will.'

'Oh, spare me. Like that makes it any better. Actually, it just makes you even more of a pig. I heard what Sue said. Amber was in love with you.' She paces around the kitchen. 'And as much as I hate her for what she did, I almost feel sorry for her. Poor deluded kid!'

Emma stops prowling, perches on a stool opposite Ryan and studies his face, which is now a mask of abject misery. She takes a deep breath. 'Look, you're not the first married man to have a fling at work and you won't be the last. But here's the thing: I specifically asked you if you were having an affair months ago, after your so-called business trip to Bristol. And you lied. You looked me in the eye and accused me of being jealous and paranoid.'

Ryan buries his head in his hands. 'I'm sorry. I panicked... I made the wrong call. Em, I didn't – I *don't* – want to lose you. It was already over by then and we wouldn't even be having this conversation if bloody Sue hadn't opened her—'

Emma springs up off her stool. 'Give me strength! So now it's Sue's fault? *Everyone* is to blame but you, Ryan.' She crosses her arms and hugs herself, feeling sick and exhausted. 'There's nothing more to say. Pack some things and go, will you? Before Callie gets back, I can't have her coming home to this.'

'Emma, please, darling, don't do this,' Ryan begs, tears shining in his eyes. 'Where will I go? We can't leave things like this. I love you. I love Callie, we're a family.'

The sheer horror in Ryan's eyes and the pain in his voice creates a tiny thaw in Emma's heart. She softens her tone. 'Check into a hotel this week and we'll speak again in a few days. I need time and space to think, surely you can understand that? I'll tell Callie you're working away for a while and that you'll phone her every night at bedtime. Can you do that?'

Ryan nods slowly, gets to his feet and goes upstairs to pack.

When it's time for Ryan to leave, he tries to hold Emma, but she recoils and shakes her head. 'No. Don't make things any harder than they are already. We'll speak soon. Bye, be careful,' she says, her voice catching. Then she turns away to hide her tears, waits for the slamming of the front door and the sound of Ryan's car engine driving away before collapsing onto the kitchen sofa and shedding hot, frightened tears.

Ten minutes before Meghan is due back with Callie, Emma goes upstairs and repairs her face, ready to greet her daughter.

It is shortly after one when Callie arrives, her cheeks flushed with fresh air and excitement. She hugs Meghan goodbye at the front door, then trots through to the kitchen, chatting about her morning spent at the children's playground. 'And then we had an ice cream, Mummy, which was lovely except that my flake fell out and landed on the floor, so we left it there for the birds,' she adds earnestly, as though dropped chocolate is the worst thing she can imagine. Finally, she registers Ryan's absence.

'Where's Daddy?'

Emma digs her nails into her palms and wills herself not to cry. 'Daddy's gone away for a while. The reason we were arguing is because the company he works for are sending him away to do an important job. The thing is, sweet pea, he forgot to tell me – which is why I was cross – and he was sad because he'll miss us. But he'll be back soon and you can tell him all your news, okay?'

Emma holds her breath and waits for a battery of questions, or even tears. She's relieved when Callie accepts her version of events with a resigned little shrug.

That evening, after eating in front of the TV and putting Callie to bed an hour later than usual, Emma pours herself a glass of white wine and, driven by curiosity, wanders into Ryan's study.

His fragrance still hanging in the air and the sight of one of his old hoodies draped over the back of his chair causes a knot of pain to throb behind her sternum.

How could Ryan *do* this to her after all their years together? It seems ridiculous and surreal, like a bad dream, or a low-budget clichéd TV drama. At least he'd seemed genuinely regretful and ashamed, and sad to the point of being broken.

Had she been hasty in throwing him out? He'd alluded to it being Amber who'd done all the chasing – what were the words he'd used to describe her? *Needy and obsessive?* Perhaps Ryan had merely been weak rather than treacherous.

Emma walks round to the far side of his desk, sits in his chair, her breath catching as the smell of him intensifies.

She looks around, taking in the neatness of Ryan's filing system, her eyes settling on a framed photo of the three of them taken last summer at a neighbour's barbeque – all sun-kissed and smiling. They'd been happy then – or so she'd thought...

For heaven's sake, what is she even *doing* in here and what, if anything, is she looking for? Emma stares at Ryan's almost empty desk, his laptop having departed with its owner, and begins rifling through his drawers, knowing that she's torturing herself and twisting the knife unnecessarily, yet unable to stop.

She wonders if there are any photos of Amber in Ryan's desk, then laughs dryly at herself for being old-fashioned. Nobody keeps photographs anymore; any pictures he has will be on his phone. Regardless, Emma continues to hunt through Ryan's things and is astonished to find an old tablet he rarely uses. She presses the power button but the screen remains dark. A few minutes later, hidden beneath a pile of ancient bank statements, she finds its charger, links them together and plugs it into a nearby socket.

Then she finishes her wine, pads through to the kitchen and refills her glass from the fridge before going into the sitting room with the intention of watching TV. Forty minutes and another glass later, unable to settle, Emma goes back into Ryan's study and switches on his tablet, surprised to find it unprotected by passwords or pin numbers. She swallows hard, daunted by what she might find.

Soon, she is trawling through photo files; mainly technical images of property renovations that Ryan has project managed. She keeps scrolling but there's nothing personal, nothing that satisfies her curiosity about Amber. As she continues to hunt around blindly, a box pings onto the screen, asking if she wishes to *sync emails to other devices*. She pauses before clicking YES, then watches as hundreds of emails begin to download into Ryan's inbox; emails that presumably he himself has already read and dealt with.

Feeling guilty and duplicitous, Emma waits for the huge download to complete, then scrolls through looking for Amber's name. It isn't long before she finds half a dozen messages from *Amber J Rutherford*. Breathing hard, she carries Ryan's tablet back to the sitting room, settles on the sofa, her feet curled beneath her, and begins to read.

CHAPTER FORTY-TWO

NOW

After bundling Callie into the back of the car, examining her thoroughly for signs of physical injury, and gratefully finding none, Emma hugs Callie close, smoothing her matted hair and showering her tear-stained face with kisses.

'Why didn't you come? I was waiting and waiting,' Callie cries, wrapping her arms around Emma's midriff.

Ryan grips the steering wheel, his hands shaking as he speeds along the main route towards Mahon. He eyes his daughter in the rear-view mirror. 'Baby, we're so sorry; we wanted to come, but we didn't know where you were,' he splutters. 'But you're safe now, and nobody will ever take you from us again. Do you understand?'

'Yes, Daddy. It's not my fault; I didn't want to go but Teddy woke me up and said he needed me to help with Diesel.'

From the back seat, Emma meets Ryan's eyes in the mirror.

'Teddy? Do you mean Max's friend, who was at the party?' Emma asks, shocked and relieved in equal measure that Callie's abductor is someone she can at least picture, rather than a faceless thug.

Callie nods. 'Yes, Mummy, *that* Teddy.'

'Did Teddy hurt you, sweet pea? Did he touch you?' Ryan asks hoarsely.

'No,' Callie answers, burying her head against Emma's chest.

'And, darling, who's Diesel?' Ryan probes.

'Teddy's doggie. He's only little now, but Teddy says he'll grow big one day.' She shrugs matter-of-factly. 'I helped to feed him and take him to the toilet on the roof.'

It takes Emma and Ryan another fifteen minutes of gentle digging to form a picture, before Callie, exhausted by her *adventure*, snuggles beneath the duvet across Emma's lap and falls into a deep sleep.

'I'm going back,' Ryan says in a low voice, surprising Emma by pulling to the side of the main road. 'There's no way those bastards are getting away with this.'

'Ryan, no! We agreed to find a hotel near the airport and leave on the first flight possible. We have to get off the island, it's not safe,' Emma says, panic rising.

'Actually, it is. The whole thing was a sick and elaborate prank – an act of revenge against me. Well, I'm not having it. How dare those people take us for every penny we've got – I'm going to get our money back if it kills me.'

'Ryan, stop. Don't even talk like that. We could have lost Callie, but we didn't. It's only money and I couldn't care less... we can sell the house when we get back, buy a smaller one... none of it matters except that our baby's okay.'

'But aren't you curious, Em? About how they did it?'

'I don't *care* how they did it. I just want to leave Menorca and never come back. Please, Ryan, let's stick to the plan: find somewhere we can rest for a few hours, then get to the airport as soon as it opens.'

Ryan considers their options, his fingers drumming on the

wheel. 'Okay. Maybe you're right,' he says through gritted teeth, pulling back onto the road and resuming their journey.

The hotel's night manager peers over the rim of his glasses, taking in Ryan and Emma's unkempt appearance and the fact that the child Ryan is carrying appears to be comatose.

'Is very late, to be checking in, no? May I see your passports, please?' he says.

Ryan offers him a reassuring smile. 'You could say that. I'm afraid we had a last-minute change of plan and had to vacate the villa we were staying in. We'll be leaving for the airport first thing. Any room you have is fine for us; our little girl can share our bed.' He waves his debit card, then presents all three passports for inspection.

'Yes, any room, however small,' Emma echoes. 'We just need to rest for a few hours.' She looks around the pleasant reception area where even the sofas look inviting in her desperation.

'One moment, please.' The receptionist examines their passports, then strikes a few keys on his computer. 'We have a room on the second floor. It has one double and one single bed. Breakfast is from seven thirty and we can deliver to your room,' he says, eyeing Emma kindly.

'Thank you so much, that's perfect,' Emma says, almost tearful with relief.

Ryan had expected to pass out from exhaustion, like Emma and Callie, sprawled beside him. Instead, he lays wired and sleepless, his limbs buzzing with adrenalin, his head replaying the night's events on a loop. Callie sleeps deeply, secure and happy, curled between her parents, as if nothing bad had ever happened in her world.

Gently, so as not to disturb his family, Ryan reaches for his mobile, appalled to find it is already five fifteen. Shit. In under three hours, they'll be inside the airport, ready to pounce on the first available flight back to Gatwick, which is not a foregone conclusion by any means, especially in August, in the middle of the school holidays.

Christ, what a white-knuckle ride this so-called holiday has turned out to be. He grunts in the darkness. Well, it's not over yet. Because whilst he has every sympathy with Emma's desire to escape the island and its distressing associations, the only real danger at this point is that he'll be tempted to choke the vile, crazy old couple who did this with his bare hands.

Ryan exhales slowly and tries to calm his racing heartbeat.

First things first: get up in a couple of hours, shower, have breakfast, then pile into the car for the ten-minute drive to Mahon airport, where they'll head straight to departures to check availability.

Then, assuming they can secure seats home within the next day or two, *surely* Emma won't object to him driving back to Santa Martina to confront the John and Max with the objective of getting their money back.

'Daddy, are you awake?' Callie whispers, bringing her face closer so he can feel her breath on his cheek.

'I am, Cal,' Ryan whispers, swallowing the lump in his throat.

'I didn't like it at Teddy's house and I'm not going again,' she says, before closing her eyes and drifting back to sleep.

CHAPTER FORTY-THREE

Emma finishes reading Amber's emails to Ryan and sets his tablet down.

What had Ryan called her? *Needy and obsessive?* Well, if her messages were anything to go by, he'd been telling the truth about that much at least.

Sentimental and self-pitying, Amber's emails to Ryan were loaded with emotional blackmail. By contrast, it was clear from his cool, terse replies that, just as he claimed, Ryan had no feelings for the young woman at all.

Not that Ryan's lack of emotional connection excused his appalling behaviour; he'd still cheated on her by sleeping with Amber, and on several occasions at that. But the fact that he'd never been *in love* with her, that he'd never wanted to leave his family and be in a legitimate couple with the scheming little bitch, made it bearable somehow.

Emma recalls the walk she, Ryan and Callie had taken together at their local country park just after Christmas. He'd been distant and miserable throughout the holidays, but on that particular day, he'd talked about getting away and starting again in a new town where nobody knew them. Clearly, he'd felt trapped by Amber then and had wanted to escape, but *with* his family, not *from* them.

She sits up straighter, sobered by the thought that if she keeps on the same trajectory, she'll be a divorced single parent by the time she's forty. Short of money and short of time for Callie – assuming she'll need to work more hours, just to cover their outgoings.

She longs to confide in her mum, then pictures Deirdre, wearing her best I-warned-you-but-you-wouldn't-listen face and shuts that idea down.

Because at this juncture, she and Ryan have been separated for less than twelve hours, and nobody on Emma's side of the family knows the first thing about it. Yes, some of Ryan's colleagues are aware of his office fling, but if Sue and Pete Robson's reactions are typical, they disapprove of Ryan and think him an idiot.

Perhaps she has been too hasty in throwing Ryan out of the house and calling time on their marriage. Maybe a better strategy would be to make him sweat, to give him time to miss her and Callie – not to mention their cosy, comfortable family life together. Living in a cheap hotel or squatting in somebody's spare room would soon kick him into touch.

Then, after he's had time to reflect on his huge mistake, she could grudgingly take him back, no doubt with his tail between his legs and a heartfelt assurance that it would never, *could* never happen again.

And who knows, their marriage might even be stronger for it.

Emma exhales, aware that for the first time in twenty-four hours, she feels a tiny glimmer of hope for the future.

CHAPTER FORTY-FOUR

In the hotel bar, feeling like a rubbernecker at a car crash, Ryan sips his second glass of Malbec and surreptitiously watches a couple in their late forties.

Something about their frequent brushing of hands, forearms, and knees, and the way they laugh too loudly at each other's jokes, tells him they are not married, nor will they be any time soon.

His theory gains traction when the woman, teetering on vertiginous heels, goes in search of the cloakroom, providing a window of opportunity for the man to text someone who is almost certainly his wife.

'Hope she's worth it, fuckwit,' Ryan mutters under his breath, just as the man looks up, catches his eye and guiltily pockets his phone in time for his mistress's return.

Ryan's thoughts turn to Emma and his heart stutters painfully as he pictures her with Callie, eating together in front of the TV as is their Saturday night ritual, one he's unlikely to be included in again.

How the hell had he let it happen?

He'd fallen for the triple whammy of adulterers' stupidity: stupid once in that he'd had an affair in the first place; twice because he'd got caught; and stupid three times over because he'd lied to Emma's face months earlier when she'd confronted him.

Well, at least Emma doesn't know about the baby or Amber's subsequent abortion, and she never will if he's got anything to do with it.

It's almost nine o'clock when the rumbling of his stomach reminds Ryan that he hasn't eaten all day. He longs for a juicy steak in the restaurant but can't face eating alone. After finishing his wine, he walks up to the bar, currently manned by a lone guy in his twenties.

'Hi,' Ryan says, leaning in. 'Do you have a room service menu, please?'

The barman nods and hands him a laminated card. 'We do, sir. Just order at reception and they'll get it sent up.'

Ryan thanks him.

'Pleasure, sir. Enjoy your stay,' the barman says as Ryan turns to leave.

Forty minutes later, propped up against pillows on the king-sized bed, Ryan chews his way through an indifferent club sandwich. The TV is on but nothing grabs his attention, and he channel surfs as he eats, wondering for the umpteenth time what Emma is doing at home.

Then, thirsty and bloated, he raids the minibar for bottled water, undresses down to his underwear and scrolls through his phone. He's desperate to call Emma, to beg her forgiveness, to tell her he loves her, that he'll never do anything like this again. Ever. Except she'd asked him not to ring over the weekend. Too upsetting for all of them, she'd said, adding that from Monday, he should call every night to chat to Callie.

'You idiot,' he says aloud. 'You prize fucking moron.' Tears of self-pity well in his eyes. 'You have to take me back, Emma,' he mouths, putting his head in his hands. 'You just *have* to.'

Sunday morning dawns as grey as the room he's woken up in. Ryan showers, goes downstairs to the restaurant, drinks two cups of stewed filter coffee and forces down some granola and a croissant. Nothing tastes good or fresh. Come to think of it, nothing tastes of anything, period.

No way can he hack this bland budget hotel for more than a couple of nights. Tomorrow, he'll spend his lunchbreak online, looking for an Airbnb.

With a twinge of guilt, he recalls being unsympathetic to Robbo when his wife had thrown him out and he'd been forced to sleep on his brother's sofa for months on end. To his shame, Ryan realises that it's been weeks since he asked Pete how things are going in his personal life. Now, here they are, in the same position: two cheating husbands out on their respective ears.

He shudders, appalled to have so much in common with someone he openly ridicules.

'Good Lord, you look rough,' Sue says, eyeing Ryan up and down. 'Heavy weekend?'

He glances around the office, hoping nobody has overheard Sue's caustic remark and is thankful when he realises it's only eight thirty and they are the only ones in the office.

It's on the tip of Ryan's tongue to say something cutting in reply, blaming Sue for her part in his misery. But it's been a weekend of harsh lessons, and he shrugs mournfully.

'Actually, Sue, it's been an awful couple of days.' His shoulders drop. 'Just dreadful.'

Sue's expression softens. 'Why? Are you okay? You don't look well, now that you—'

'Emma and I have split up. Specifically, she's thrown me out.' Ryan hangs his head and massages his temples.

'God, that's awful, I'm so sorry.'

'Are you though, Sue? Because from what you said on Friday night, it's clear you think I deserve it. The thing is, Emma was there at the end of the evening. She heard our whole conversation. Everything we talked about.'

Sue's eyes widen and pink spots appear on her cheeks. 'Oh, Ryan, I'm so sorry. And no, I *don't* think you deserve it at all. Nobody deserves to lose their family overnight.'

The front door clatters open and shut as people start arriving for work. Ryan puts a finger to his lips. 'Not a word to anyone, please. I'm devastated and I'm not ready to share this yet. Today's priority is finding somewhere to live. Longer term, I've promised to give Emma some space. But after a break, I'll be on a mission to get her back.'

He nods at Raj and Paul, who walk in together, regaling each other with stories from Friday night. 'Morning,' Ryan says, keeping his head down and going straight to his desk and opening his inbox.

Ten minutes later, an email arrives from Sue with the words *read and delete* as the subject heading. He scans the message, which is brief and to the point.

```
Ryan, you can have my spare room. Least
I can do. Let's grab a sandwich together
at one o'clock to sort logistics. Sue x
```

He lifts his head to find Sue looking straight at him. *Thank you*, he mouths, placing his hands together as if in prayer and feeling unusually grateful.

CHAPTER FORTY-FIVE

NOW

Mahon airport reeks of cologne, sweat and stress as people mill from one area to another, tired and confused. The check-in lines straggle into one amorphous mass and the cafés are full to bursting – and it's only nine o'clock.

'Please, help us,' Emma begs the crimson-lipped ticket agent. 'We *have* to get home today; we've had a family emergency.'

Ryan frowns. 'My wife's right. We need to leave today. Any airline, any route, any price. Surely you can squeeze us onto a flight this evening?'

The red mouth becomes a tight line as the woman's matching nails fly over her keyboard.

'No, I'm sorry. It's impossible,' the check-in attendant says, looking up from her screen. 'The soonest I can give you is seven fifteen tomorrow morning, changing at Barcelona. August is very busy as you can see.'

Ryan hesitates, puffs out his cheeks. 'Fine, we'll take it. Book it up, please.' He presents his debit card and all three passports for inspection. 'It's fine, Em,' he says in a low voice. 'We'll find a nice hotel where we can relax and decompress.'

Emma grips Callie's hand tighter. 'Relax? After everything we've been through?'

'Don't make a scene,' Ryan whispers, not wishing to distract the check-in attendant, who is busily confirming their flights.

After a few minutes she hands Ryan all three passports and their travel documents.

'All done for you.' She smiles. 'Have a pleasant journey home.'

'Okay, well at least that's sorted,' Ryan says. 'This time tomorrow, we'll be in the air. And did I mention, I've extended our car hire for another twenty-four hours,' he says as they walk back to the SUV, which is thick with dust and grime. 'I used the app on my phone – it was simple enough. Question is, what are we going to do today?'

Emma shrugs. 'I don't care. In case you need reminding, our holiday's over. As far as I'm concerned, we're here under duress. Let's just find a decent hotel and try and get a good lunch down Callie. God alone knows what she's been eating.'

'Agreed. Let's head into town, maybe we can get a room in one of the hotels overlooking the harbour. Sod the expense, it's only for one night.'

An hour and a half later, after trawling round several big international hotels and being told by their polite but unyielding receptionists that there are no vacancies, hungry and deflated, they stop at a café with a view of the bay. Despite the picture-perfect scenery, the glorious weather, and the delicious coffee and Menorcan cake they've ordered, Emma's anxiety is beginning to boil over.

'What are we going to do, Ry? We can't just drive around all day – Callie needs to rest and recover. She needs to eat properly. We all do.'

Ryan dusts icing sugar from his fingers and swallows the last mouthful of cake. 'There's bound to be somewhere with a free room. We need to stay calm and keep trying.'

'Stay calm? Are you joking?' Emma says, her tone shrill.

'No, I'm not joking. Nobody knows the situation we're in better than me, I can assure you, but come on, Em, not in front of Callie,' he says quietly.

There's a beat of silence before Emma's eyes light up as an idea strikes her. 'Hey, do you remember the spa hotel I went to with Sheena? Well, that was off the beaten track – in the middle of nowhere, actually. Why don't we give them a call, see if they've got room for us? They've got two lovely swimming pools – an indoor and an outdoor one – it might be a real lift for Callie to swim and play in the water; a distraction from the trauma she's been through.'

Callie's head whips round. 'Ooh, yes please, Mummy. I'd love to go swimming.'

Ryan rolls his eyes. 'Now look what you've started. You said the magic word. Let's hope they can accommodate us after getting her hopes up,' he says, scrolling through his phone for the hotel's number.

'I can't believe they're giving us a suite for the price of a regular room,' Ryan says, some of the tension leaving his face as they drive towards the spa hotel.

'It must have been the only room they had free and I guess it's better than turning business away,' Emma says. 'God knows we needed some luck.'

Soon they are pulling into the hotel's car park, which, true to Emma's memory, is filled with sleek expensive-looking vehicles.

Passing through the glass doors and into the pale serenity of the hotel's foyer, Emma feels some of the angst leave her.

'This is just what we need,' Ryan agrees, signing them in at reception before being shown to their room by a male porter in spa scrubs.

Then it is just the three of them, alone in the opulence of their suite, with its vast super-king bed and adjacent pastel sitting room complete with wall-mounted TV and a minibar stocked with healthy drinks and snacks.

'This is surreal,' Emma whispers while Callie is in the large marble bathroom. 'This time yesterday our daughter was missing and we had no idea if we'd see her again. It could all have ended so differently.' She shudders and rubs the goosebumps that have sprung up on her arms. 'As soon as we get back, we're taking Callie to the doctors' – get her fully checked over. I know she seems fine, but we've no idea what happened to her. Maybe we should have some family therapy sessions, or—' Emma stops speaking abruptly and smiles as Callie emerges, talking about the lovely taps and tiles and how it reminds her of a TV show she's seen.

Ryan opens his arms. 'Does it, sweet pea? That's nice. Come and give Daddy a big cuddle. We missed you so much,' he says, squeezing her tightly and beckoning Emma into a group hug, until Callie wriggles free and marches over to the stack of holdalls in the corner of the room.

'Where's my costume, Mummy? You said we could go swimming.'

Ryan grins. 'That's right, Cal. Why don't we all go? Some fresh air and exercise will do us all a world of good.'

Emma looks doubtful, given that it's two thirty in the afternoon and nothing more substantial than breakfast and cake has passed their lips all day. She shrugs. 'Okay, let's go have some fun in the pool and maybe we can have an early dinner on the terrace tonight.'

With all three of them dressed in swimwear, sarongs and flip-flops, they make their way across the tiled sun deck with its huge kidney-shaped pool. Emma jumps when Callie lets out a shriek of excitement. 'Look, Mummy, I can swim with Lucas,' she cries, breaking into a skip.

'Bless her, she's getting confused, remembering the old pool,' Emma tells Ryan as she quickens her pace. But then she really looks towards the pool, pausing mid-step when she spots a woman's sleek chestnut head beside two little boys as all three tread water. She gropes for Ryan's hand. 'God, it really *is* Lucas. Look, there's Sheena with the kids.'

Ryan shields his eyes against the sun. 'Oh no. That's all we need. We didn't exactly part on good terms, did we?'

But Callie is already at the edge of the pool, waving and calling out to Lucas and Leo.

On her heels, Emma's heart swells as Sheena turns to look, confusion darkening her expression for a moment, only to be replaced by a beaming smile.

'Callie! Oh look, boys... it's our friends,' Sheena cries, wading to the side where Callie sits down happily and dangles her feet in the water.

Emma drops beside her. 'Sheena! Hi... what are you doing here? How are you all? We've got her back. We've got our baby back and she's fine,' she says, her voice catching.

Sheena heaves herself out of the pool and envelops Emma in a hug, drenching her as the women fall against each other, crying with raw emotion as Sheena fires questions that for now need no answers.

Hovering awkwardly to the side, Ryan nods to Sheena. 'Hello. Is Jack here, too?' he asks gruffly.

'Yeah, he's getting drinks at the bar.' Sheena wipes her eyes. 'Why don't you give him a hand?'

Ryan hesitates.

'Go on. I guarantee he'll be pleased to see you,' Sheena says, glancing over to where all three children are huddled at the side of the pool, yelling over each other in their excitement.

Callie folds her arms. 'Mummy, *please*! You said I could.'

Emma lowers herself and her daughter into the pool while Sheena jumps in beside her.

The women stand in chest-deep water, watching the children splash and play as though they've never been apart.

Emma's eyes meet Sheena's. 'We owe you and Jack a huge apology. I can't believe we thought you were involved when Callie went missing. Please forgive us. It seems completely ridiculous to me now.'

Sheena waves a hand. 'Hon, it's fine. It was the stress talking. And *fear*. Every parent's worst nightmare actually happened to you and Ryan.' She grins at Callie. 'Not that you'd know to look at her! It's incredible; kids are so resilient, aren't they?' She lowers her voice. 'Emma, I don't want to pry but when you're ready, I'd love to know what actually happened and it might help you to talk it through, you know?'

'Of course. We'll tell you everything,' Emma gives herself a little shake, 'although I still can't quite get my head around things.'

Sheena nods. 'Understandable. Tell you what, why don't we put all three kids in the Four o'clock Club; it's an hour of supervised play; the boys love it. We can watch from the sidelines while you tell us all about it.'

'All right. As long as I can physically see Callie. I couldn't bear to let her out of my sight,' Emma says.

'Great. Here come Jack and Ryan with our drinks and by the look of it, they've patched things up as well,' Sheena says. 'Honestly, Em, we *were* a bit upset that you suspected us, but mostly we were terrified there was a lunatic on the loose and we were desperate to protect Leo and Lucas. I hope you understand why we took off so suddenly?' She grimaces. 'I even deleted my holiday posts from Instagram. All those photos of us having a great time, including some lovely ones of Callie playing with our two, while you were going through utter hell... it seemed so wrong and inappropriate, you know?'

'Of course. I get it,' Emma says, reassured by Sheena's warmth.

CHAPTER FORTY-SIX

Emma cups Callie's face in her hands. 'Mummy and Daddy will be right here, having a chat with Leo and Lucas's parents, okay, angel?'

Callie pulls away impatiently and runs to join the other children for the four o'clock play session that is about to start.

Marvelling at her daughter's resilience, Emma turns to Sheena. 'Did you see that? She practically rolled her eyes at me. Sometimes I think she's six going on sixteen.'

'Aww, she's amazing. You'd never know that she'd just been...' Sheena trails off and glances at Jack.

'What you went through in Santa Martina is unbelievably shitty,' Jack says. 'If you can bear to talk about it, put us out of our misery and tell us what happened.'

Ryan shifts uneasily in his seat and takes a sip of his beer. 'I'm not sure you need all the details.' He glances warily at Emma.

'It's fine. No more secrets,' she says simply.

Ryan exhales. 'You won't believe this, but it was John and Max who staged Callie's abduction. It was all an elaborate hoax to get back at me.'

Jack's eyebrows fly up. 'What?! Mate, I'm sorry. I didn't see that coming. Why the hell would they do that?'

Ryan shoots another look at Emma; she nods.

'A while back, I had a fling at work with a young intern. Oh, Emma knows all about it and thank God she's forgiven me. Anyway, it was nothing really, to me at least. But when I ended it with Amber, she couldn't accept it. She took it badly and went on a bit of a spree, drinking too much, mixing medication with alcohol, and generally neglecting herself by all accounts. Turns out she had a history of depression but needless to say, she hid it well at work.'

Sheena frowns and nibbles her thumbnail. 'I think I know where this is going.'

Ryan sighs. 'Thing is, after our... after we'd stopped seeing each other, Amber left the company where I work and we lost touch, which was fine by me as you can imagine.' Ryan pauses, the cleft between his brows growing deeper.

'What happened to her?' Sheena asks gently, looking from Ryan to Emma.

'She, er... she was killed in a car accident.' Ryan stares into the middle distance over Sheena's shoulder. 'She hit a tree while driving drunk, according to her parents.'

'Amber was John and Max's daughter,' Emma says, hugging herself as a chill washes over her despite the heat. 'They had her late in life. Max called Amber her miracle menopause baby.'

There's a moment of stunned silence.

'So they blame you, Ryan, for her death, even though it was an accident,' Sheena says, breaking it. 'Because as far as John and Max are concerned, you took their daughter. So they took yours.'

Ryan flexes his hands then balls them into fists. 'Yeah, that's about the long and short of it. We lost a hundred grand and had the worst forty-eight hours of our lives.'

'Mate, that's terrible,' Jack says, shaking his head. 'The whole thing with their daughter is heartbreaking – no one should ever have to bury their child – but it was an accident and unless you were there, pouring booze down her throat, you're not to blame.'

Ryan nods slowly, rubbing his chin. 'Obviously, I deeply regret everything that happened – I always will – but now Callie's safely back with us, all I can think about is confronting them and trying to get the money back. Nothing will bring Amber back and we're talking kidnap and extortion here.'

'You should go straight to the police,' Sheena says, her face set. 'I mean, I'm sorry for their loss, but what they did to the two of you is beyond despicable. Putting you through all that for the sake of revenge: it's inexcusable, not to mention illegal. And what if things had gone wrong? What if there'd been an accident and Callie wasn't sitting over there now, playing games with our two?'

Emma shudders. 'Don't. Look, I hear what you're saying. But if the police get involved, the whole thing will get blown up even bigger than it is already. I just want the three of us to get on that plane tomorrow morning and get back to normal.'

'Normal?' Ryan says. 'How's that going to work then, Em? Those bastards cleaned us out of every penny we had – and then some. I've got a loan to pay back as well, remember?'

'But it's only money. Callie's safe, I just think—'

'Emma, tell me to mind my own business,' Sheena says, placing a hand on Emma's forearm, 'but I agree with Ryan. Cala Savannah is only twenty minutes from here. I think we should *all* go, tonight. Catch John and Max by surprise.'

'Sheena's right,' Jack says. 'We'll go together. Tell them you want the money back or you're going straight to the police. Simple as that. What have you got to lose?'

It had taken almost two hours to feed and bathe the children before corralling them into two separate cars and setting off for the short journey to Cala Savannah. Eyes fixed on the road ahead, Ryan says little, his expression grim. By contrast, Emma nervously attempts small talk in an effort to distract Callie from why they're going back to their *old house*.

'Daddy just wants to chat to John and Max. You remember them, don't you, sweet pea?'

Callie nods. 'Of course I do. Are they having a party like before? Will Teddy be there with Diesel?'

Alarmed, Emma glances at Ryan, who by now is grinding his teeth. She gives him a warning look. 'No, Cal, it's not a party. We'll wait in the car while Daddy has a quick chat, then we're going back to the hotel for one more sleep before we fly home in the morning. Is that okay?'

'Yes, Mummy.' Callie yawns, totally unfazed.

It's seven forty by the time they reach Cala Savanna, with its ribbon of blue sea to one side and the bustling strip of shops, bars, and restaurants to the other. The pavement cafés are packed with tanned relaxed holidaymakers, enjoying drinks and tapas, or already having dinner.

Emma gazes from the car window, a rock of sadness weighing on her chest. 'I was so happy when we arrived on that first day,' she says in a low voice. 'I thought it would be the perfect holiday.' She inhales sharply. 'Ryan, we are doing the right thing, aren't we? What if they—'

Ryan glances at Callie in the rear-view mirror. 'Emma, whatever they've done, we're not dealing with criminal masterminds or violent gangsters here,' he says quietly. 'They're just two vindictive old people who had a point to make.'

'They're also grieving parents who'll never see their daughter again,' Emma reminds him.

As they slow to a crawl before turning and passing under the arch for the Santa Martina development, Jack and Sheena pull up behind them. Then, driving slowly, Ryan pulls up outside the Rutherfords' villa and waits for Jack to park behind him.

He takes a deep breath. 'Right, this won't take long. They've had their fun with their vile little stunt, so I'm expecting them to co-operate. Lock the doors and I'll be back before you know it,' he says, getting out of the car and giving Jack the nod. Then Emma watches, her heart in her mouth, as shoulder to shoulder, the two men pass into John and Max's lush garden, knock on their front door, and disappear inside.

She glances behind her, sees Sheena through the back windscreen, slouched low in her seat, her face half hidden by sunglasses.

'Mummy, aren't we going in?' Callie asks.

'No, sweet pea. I told you. Daddy won't be long and then we're leaving, okay?'

With a pounding heart, Emma fixes her eyes on the Rutherfords' villa and is astonished when a few minutes later, Ryan and Jack emerge. There's a brief exchange between them before Jack gets into his car and Ryan rejoins Emma, looking furious.

'I'm sorry, I tried, but they completely clammed up and they'll only speak to you,' he says flatly.

'What? Why? Ryan, I can't. Surely you don't expect me to go in there on my own?'

Ryan closes his eyes briefly. 'Em, for what it's worth, they were both completely calm and I suspect you'll get a lot further than Jack and I did. Please, just go and talk to them. At this point, we've nothing to lose.'

'Okay, I'll go,' Emma says after a few seconds have ticked by.

'I'll talk to them.' She takes a deep breath, feels her hand shaking as she fumbles with the car door handle, then she walks purposefully up John and Max's garden path.

CHAPTER FORTY-SEVEN

THEN

'Thanks, Sue. I really appreciate this,' Ryan tells her, as they sit eating pasta crema funghi in her spotless modern kitchen.

'No problem.' Sue waves a hand. 'You're welcome to stay here until you can sort something more permanent. I feel really bad about letting the cat out of the bag, even though it was an accident.' She tops up Ryan's glass with Pinot Grigio and laughs. 'You needn't think I'm feeding you every night though, I'm not your mum.'

'No, of course not. Thanks again for cooking tonight.' Ryan puffs out his cheeks. 'And don't even mention my mother. She's no idea that Emma and I have split up. I can't face telling her, she'll be devastated. In fact, she'll probably disown me.'

'Maybe she doesn't have to know just yet. See how it goes. It's only been a few days. Give Emma some space. You've hurt her and broken her trust, but I'm willing to bet she's missing you as much as you're missing her.'

'Do you really think so?' Ryan asks, hope surfacing for the first time since leaving home.

'All that love, all those years of being there for each other, you can't just switch it off overnight. Trust me.'

'You sound like you're speaking from experience. Are you still in touch with your ex-husband?'

'Not a chance. Our divorce was too bitter, too toxic. Not only did Michael cheat on me, but he rubbed my nose in it by sleeping with my best friend. It was never going to end well, was it?'

'But you said—'

'The point I was trying to make, is that for the first year after we broke up, I still loved him. And I'd have taken him back even after everything he'd done, if only he'd been sincerely sorry.' Sue sighs heavily. 'But he wasn't. He'd fallen out of love with me and that was that.'

Ryan swirls the wine around his glass and takes a sip. 'For what it's worth, I *am* sorry. Truly. And not just because I got caught. I've apologised and I will keep apologising until Emma believes me.'

Sue purses her lips. 'Yeah, well. Controversial this, but I think you should also say sorry to Amber. Last time I spoke to her, which admittedly was a month ago, she was still pretty upset. Even more so because you'd cut her off without a backward glance. She said I didn't know the half of it, about what happened between you.' She kneads her napkin. 'And I don't want to know – it's none of my business.'

It's on the tip of Ryan's tongue to ask Sue whether she knows about the baby, but it's a huge gamble and he decides against it. Finishing his food, he puts his knife and fork together. 'So you think I should talk to Amber? Won't that confuse things – give her hope when there is none?'

'Not if you handle it right. Ryan, you really hurt her, saying sorry might give Amber closure and restore her self-worth. As far as I'm aware, she's not long back from visiting her parents abroad. They live in Spain, I think. Hopefully the break has done her good and she'll feel more upbeat after a change of scene.'

'Okay. Leave it with me, I'll speak to her. Maybe I'll message her tomorrow in my lunch hour. Can't say I'm looking forward to it though.'

'Yeah, well, that's life. And sometimes it feels made up of things we don't want to do.' Sue smiles wryly. 'Speaking of which, how about I load the dishwasher and you handwash the saucepans. Deal?'

'Deal,' Ryan says, getting to his feet.

Wednesday morning races by in a blur of internal meetings and needless emails, and by one o'clock, Ryan is ready for a break.

'Just popping out. I'll be about forty-five minutes if anyone's looking for me,' he tells Nancy, the receptionist, who barely looks up.

The mid-April sunshine is cool and tentative, nevertheless, craving privacy, Ryan orders chicken and sweetcorn on brown and a latte from the nearest sandwich bar, and heads to the local park.

Scanning for a quiet spot, he finds a bench overlooking a pond. Apart from a trio of buggy-toting young mums, preoccupied with pointing out fluffy ducklings to their toddlers, there's nobody around, and after eating half of his sandwich, Ryan messages Amber.

> Hey, how are you? Is it okay to give you a quick call? Am between meetings so can't chat for long. Ryan x

He hits send, then reads the message back, hating himself for making excuses before they've even said hello.

He expects Amber to reply by text but instead, his phone rings. He clears his throat, wondering what kind of reception he'll get after months of radio silence. 'Amber, hi. Thanks for ringing. I was about to call you.'

'Oh, were you now? Well, that's very nice,' Amber says, her tone breathy and flirtatious. 'So, what can I do for you? It's been ages.'

He cringes inwardly, his thoughts racing. What the hell is he doing, contacting the woman who has cost him his marriage? Remembering Sue's speech about giving Amber self-worth and closure, he presses on. 'Look, I've been meaning to call you, just to say... to tell you I'm sorry for how things worked out. I'm not proud of the way I acted, and I hope you can forgive me in time.'

There's a pause at the end of the line, a small gasp of emotion. 'Thanks, but you needn't have worried. I mean, yeah, I was in a bad place for a while, but I'm much better now.'

Ryan notes her change in tone: the smile has left her voice; and she is crisper, less flirtatious. 'Good, I'm glad you're happier,' he says. 'I was chatting to Sue recently and she said you'd been away?'

'Yes, I stayed with my parents for, like, the whole of March. The change of scene and Mum and Dad fussing over me was a boost, you know?'

'Right... well, that's good,' Ryan says. 'I'm glad. So, er, what are your plans, workwise?'

Amber hesitates. 'Oh, I'm exploring a few options.' She gives a dry little laugh. 'I'm considering asking Raj and Henry for my old job back.'

Ryan's stomach drops as though he's entered a high-speed lift. 'Really? I'm not sure it's ever a great idea to go back, is it? I always think going forward makes more sense.'

'Like I said, I'm just sifting through a few ideas. I haven't actually spoken to anyone at Sutton & Singh yet.'

The thought of Amber reappearing in the office, reopening old wounds and acting smug now that his marriage is in tatters sickens him. He clams up, unable to think of anything neutral to say.

'You wouldn't have a problem with that, surely?' Amber goes on, filling the vacuum. 'Because clearly you don't have any feelings for *me*, and don't flatter yourself, Ryan – I am well and truly over you.'

The hard bitter edge to her voice is unmistakeable now. So much for Sue's theory.

'Actually, I've got to go,' Ryan says. 'I'm due in a meeting and I need to print some stuff off first. Great to catch up though, and I'm pleased to hear you're back on form,' he adds with forced heartiness, ending the call a moment later.

That went well. Not.

Ryan eats the other half of his sandwich and watches the young mums, irritated by their shrill voices and saccharine baby talk. To think he could have been a father all over again if he hadn't insisted on Amber having an abortion.

He pictures Callie looking up at him, her dark eyes so like his own, full of love and trust, and almost chokes on the last mouthful of his lunch. *What an utter shit I've been...*

On impulse he phones Emma, but his call goes straight to voicemail and he realises she'll be at the salon and unable to talk. He blathers his way through a voicemail, can hear the wheedling begging note in his voice as he rounds off the message by telling Emma how much he loves and misses her.

Feeling defeated, he tosses his rubbish into a litter bin and walks back to the office.

It's around six when Sue wanders over as their colleagues are packing up and preparing to leave the office for the day.

'Everything all right? Good day?' she asks, perching on the edge of his desk, her arms folded.

Ryan sighs heavily.

'Oh, as good as that?' The smile she gives him is loaded with sympathy. 'I don't know what your plans are this evening but I'm going out with a friend, so please make yourself at home, okay? Use the washing machine if you need to, cook some food, whatever. I'll be back around ten.'

'Thanks, Sue, I appreciate it.' Ryan gives her a knowing look. 'Is it a date, by any chance?'

'God, no! I'm having a bite to eat with my friend Sarah. We try to meet once a month. We'll probably go for Italian or Thai.' Her eyes dart around the room and she lowers her voice. 'Don't suppose you made that phone call, did you?'

'I did,' Ryan says. 'I did exactly as you suggested. I wished Amber well and sincerely apologised. I'm not sure it helped much.'

'Well done, that can't have been easy.' Sue glances at the wall clock. 'Right. I'm off to meet Sarah. See you later.'

After a pitstop at Tesco Express to pick up a ready meal, Ryan drives to Sue's modern semi in its neat close full of similar houses, relieved that for the next few hours, he'll have total privacy.

Once there, he changes into tracksuit bottoms and an old sweatshirt, then heads downstairs to the kitchen where he microwaves the cottage pie he's just bought. He's about to dig into his meal when he notices the time. Scrabbling for his phone, he calls home.

'Another five minutes and Callie would have been in bed,'

Emma snaps coldly without preamble or pleasantries. She calls out to their daughter. 'Daddy's calling to say goodnight, sweet pea.'

The sound grows muffled as the handset is passed to Callie, followed by her sweet high voice. 'Hello, Daddy. When are you coming home? I've got lots to tell you.'

Ryan can hardly speak for the lump filling his throat. 'Soon, angel. I'm just working away for a bit. So, what have you been doing today...?'

He listens while Callie tells him about a little boy in her reception class who has a tortoise *and* a puppy, and why can't *she* have a puppy but maybe not a tortoise as they sleep all winter before Emma cuts her short and tells her it's bedtime.

'God, I miss her. And I miss you, Em, so much,' Ryan says, choked up as Emma reclaims the handset. 'Did you get my message today? I meant every word. I'll do whatever it takes to put things right. Just tell me what to—'

'Ryan, I've already asked you for space and time. That's what I want.' Emma sounds weary and resigned rather than angry. 'Look, I have to go. Speak soon, night.'

'Night. I love you,' Ryan whispers as the phone goes silent in his hand.

CHAPTER FORTY-EIGHT

NOW

Max leans in the doorway, her expression bemused, one arm extended as if to draw Emma inside.

'Come in, Emma. I won't bite,' she drawls, the ghost of a smile on her lips.

Emma hesitates, unwilling to enter the older woman's lair.

'Please. I can assure you, I only want to talk.' Max steps back, allowing Emma to pass.

Emma lifts her chin. 'Okay, but whatever you need to say, please make it quick. Ryan and Callie are in the car, and we're all exhausted after everything you've put us through.'

Max raises a hand. 'Just hear me out, that's all I ask. Then I imagine you'll have a few questions of your own. Now, come and sit down. Would you like a drink?'

Emma shakes her head, incredulous. 'No. Max, this isn't a social occasion. Please, can you just get to the point?' She follows Max through to the sitting room, expecting John to be there too.

'It's just us,' Max says as if reading Emma's mind. 'John's upstairs reading. This conversation is between us: woman to woman, mother to mother.' She sits in a large soft armchair and indicates that Emma should take the sofa opposite.

Emma perches on the edge and glances around nervously. The dark wood floors, heavy furniture and Moorish lamps highlighting original artwork on the walls had once seemed stylish and exotic, but now they appear oppressive and claustrophobic. She takes in Max's own appearance, sees clearly for the first time that devoid of flamboyant clothing and jewellery, and without make-up, she is smaller, frailer, and older than she'd realised. There's a slight tremor to her right hand as she reaches for her glass, causing the ice to rattle in her gin and tonic.

'So what do you want to talk about, Max?' Emma asks as the threat of danger seems to recede.

Max sips her drink, then clutches it in both hands like a comforter. 'I wonder how well you know your husband,' she says conversationally.

Emma stops short of rolling her eyes. 'We've been through all this. I told you, Max, there are no secrets between Ryan and me. I know all about Amber and their grubby little fling. But that's all it was – a fling – and I've forgiven him.'

'Ah, standing by your man. How old-fashioned of you, Emma. But I doubt you know *everything*,' Max says tartly. 'Did Ryan tell you that he got Amber pregnant? That he bullied her into having an abortion she didn't want?'

Emma gasps, her hand flying to her mouth as the ground seems to slide beneath her.

'I thought as much,' Max says, her tone triumphant.

'Obviously, I've only got your word for it,' Emma says eventually, determined to keep strong in front of her opponent.

Max narrows her eyes. 'Why on earth would I lie about a thing like that? The day your husband marched Amber into that clinic, he took *everything* away from her: the baby she wanted; a new job she was enjoying; and, worst of all, her confidence and self-belief.'

Emma shakes her head. 'Oh come on, Max, you talk as though Amber was an innocent bystander. And it's just not true. Seems to me you're completely in denial about the kind of woman she *really* was. Amber made her own choices and decisions – and one of them was to sleep with my husband, so you'll forgive me if I'm unsympathetic, won't you?'

'Your *husband*,' Max says with emphasis, 'not only robbed John and I of a daughter, but of our first grandchild.' She stares into the distance. 'Amber couldn't accept it, you see – the guilt and shame of getting rid of an innocent child. She'd always been sensitive and prone to depression, but after the abortion, she plummeted to new depths of despair.'

There's a beat of silence, before Max's eyes snap back to Emma's. 'Do you know what the coroner's report said? The likely reason Amber crashed her car was because she'd mixed Zammertil with alcohol. Imagine! What state of mind must she have been in to mix anti-psychotic pills with alcohol and then take a drive in the countryside? She wasn't even wearing a seat belt when they found her. It was practically suicide.'

Emma takes a ragged breath as shockwaves travel through her. 'I'm genuinely sorry for your loss, Max,' she says, composing herself. 'When did the accident happen?'

'It was on a Tuesday afternoon, 26th April. That date is stamped on my heart forever. A part of me died that day, too.'

Emma clears her throat. 'I don't want to fight with you. You and John have been through a lot... *so* much. But you must understand, so have we. You kidnapped a six-year-old little girl – actually took her out of her bed – and you stole a hundred thousand euros from us, so don't sit there and guilt trip *me* because it won't work.'

Emma gets to her feet and squares her shoulders. 'Max, either you return the money at once, and we call an end to this, or Ryan and I are going straight to the police. The choice is yours.'

She's astonished when Max begins to laugh, spluttering as she gulps the last of her gin. 'Oh dear, that's so funny... you haven't a bloody clue, have you?'

Confused, Emma is torn between humouring Max in an attempt to get the money back or fleeing back to the car and escaping with her family.

Max stops laughing abruptly and eyes her coldly. 'Oh for God's sake, sit down, will you?'

Reluctantly, Emma sits.

'So, you're planning to go to the police? Well, good luck with that,' Max sneers. 'They take a pretty dim view of time wasting.'

Emma frowns. 'You really have lost the plot, haven't you?'

'Far from it. *You'll* be the one looking like a paranoid fantasist because I think you'll find that no crime has been committed.'

'Where do I start? Let's kick off with breaking and entering—'

Max waves a hand. 'John and I *own* the house you've been staying in; in fact, we own all three houses here. So I simply gave young Teddy a key to the back door, and he let himself in.'

Emma recalls bickering with Ryan about forgetting to lock up properly when all along Teddy had slipped in using a key. 'For God's sake, Max, how the kidnapper got into the house is splitting hairs: you arranged to have my child *taken*. How is that *not* illegal?'

Max makes a face. 'Define taken. Teddy merely asked Callie if she'd like to meet his uncle's sweet but rather gormless young Labrador. Needless to say, Callie was excited by the idea

– after all, what child can resist a puppy? So, you see, no force was used: your daughter was a willing guest at our friends' rather charming flat above the shop, where Teddy has been staying quite comfortably all summer. And I have to hand it to you, Emma, you raised a very sensible and gutsy kid. I'm assured there was absolutely no whining, just a degree of curiosity about when you and Ryan would be joining her.' Max's eyes glitter darkly. 'I could tell at once she was a tough little cookie, the way she handled herself around that whinging brat, Leo.'

Emma shakes her head. 'I can't believe I'm hearing this rubbish. Let's not forget you *drugged* me, Max. It's obvious that John put something in my drink that night. No wonder I was all over the place and passed out until morning. Anything could have happened; I could have choked in my sleep.'

Max tilts her head. 'Ahh, but you didn't. And you'll prove you were drugged *how* exactly?'

'What about the money? That's extortion,' Emma says, her chin jutting, 'so good luck tap-dancing your way out of that one.'

Max smirks. 'You insult me if you think a hundred thousand euros means anything to John and I. Ha! It's not even the going rate. We only set the bar so low because we knew you'd struggle to raise a penny more.'

'Then give the money back and we can call a truce,' Emma says wearily.

'Have you checked your bank account lately? The money was sent back by return. This was never, *ever* about money, can't you see that?'

Emma feels limp and deflated. 'All that plotting and scheming. All powered by hate. What a sad, twisted woman you are, Max. I feel sorry for you.' She pauses. 'How did you get us out here in the first place?'

Max adopts a manic grin. 'Congratulations, you have won first prize in our super summer competition,' she sings. 'Ring any bells?'

Emma recalls the flyer; its professional-looking photography, its call to action: *contact your participating travel agent to redeem your prize.* 'How did you get the travel agent to go along with it all?'

Max's smile is shark-like. 'Oh, it's a family business. My daughter Lyndsey is the owner; her role was to convince you that the prize was authentic and not a scam. And to book your flights, of course. I didn't need to ask her twice. She lost the little sister she adored, after all.'

Emma bites her lip. 'Callie's tablet ending up in the pool and that disgusting dead rat in her bed? That was you, too, wasn't it?'

'Yes – and no. I couldn't quite bring myself to touch the rat. John sorted that little task for me.' Max raises her eyebrows. 'There are limits, you know.'

Emma feels sick to her stomach. 'I need to go,' she says, her voice hoarse. 'I need to get out of this madhouse and get back to my family.'

'Well, lucky you that you still have a daughter. Because thanks to your shitbag of a husband, I lost one of mine. You can see yourself out,' Max says, not budging from her armchair.

Emerging into the fresh air, Emma is struck by the glowing embers of a beautiful sunset after the oppressive shadows of Max's villa.

She gets into the car beside Ryan and stares straight ahead, her eyes stinging with unshed tears. 'We've got the money,' she whispers. 'It's over. Just drive. As fast as you can.'

'But what happened? Are you okay?' Ryan touches her arm but Emma flinches as though scalded. 'Not now. Just go. GO!'

She's aware of Ryan opening the car door and calling out to Jack and Sheena parked behind them; of Callie asking *why is Mummy crying?* Then she closes her eyes, clasps a hand over her mouth to muffle her sobs, feeling older and sadder than ever before.

CHAPTER FORTY-NINE

THEN

After two weeks of feeling stressed, exhausted, and desperately lonely, Emma caves in to Ryan's frequent begging and allows him to come home.

'You won't regret it, Em, I promise,' Ryan says over coffee drunk sitting at the kitchen island while Callie chats happily, showing him new toys, drawings she's done and things she's made at reception school.

'Things have to change though, Ryan,' Emma says, watching their daughter, as she tears around, shrieking with excitement. 'No more secrets, no more lies. If I suspect for one minute that you're keeping something from me, we're done. Do you understand?'

'Emma, do you really think I'd screw up again? This whole sorry situation has been a massive wake-up call. I swear on Callie's life that I've learned my lesson.'

'Okay. Why don't you unpack properly, stick a wash on, and then we'll take Callie to the country park for a walk. The sunshine and fresh air will do us all good.'

'Sounds perfect.' Ryan gets up, drops a kiss on Emma's forehead and goes off to unpack.

Callie skips ahead, hair flying, cheeks flushed. 'Look, Mummy and Daddy, a robin. He's following us,' she squeals, delighted by the little bird as it bounces from bough to branch as they walk alongside the scented hedgerow.

Feeling more hopeful and relaxed than she has in weeks, Emma tucks her arm into Ryan's. 'It's wonderful to see Callie so happy. Exactly how things should be.'

Ryan snuggles against her. 'Yeah. I have a good feeling about the future, Em. You know, I wouldn't be against trying for another baby if you thought that—'

Emma's eyes bulge. She laughs out loud. 'Whoa! Where did that come from? Can we not just enjoy a bit of calm and normality? I mean, never say never, but another child isn't top of my wish list right now.'

Ryan smiles, his eyes crinkling at the corners. 'I just meant if and when you're ready, then I am too. Your happiness is my priority now.'

'The main thing is that we're really honest with each other, you know?' Emma says, leaning her head against Ryan's shoulder.

Ryan stops walking and faces her, his expression serious. 'Of course. Which is why I need to tell you something. It's nothing to worry about but just in case you see her name in my calls list, I spoke to Amber recently.'

A look of hurt and confusion clouds Emma's eyes. 'Why? Why would you do that?'

'Not sure now, to be honest.' Ryan sighs. 'Actually, it was Sue's idea. She seemed to think it would help all of us to move on if I apologised to Amber.'

Emma purses her lips, a nugget of hardness forming in her chest. 'Right. And did it? Did it help you or Amber? Because it sure doesn't help me. I couldn't care less about the treacherous little bitch,' she hisses, glancing to where Callie stands beating the hedge with a stick she's found.

Ryan shrugs. 'Probably not. It was awkward. Neither of us had much to say. Em, I'm only telling you this because we said no more secrets: Amber mentioned that she might ask for her old job back. I can't imagine it'll happen, and frankly I couldn't care less, but—'

'God, Ryan. Can't you see? She's still in love with you. She'll try and lure you back, I know it.'

'I disagree, Em. I think the opposite is true and she's only considering returning to Sutton & Singh because there's absolutely nothing between us, on *either* side. You have to believe me. Please, Em – trust me.'

'I want to, but it's hard after everything...' Emma blinks back sudden tears. 'Let's go home,' she says, aware that their lovely mellow mood has been shattered.

On Sunday morning, Emma wakes to the clatter of crockery and the unmistakeable smell of frying bacon.

She stretches languorously, aware that Ryan is pulling out all the stops. She can hear Callie chatting away to him and attempting to help. Then they're on the stairs, and bumping the bedroom door open, beaming smiles on their faces.

Emma sits up slowly and feigns surprise. 'Wow, what's all this for? It's not my birthday.'

'Can't a bloke spoil his lovely wife once in a while?' Ryan says, setting down a tray laden with tea, and bacon sandwiches.

Emma salivates. 'These look good. Thanks, I could get used to this.'

Ryan and Callie gently climb onto the bed. 'Eat up before it gets cold,' Ryan says, taking a sip of tea. 'Oh, and I thought I could take us all out for Sunday lunch today – maybe that pub with the atrium at the back... what's it called?'

'The Fox,' Emma says, taking a bite of her sandwich, 'but honestly, there's no need. Let's eat at home. I'll roast a chicken. You can give me a hand if you like.'

'Sounds perfect.'

Bored now that the surprise has concluded, Callie gets down and scampers off to her own room, leaving Emma and Ryan alone.

Emma smiles. 'You don't have to do this, you know? Breakfast in bed, meals out. It's lovely, but we need to get back to normal – try and get past what's happened and move on.'

'I just want you to know how much I love and appreciate you. How grateful I am for my family,' Ryan says, his voice catching.

'And I get it, but you don't need to try so hard, there's no need to reinvent the wheel. Hey, fab bacon sarnie, though – just the way I like it,' she says, leaning in for a greasy kiss.

The following day, Emma waves Ryan off to work, drives Callie to school, sorts through a mound of laundry, and vacuums the carpets. The usual Monday routine that rarely differs, given that for the next three days she'll be at the salon and domestic chores will have to take a back seat.

By twelve thirty, she collapses onto the kitchen sofa, relieved that the house is tidy and fragrant and that everyone has enough clean clothes to see them through the week. When her stomach rumbles, her thoughts turn to lunch and she wonders idly what Ryan will do today; whether he'll grab a sandwich and eat at his desk or pop out to one of the many cafés nearby with Pete, Sue or one of the others: *others* that might soon include Amber, should she return to Sutton & Singh.

The image of Ryan and Amber ensconced in a dimly-lit café, heads bowed in intimate conversation, knees brushing beneath the table, slides into her mind. She checks herself, pushes the thought away and gets up to make a sandwich from yesterday's leftover roast chicken.

But later, thoughts of Amber return and she goes into the study, opens the desk drawer, and retrieves Ryan's forgotten old tablet. She remembers snooping through Ryan's emails the day she'd thrown him out a little over two weeks ago: how she'd read through Amber's messages to him – persuasive, flirty and emotional, compared to his succinct replies.

Once again, she searches Ryan's inbox by *sender* and waits for Amber's emails to reappear.

Bingo. Just as she'd hoped. There, at the bottom of each one, as part of Amber's signature is her mobile phone number. Grabbing a Post-it note and pen from the desk, Emma jots it down, then switches off the tablet and puts it back in the drawer.

CHAPTER FIFTY

NOW

The journey home is long and arduous, not least because of the two-hour stopover in Barcelona, which, like Mahon airport, is packed with irritable tourists.

Numb and exhausted, Emma sleepwalks her way through both flights, seeing to Callie's needs, but feeling oddly detached from Ryan, who keeps staring at her with a haunted look.

'I'm just tired,' she says when he asks her for the fourth time what went on in Max's house and whether she is okay. 'We'll talk properly when we get home and I'll explain exactly what happened.'

But with some omissions, Emma thinks, trying her best to keep it together when all she wants to do is curl up in a ball and cry.

The night before, they'd said an emotional farewell to Jack, Sheena and the boys, promising to stay in touch. 'I have a feeling I'm soon going to need all the friends I can get,' Emma had whispered to Sheena as they hugged goodbye.

Rounding the corner into Wisteria Close, which today looks picture-perfect against a deep blue sky, Emma feels a brief surge of relief and happiness.

She wrinkles her nose on entering the house; the plug-in air freshener in the hallway smells sweet and cloying – thanks to the doors and windows being sealed up for the best part of three weeks – and a mound of post and junk mail is strewn on the mat. Pushing it aside, she and Ryan march back and forth to empty the car, piling their bags in the hallway, both gasping for a *proper* cup of tea.

After sorting the luggage, they collapse in the kitchen together, mugs of English breakfast tea in hand, French windows thrown open to let the sun and fresh air stream in, commenting on how much the grass has grown and how the flower beds are looking choked with weeds.

'Maybe I'll take a couple more days off work,' Ryan says, 'get it all looking ship-shape. I'll have to speak to Henry, of course, find out what's been going on in my absence.'

Emma doesn't answer, unable to think of anything beyond getting through the next few hours.

'Takeaway tonight?' Ryan presses on. 'We'll do a big online shop tomorrow, shall we?'

'Probably,' Emma says, turning away to hide the tears that have sprung into her eyes.

'Can I go up to my room, Mummy?' Callie asks.

'Of course, sweet pea,' Emma says, relieved that she and Ryan will finally be alone.

'Em, you've been incredibly quiet all day,' Ryan says, his brow furrowed. 'Are you going to tell me what happened between you and Max? I mean, it's brilliant that you got the money back – I couldn't believe it when I checked my banking app and found the money in our joint account – what did you say to make it happen?'

Emma pushes the kitchen door to, sits up at the island and asks Ryan to join her. 'I'll tell you what happened, but quietly – no outbursts or yelling – Callie's been through enough.'

A look of consternation crosses Ryan's face. 'That sounds ominous.'

'Talking to Max was interesting,' Emma says softly, 'and illuminating.'

'Really?'

'You see, Max told me all about the baby. Amber's baby. The child *you* fathered, Ryan. The baby you made her get rid of.'

Ryan gulps and bows his head. 'Emma, I wanted to tell you. Really, I did, but I couldn't find the right time.'

Emma shudders and hugs herself. 'The right time would have been somewhere – *anywhere* – between you finding out about the pregnancy and the day you moved back in after our brief separation. The day we decided to put the past behind us and work on our marriage. *No secrets*, remember? You swore to me, Ryan, on our daughter's life.' She pauses and shakes her head sadly. 'Did you know that Amber was dead, before Max and John told us about the accident?'

Ryan shakes his head. 'No, I didn't. I had no idea. I was relieved when I stopped hearing from her – it suited me just fine.'

He reaches for Emma's hand. 'Love, all this happened a long time ago and we've been through worse since, haven't we? For what it's worth, if I could turn the clock back, I'd do it in a heartbeat but we can't let this come between us. Not now, not after everything that's happened.'

Emma gets to her feet. 'It's too late. We're done, Ryan, everything's broken. Look at our track record. The trust simply isn't there. Even on holiday, *before* Callie was taken, I thought you wanted Sheena, just because she's youthful and attractive.

Don't you see? There'll always be an Amber or a Sheena. I'll always have my heart in my mouth, wondering if you've met someone else, or whether you're about to. Once a cheat, always a cheat. It's in your DNA. You can't help it.'

'That's not true. And nothing happened with Sheena, you know that,' Ryan says, his eyes wide with panic.

'But it might have. There'll always be someone who catches your eye, someone who makes me feel like rubbish. I don't want a life spent trying to tame you. You are who you are, Ryan. And it's okay. You're a brilliant dad to Callie and you can see her whenever you want. I'm not going to be the kind of ex-wife who weaponizes a child. But you and me are over.'

'Emma, please. We need to talk about this. You can't just decide—'

'My mind's made up. I'd like you to leave tomorrow, the sooner the better really. I'll take Callie to see my parents for the day so you can pack and go without her watching and getting upset.'

Ryan holds up his hands. 'No. Absolutely not. I'm not going anywhere. I belong here, with you and Callie.'

'No, you really don't. Not now,' Emma says, getting up and refilling the kettle. She sighs, too weary to cry. 'I need another cup of tea; would you like one?'

Ryan nods mutely, his hands shaking as he wipes his eyes.

CHAPTER FIFTY-ONE

THREE MONTHS LATER

Emma glances at the kitchen wall clock; it's nine fifty.

'Are you ready, sweet pea?' she calls from the bottom of the stairs. 'Daddy will be here in ten minutes.'

There's a drumming of feet before Callie descends, dressed in jeans and a stripy hooded jumper, her pink unicorn rucksack dangling from one arm.

Emma gathers her in for a hug and straightens the waistband of her jeans. 'Are you going to be warm enough? It's really cold today.'

Callie rolls her eyes. 'It'll be warm in the cinema, and after, we're going for chicken.'

'All right, as long as you wear your parka on top when you're in the street,' Emma says, doubtfully.

'Daddy!' Callie shrieks as Ryan's car pulls up outside. She dives into the cloakroom, muttering that she needs a wee.

A moment later, he's at the door, wearing a navy peacoat Emma has never seen before and stylish new boots. His hair is a little longer than usual, giving him a rakish air. In spite of everything, her stomach flutters at the sight of him.

'Hey, come in. Almost ready,' Emma says.

Ryan nods, his expression serious. 'So, how are you, Em?' he asks in a low voice. 'Only, don't take this the wrong way, but every time I see you, you look thinner and more exhausted. Are you okay?'

'Well, thanks for that!' Emma laughs. 'How to make a girl feel fabulous. I'm fine, we both are – touch wood.' She taps the newel post. 'How are you? Have you had a busy week at work?'

Ryan rubs the two-day old stubble on his chin. 'Yeah and it's about to get crazier, not least because Robbo left yesterday. He's starting at another practice next week. I can't believe I'm saying this, but I'll miss him.'

Callie explodes from the cloakroom and throws her arms around Ryan, ending the stilted conversation, the same predictable, box-ticking questions they ask each other most Saturday mornings. *Polite small talk between strangers*, Emma thinks, ruefully.

'Daddy, I missed you,' Callie says, burying her face in Ryan's jacket.

Ryan and Emma's eyes meet as a look of tacit understanding passes between them.

'I missed you, too, stinker. Right, are you ready? I thought we could go shopping before the film starts.'

'Ry, I know you love spoiling her but she doesn't need anything right now, do you, sweet pea?' Emma says.

Callie's eyebrows shoot up. 'Mummy, how can you say that? I need new trainers. My old ones are too little. It's not *my* fault I'm getting bigger every day.'

Emma raises her hands. 'Okay, I stand corrected. Have a great time, both of you.' She bends to hug Callie. 'Bye, baby. See you tonight. And not too many sweets, please,' she adds, waving them off at the door.

Emma makes herself a coffee, carries it to the sofa and gazes out at the garden. Outside, November's drab palette matches her mood. The vibrant russets and golds of early autumn are long gone and the grass is waterlogged from two weeks of endless rain.

She hunkers down and catches sight of her reflection in the mirrored microwave. No wonder Ryan noticed that increasingly she looks like shit – and that's just the outside...

Thank God he can't see the maelstrom flowing inside her tormented, exhausted head. That he's clueless to the guilt, shame and self-loathing that chugs on, like an endless freight train, impossible to stop or derail.

If only Ryan knew the dark, fetid secret she keeps, the one that has robbed her of sleep since Max Rutherford's one-to-one pity party on the night Emma learned the exact circumstances of Amber's death.

No wonder sleep evades her and food sours in her mouth.

And yet, apart from the physical toll her guilty secret takes on her body, Emma hides it well and is becoming quite an actress.

Keeping up with the lively banter at the salon three days a week, chatting to the other mums at the school gates, and good-naturedly joining in with the cynical but amusing 'all-men-are-bastards' brigade. Happy to soak up the camaraderie that goes with being a nearing-forty, hardworking, soon-to-be-divorced mum who has been betrayed and let down by another rubbish bloke; even lapping up the envious compliments about her dramatic weight loss.

Oh, but the reality...

Emma lays in bed at night, replaying the events of that cloudy afternoon in late April, like watching film footage on a loop – forever wishing she could change the ending.

CHAPTER FIFTY-TWO

THEN

Perched on the kitchen sofa, Emma's heartbeat quickens as she grips her mobile phone and stares at the number scrawled on the yellow Post-it note.

Is she, Emma, usually so placid, so patient and so risk averse, really doing this?

'The hell I am,' she says aloud. Then, propelled by a quiet seething rage that burns from somewhere deep within, she opens the text icon, and begins to type.

> Hey, Amber, Ryan here. I lost my phone, hence the strange number. Sorry about our awkward phone call the other day. Can we meet? Would hate things to be weird if you come back to work at S&S. Are you free tomorrow lunchtime (Tuesday)? One o'clock at The Pear Tree, M20 Junction 8? Let me know. Looking forward to a proper chat. xx

She rereads the message, ponders on whether it's a good or bad thing that she's been to the pub before – once, with Ryan and Callie for Sunday lunch. She remembers it being comfy and traditional, popular with families and office workers alike.

She wonders if Ryan has ever taken Amber there... not that it matters now.

Nothing matters except drawing a line under their sordid affair and making it crystal clear to Amber that she is to stay away from Ryan. Permanently.

A fresh thought dawns. What if Amber phones rather than texts back? She waves the thought away. Why would she? Don't all young people swerve phone calls these days?

She stares at the screen, willing Amber to reply. And there it is: the irritating little *ping*, the bright green dot that signals the arrival of a new text. Adrenalin floods her system as she swallows hard, takes a deep calming breath, and reads Amber's reply.

> Hey. Bad luck about your phone. Been thinking the same – hate an atmosphere! Am free tomorrow. See you inside at 1.00. xx

Later, nauseous with nerves, Emma sleepwalks through the school run, gives Callie her tea and plays with her until Ryan arrives home just after six thirty. They eat together in the kitchen while Callie watches TV, and it is Ryan who puts her to bed, reading from one of her favourite storybooks until she falls asleep.

'She's out for the count,' Ryan says, his face suffused with love. 'I'll clear up, you go find one of your dramas.'

'Thanks, but we'll do it together. You need to relax, too, you've been at work all day. I told you, you don't need to try so hard. We're okay, I promise.'

Or we will be, if I can keep that vicious little homewrecker away, Emma adds in her head.

Ryan drops the tea towel he's holding, puts his arms around Emma, and kisses her. 'Am I the luckiest man in the world, or what?'

The following morning, after a fitful night during which Emma has clocked up less than four hours sleep, she limps through sorting breakfast, waving Ryan off to work, and taking Callie to school – all on autopilot, unable to focus on anything other than meeting Amber at the pub.

Once back from school, she phones work, adopts a feeble voice, and explains that she's at the tail end of a throat infection she's had all weekend. 'I'd hate to spread it around the salon,' she tells Cheryl, the owner. 'I'll dose up today and with any luck, I'll see you tomorrow.'

Cheryl sighs. 'Well, don't come back until you're better, eh? I can't have all my stylists off sick.'

The rest of the morning passes by in a blur of grooming as, anxious to keep her end up in the presence of her rival, Emma showers, makes a huge effort with her hair, and applies her make-up with more precision than usual. Then she pulls on her most flattering jeans, teams them with a spriggy print shirt and a well-cut blazer, and steps into her favourite boots.

The woman who stares back from the full-length mirror looks stylish, attractive – and far more confident than Emma feels. After a quick spritz of perfume, she gets in her car and drives to The Pear Tree, feeling as though she has a date with destiny itself.

She's purposely ten minutes early so she can park, order a drink, and find herself a vantage point where she can watch the door without being seen.

'Vodka and tonic, please,' she tells the young barman, mindful that she's driving, yet desperately in need of some

Dutch courage. *One drink won't hurt*, she tells herself, finding a table from where the door is clearly visible.

By one fifteen, Emma is sure Amber has stood her up. Correction: has stood *Ryan* up.

A blend of embarrassment and relief washes over her. Thank goodness her crazy stupid idea has, in fact, been foiled by Amber herself.

Feeling sheepish, she stands, checks her phone one last time for messages, and is hunting through her handbag for her car keys when the door opens and a deer-like red-haired woman enters.

Emma gasps. There is no dilemma as to whether the woman is Amber. She's even more beautiful than her photograph suggests, yet younger and frailer looking than Emma had expected. *Almost young enough to be Ryan's daughter*, she thinks bitterly.

Tucked out of sight, she watches Amber lift her delicate chin as she searches for Ryan in the buzzing lunchtime crowd.

For a few seconds, Emma freezes, torn between confronting Amber and leaving with her dignity intact. Then, feeling an inexorable pull into the other woman's orbit, she walks over slowly, so as not to startle her, and is only a metre away before Amber is aware of her.

'Sorry,' Amber says, assuming Emma wants to pass. But Emma stands her ground, her legs gelatinous, her heart pounding audibly in her ears.

'Hello, Amber,' she says, softly. 'Thanks for coming. It was me who messaged you yesterday. I'm Emma, Ryan's wife.'

The words are released carefully, gently, with no trace of the hate Emma feels inside.

Amber's mouth falls open, confusion clouding her face. 'Emma? Why? I mean, what do you want?'

Emma attempts a smile. 'Not sure now I'm here. I just

wanted to meet you, more out of curiosity than anything, I suppose.'

Amber's face hardens. 'Well, that's just weird. *You're* weird if you think we're going to sit and have a cosy chat and compare notes or whatever.'

'Please, Amber, come and sit down. Just for a few minutes, you're here now.'

Amber hesitates. 'All right,' she says sulkily, her eyes darting around the pub. 'You can get me a drink.'

'Of course. What would you like?'

Amber pouts. 'I'll have a Diet Coke; I'm driving, obvs.'

'Are you sure? One drink won't hurt,' Emma says, aware of the tension flowing between them.

'No thanks, I'm also on tablets, so I'll stick with soft.' She hunches her shoulders and folds her arms, looking as self-conscious as a teenager.

Emma points to where she's been sitting. 'Grab a seat there.'

She watches as Amber slouches over, marvelling that Ryan could have been in a relationship with someone so young and gauche.

'Two Diet Cokes,' Emma says, returning from the bar a few minutes later. She sits down opposite Amber, picks up her light floral scent, and realises how familiar it is.

'Thanks.' Amber frowns and fiddles nervously with the silver bangle she's wearing. 'Emma, I hope you don't mind me saying, but you texting me like that and getting me here under false pretences is pretty fucking twisted. So, I'll ask you again: what do you want?'

Emma hides her shock at Amber's directness. She'd expected a degree of contrition, a little humility at the very least. But the set of Amber's mouth as they face each other – the wife and the mistress – tells her that this young woman feels no remorse at all.

She looks into Amber's green eyes and is caught off guard by a sudden urge to slap her. She slows her breathing, determined not to create a scene and to be the bigger person.

'I suppose I came here today looking for an assurance,' Emma says. 'I hoped you'd tell me that you're done with Ryan and you'll leave him in peace. Honestly, I'm not interested in the past, it's the future I care about. And Ryan's future is with me and our daughter, Callie.'

Amber gives an irritating little laugh. 'And you're telling me this, why? Honestly, Emma, the cracks in your marriage are not *my* problem. It's not *my* fault you can't keep your husband's attention, or that you've let yourself go.'

Smirking, Amber takes another sip of Coke. 'For what it's worth, it was Ryan who did all the chasing. And can you blame him?' She casts her eyes heavenward. 'But you're in luck, because guess what? I'm not interested in Ryan anymore. I'm *bored* of him. He's old and he's dull and I can do *soo* much better. But don't expect him to be faithful, will you? He's just not the type.'

Seething, Emma imagines throwing her drink in Amber's spiteful face before walking away with her head held high. Instead, she steels herself, dignity and decorum preventing her from doing either.

'I need the loo,' Amber announces, looking around for the ladies'. 'Then I think we're done here, aren't we?'

Emma sighs. 'Probably.' Fuming, she watches Amber stalk off, then gets up and trots briskly to the bar.

'May I have a neat double vodka, please, no ice,' Emma asks the barman urgently, her debit card already in her hand. She watches him raise a glass to the optic: 'Actually, make that a triple measure, will you?'

She pays quickly using the contactless machine, then returns to her seat in time to spot Amber across the other side of the bar. In one swift movement, she pours the vodka into Amber's Coke and parks the empty glass on an adjacent table. Then she picks up a laminated menu and pretends to study it.

Amber sits; her full lips freshly glossed, her expression defiant.

Emma puts the menu down and clears her throat. 'You know, Amber, there's a possibility we'll meet again someday and I'd hate things to be awkward. Because ultimately, most of the blame lies with Ryan. He's the married party, after all.'

'You're right. It's not up to *me* to keep *your* husband on track.' Amber frowns. 'It's always women who get the blame in these situations.'

'It is and it's not right that we have to pay for men's mistakes,' Emma says, her heart beating fast. 'Would you like another drink?'

Amber shakes her head. 'No thanks, still got half my Coke – it doesn't seem to be going down.'

Emma laughs lightly. 'I know, right? Oddly enough, you never get that with a nice glass of wine!'

She attempts small talk, willing Amber to finish her drink so their miserable meeting can end, but the younger woman ignores her, silently scrolling through her phone and sipping slowly.

And for a second, Emma almost feels regretful. *Almost.*

She'd come here hoping for an apology. For the younger woman's assurance that she'll leave Ryan alone. But Amber has offered no such guarantee. Neither is she sorry for the trouble she's caused. And it's clear to Emma that Amber is arrogant, spoilt and utterly self-obsessed and what she needs is a lesson in humility.

Emma pictures her being flagged down by the police that constantly patrol the M20 and the B roads that spur off to Maidstone town centre. She imagines Amber being breathalysed; the confusion in her eyes as she swears she's only been drinking cola; the horror on her doll-like face as she is bundled into the back of a police car and taken for further questioning...

Emma feels the twist of spite in her stomach. Let that be a lesson: a driving ban, a heavy fine, or even a spell in jail will soon bring Miss Amber Rutherford down a peg or two.

Emma eyes Amber's almost empty glass and knows it won't be long before the alcohol begins to percolate in her system. She affects a warm smile. 'I guess we should head back. Thanks for coming today. I'm really glad we've had chance to clear the air.'

'Me too,' Amber says, putting her phone away and swallowing the last of her drink.

THE END

ALSO BY BEVERLEY HARVEY

Seeking Eden

Eden Interrupted

Eden Unbound

ACKNOWLEDGEMENTS

A huge and sincere thank you to the brilliant team at Bloodhound Books for bringing my sixth novel to life. In particular, my thanks go to my brilliant editor, Abbie Rutherford; to senior editorial & production manager, Tara Lyons, for her support in so many ways; to senior commissioning editor, Rachel Tyrer, for her enthusiastic response to my manuscript; to social media & PR guru extraordinaire, Lexi Curtis - and of course a massive thank you to Bloodhound's dedicated founders & publishers, Betsy Reavley and Fred Freeman for their faith in *The Villa Next Door*.

I'm also incredibly grateful to my husband, Mark, for his unending patience, kindness and encouragement, and for continuing to take my writing seriously.

A final note of thanks goes to the handful of writing buddies, whose support is always appreciated, and to my readers: please, stick with me – there's more to come!

ABOUT THE AUTHOR

Throughout Beverley Harvey's many years spent working in advertising and PR, she harboured a secret ambition to write fiction. In 2015 a creative writing course inspired her debut novel, Seeking Eden, which was published in 2017. The sequel, Eden Interrupted, soon followed. Her third and fourth novels, The Perfect Liar and Close My Eyes, saw her shift into domestic thrillers, a genre in which she plans to continue.

Beverley was born in Yorkshire – her spiritual home - and brought up in Kent, where she now lives with her wonderful husband and their gorgeous elderly terrier. When not reading or writing, you'll find her walking the dog, listening to music, or devouring TV dramas.

Visit her blog at www.beverleyharvey.co.uk or follow her on social media at:

Twitter : @BevHarvey_

Facebook : Beverley Harvey Author

Instagram : beverley_harvey_booksnstuff

A NOTE FROM THE PUBLISHER

Thank you for reading this book. If you enjoyed it please do consider leaving a review on Amazon to help others find it too.

We hate typos. All of our books have been rigorously edited and proofread, but sometimes mistakes do slip through. If you have spotted a typo, please do let us know and we can get it amended within hours.

info@bloodhoundbooks.com